Visible City

BOOKS BY TOVA MIRVIS

The Ladies Auxiliary

The Outside World

Visible City

Tova Mirvis

Visible
City

Houghton Mifflin Harcourt
BOSTON • NEW YORK 2014

For information about permission to reproduce selections from this book,
write to Permissions, Houghton Mifflin Harcourt Publishing Company,
215 Park Avenue South, New York, New York 10003.

www.hmhco.com

Library of Congress Cataloging-in-Publication Data
Mirvis, Tova.
  Visible city / Tova Mirvis.
    pages cm
ISBN 978-0-544-04774-7
I. Title.
PS3563.I7217V58 2014
813'.54—dc23   2013036041

Book design by Chrissy Kurpeski
Typeset in Adobe Garamond Pro

Printed in the United States of America
DOC 10 9 8 7 6 5 4 3 2 1

Visible City

ONE DOWN AND two across, there she was again, a lone woman in the window, pressed close to the glass. For several days, she had been there on and off, standing in front of the window, on crutches, as if wanting to be seen.

Inside her own apartment, Nina stopped to watch. She was disturbed by the young woman's presence, proprietary on behalf of the middle-aged couple whom she'd come to expect in that window, reading contentedly on their couch. The couple rarely talked to one another, but neither of them seemed bothered by the silence. Sometimes the husband disappeared from view, returning with two mugs in hand. Occasionally the wife stretched her legs toward her husband and he absent-mindedly grasped one of her feet. But once Nina had looked out as the wife started to walk away and the husband stood and pulled her closer. Caught off-guard by the gesture, the woman had nearly stumbled, and to steady her, he pulled her into an embrace. To everyone's surprise, he twirled her, and for a few minutes before resuming their quiet routine, they had danced.

Nina's living room window offered no sweeping city views, no glimpse of the river or the sky, only the ornate prewar building across the street. She and Jeremy had lived in this Upper West Side apartment for five years but still hadn't gotten around to buying shades. Even though she looked into other people's windows, she'd convinced herself that no one was, in turn, watching them. With two sleeping children, she couldn't leave the apartment, but it was enough to look out at the varieties of other people's lives. At nine in the evening the windows across the street were like the rows of televisions in an electronics store, all visible at once. Nina's eyes flickered back and forth, but she inevitably returned to watching the same square, waiting for the couple to reappear, their quiet togetherness stirring her desire to ride out of her apartment into theirs. Hoping to find them there again, hoping that this might be the night in which they looked up from their books, she didn't move, not until she was pulled away by a scream.

The interminable cycle of sleeping and waking had begun. In his bedroom, her three-year-old son, Max, was thrashing, yet asleep. His eyes were open but he saw no way out of his nightmare, no path to outrun whatever pursued him. "There's nothing to be afraid of," she whispered into Max's ear, and his crying subsided. An hour later, it was Lily. From the bassinet that was squeezed into her and Jeremy's bedroom, Nina picked her up to nurse. As soon as Lily latched on, her crying ceased. For the moment, there was nothing more her daughter needed.

Before either of the kids woke again, Nina went back to the window, hoping to see not just the outrageous or the extraordinary, but any truthful moment of small ordinary. During the day, every feeling came shellacked with protective plastic coating. The only language spoken was certainty. Outwardly, she was reciting the maxims along with everyone else: The kids were always delicious and she wouldn't miss this for the world, and there was nowhere she'd rather be, and yes, it did go so fast. On the faces of other mothers, Nina sometimes caught the rumblings of discontent, but their inner lives were tucked away. Like theirs, her hands were always occupied, but while she was making dinner or bathing a child, while pushing one of them in a swing, rocking the other to sleep, her thoughts had begun to rove.

In the window across the way, there was still no sign of the couple reading. Once again, it was the young woman on crutches looking out, and Nina was tempted to wave. But that would end the illusion. Curtains would be pulled shut, lights switched off, the city's windows suddenly empty and dark. Instead, Nina stayed hidden, and from the shadows, she watched as a young man dressed in jeans and a black T-shirt emerged from another room and joined the young woman. Wide awake for the first time all day, Nina craned her neck, watching as the couple began to argue, their gestures sharp, their bodies taut. The man tried to hug her but the woman wriggled from his grasp, put her hands over her face, shielding herself from what he was saying.

The woman turned away from the man, but he wasn't dissuaded by her anger. He came up behind her and pressed against her. He took her crutches from her and she leaned into him as he entangled his hands in her long dark hair, ran his lips down the nape of her neck, cupped her breasts in his hands. Nina felt the woman's resistance subsiding and she wished there was a way to draw closer to them still.

Surely they realized they were before an open window; surely that was part of the pleasure. Could they see her breathing their every breath, feeling their every touch? The woman turned around, her back now to Nina, as the man carefully helped her to the couch where he knelt in front of her and pulled down her pants. As their dark clothes unpeeled, giving way to pale flashes of skin, Nina was inside her own body yet inside theirs as well. The woman's earlier reluctance was gone. She wasn't held back by her injured foot. Her thin body wriggled out from underneath and she climbed astride him. Her back arched, her body bare, she turned her face to the window, looking directly at the spot where Nina was standing.

She saw the look of defiance and understood the bold exhibitionist plea. But it was something else that made her want to press herself to the glass pane and move closer still. This woman was trying to let her know, *I see you, I know you are there.* In response, she wanted to reach her hand across and loosen the constraints of her own life as well. The city had cracked momentarily apart, a slivered opening in the larger night. Nina might be home with her kids, another interminable night with Jeremy at work, but she was also outside, part of the thrumming city. Nina waited for the reading couple to emerge from some back room where they'd been hiding and join the younger couple on their couch. She waited to see everyone's inner thoughts transmitted in flashes of light long and short. For every apartment in every building to light up. For neighbors everywhere to strip down, lay themselves bare. For the couples across the way to raise their windows and invite her in.

THE BEDROOM WINDOW faced the construction site next door, so close that on the loudest days, the glass rattled and a layer of dust covered every surface. The city had emerged from a harsh winter into a springtime of construction, the streets now blooming with the branches of cranes and metal vines of scaffolding.

Claudia went to the window where she struggled to lift the heavy wooden sash.

"Shut up," she screamed. "Shut up. Shut up. Shut up!"

It was a strange pleasure and so unlike her, yet what harm could it do? How different was she from the opera singer who practiced every evening, from the trombone-playing teenager who lived beneath them? She was one more voice in the city's cacophonous orchestra. In whatever form, whatever language, everyone had something to say.

"Shut the fuck up!" Claudia screamed, harboring the fantasy that when she stopped, nothing would move, speak, rattle. The city would take on the quiet of North Easton, Massachusetts, where she'd grown up. The cars on Broadway, the hordes of pedestrians, would all stand still, the Walk signs commanding Don't Walk, the traffic lights turning red.

"Do you feel better?" Claudia heard, and turned in surprise.

Leon was watching from the doorway, staring with what seemed to be admiration. But before she could decode his expression, let alone enjoy it, his face darkened to bafflement: a crazy stranger had taken the place of his wife. It wasn't the first time she'd screamed at the construction workers, but never when Leon was home.

"I didn't say anything," Claudia joked, hoping to restore herself in both Leon's mind and her own. She considered telling him how overwhelmed she felt by the noise, but he wouldn't understand that in order to survive the emotional and physical saturation of living here, she had begun conjuring imaginary paths of escape: were she to walk deeper into Riverside Park, she'd arrive not at the highway or river, but at a bucolic green field. But with the noise, those pathways were sealed off. The walls closed in.

"They're building a thirty-story building outside our window. You should be used to it," Leon said as she flipped through the blue pages at the front of the phone book to find the number for the local precinct.

"I'd like to make a complaint," Claudia said to the desk sergeant who answered. When she explained the problem to the person on the other end of the phone, she was told to call 311, the number for non-emergency situations. When she did, a recording informed her that she'd reached the City of New York and invited her to leave a message. Unwilling to give up, she called the local precinct again, and this time the officer asked for the location of the site. A rush of optimism: There were people to call when something was wrong. Someone out there was still in charge.

"You're going to wake Emma," Leon said.

"I don't think so. She had a hard night. I heard her and Steven fighting."

"Did he leave?"

"Yes, but I would think that he'd at least offer to stay for a few more days," Claudia said.

"It's a broken ankle. She's going to be fine."

"It's more than that," Claudia said.

Their daughter, Emma, had called a week earlier to tell them that she'd broken her ankle jogging and wanted to stay with them until it healed. Her fiancé was going to be away for most of the summer at a writers' colony, where he planned to finish a novel. Claudia was happy to have Emma home, but she was unable to allay her concern that something more was wrong.

After giving her a few more baffled looks and offering further reassurances that Emma was fine, Leon left the bedroom. Claudia thought about calling him back, to talk more about Emma or explain her behavior, but having another conversation about their daughter would only make her feel more concerned; instead of feeling Leon had understood her need to scream, she would only feel embarrassed.

Claudia went back to the window, which was now vibrating from the level and proximity of the noise. She screamed once more, though this time any feeling of relief eluded her.

In the living room, Leon was talking to Emma, and Claudia strained to hear their conversation, both relieved and disappointed when they failed to mention her screaming. She went closer to the living room, standing quietly outside the entryway.

"What time is it?" Emma asked as Leon opened the front door, surely trying for a quick escape.

"The crack of dawn," he said.

"No, really."

"Were you out here all night?" he asked, and Claudia had to hold herself back from rushing into the room with her own list of questions.

"I couldn't sleep," Emma said.

"Why not?" Leon asked.

"My ankle was hurting. You wouldn't believe how tight this cast is. It hurts worse than the break itself."

On the surface Emma's voice was light and cheerful, and Leon fell for it. He might be the therapist but Claudia knew her daughter better than that. Leon walked out of the apartment as though nothing was wrong, in a hurry to perform the bizarre urban ritual of alternate-side parking. "You'd sit in your car even if you didn't have to," Claudia once quipped, and he'd had to agree. If there were no law requiring him to move his car to make way for the street cleaners, he'd need to invent one. Once she had asked him what he did while he sat in the car. "I read the paper. I watch people," he had said. She'd always understood that he preferred to see people this way, from an observational perch, or else in his office where clear boundaries were in place. Though Emma had both their last names—hyphenated as though it were so easy to connect two people— Leon deftly stayed on the outskirts of any family issue. She had long ago accepted the fact that she bore primary responsibility.

"So when did Steven leave?" Claudia asked, entering the living room where Emma was sprawled on the couch.

"I was asleep. He didn't want to wake me."

As Claudia scrutinized her daughter's face, her worry flared once again. Her daughter looked uncharacteristically withered, pale and skinny even by Manhattan standards. She had been wearing the same black sweatpants for days, a departure from her typically colorful ensembles. Even the brightness in her eyes was dimmer, and her long curls, which usually haloed her head and boldly announced, *Here I am,* seemed deflated.

"I thought we could go out later. Have you been to Georgia's, that new café on Broadway? I'll call Dad. Maybe he'll come too," Claudia said. She wanted to grab her daughter into a hug and tell her how much she loved her, but Emma would take this unexpected gesture as a declaration of overbearing concern.

The prospect of a plan roused Emma. Sitting up, she shook off some of her weariness, and a glint of the old Emma peeked out. Claudia was used to her daughter full of action and energy. After a few post-college years spent finding herself, Emma had decided to pursue a PhD in French literature at Columbia, which Claudia took as an affirmation of her own academic work, as though by following in her footsteps her daughter had purposely paid her the highest of compliments. She had to restrain herself from asking to read the dissertation chapters Emma had written or offering too much advice about the best way to tackle so large an endeavor. But nothing could quell her pride in her daughter's accomplishments. Claudia's own career as an art historian had been marked with disappointment and struggle, but it was clear that Emma was destined for success.

Feeling more hopeful as well, Claudia helped Emma to her bedroom where clothing was strewn on the floor. Unwashed plates were piled on the dresser, the kind of chaos that Emma's presence had always generated. They had grown used to the way she swept into the apartment, in the throes of conversation, upending everything in her path. When Emma was young, Claudia used to go into her room at night and create order so that Emma awoke to her clothes and toys returned to the shelves, night the great restorer of all that had come undone during the day.

"Did you and Steven discuss the possibility that he would stay home until you were better?" Claudia couldn't help asking. Steven had been the latest in a long string of boyfriends, but this was the first whom Emma hadn't tired of after a few months. She hadn't been surprised when they announced their engagement—this was the first time her daughter was so visibly smitten. She liked Steven as well and was proud at the prospect of having him as a son-in-law. When Emma first told her whom she was dating, she had hurried to read his short story collection, published when he was only twenty-seven, because how often did you get such uncensored access to your daughter's boyfriend?

"I wanted him to go," Emma said.

"I would think you'd want him with you."

"Mom," Emma scolded.

"I was just wondering," Claudia said, while folding two of Emma's shirts.

"You know that's not what you were doing," Emma said, but her expression clouded. Wishing to believe what her daughter was saying, Claudia had a moment's yearning for the young Emma who always told her exactly what she needed. With her small hands on her face, Emma had looked her in the eye and said, "I love you the whole world." By the time Emma was two, she sat with them at restaurants, sampling whatever they placed before her. It had been hard not to treat her like an equal member of their threesome, Emma between them, a hand in each of their hands. Even years later, when she and Leon walked down the street with her, Claudia couldn't hold back a stir of pride: *This is who we are. This is who we have made.*

"Emma, honey, are you and Steven okay?" Claudia asked.

"Of course we're okay," Emma said, trying for a smile but not meeting her eye. She pinched her mouth shut, and Claudia was certain that if Emma's ankle had allowed, she would have jumped up and fled.

I N THE MORNING, both couples had disappeared from view. The only signs of life were the sounds of jackhammering from the construction site across the street, then a voice screaming, *Shut up, shut up, shut the fuck up!* Nina looked out the window, hoping to catch a glimpse of the face behind the rage. Once again, she was alone with the kids. Jeremy had come home sometime during the night and by the time she woke up, he was already gone for the day. Last night, like every night, he'd promised to leave work earlier yet was delayed for one reason or another. She had grown accustomed to a phantomlike figure coming into the darkened apartment, slipping beside her into bed when she was already asleep.

She was pulled away from the window by an eruption of need, Max wanting his truck, Lily needing to nurse. One demand let loose a cacophony of other demands. Nina picked up Lily with one hand, while with the other she foraged among the pile of toys for the missing truck. Hungry now as well, Max began pinching Lily's foot; Nina detached Max's fingers from Lily's toes and pulled the red battery-operated truck from under the couch. As Nina latched Lily onto her nipple, Max grabbed the truck and drove it across her lap, over her shoulder, into her hair, which became entangled in the mechanized wheels.

"Is my truck broken?" Max asked as the truck dangled from her hair. "Did you break it?" he screamed.

Was it too late to call her law firm and beg for her job back? She'd worked until Lily was born and then, instead of returning after her maternity leave, had given notice of surrender. Nina ripped the truck out of her hair and handed it back to Max. A tuft of hair was wrapped tightly around the wheels, but it would take a better mother than she to patiently pick out each strand.

She had to get outside. She would walk them to sleep, to the end of Manhattan if necessary. After packing up the kids, Nina maneuvered the double stroller into the elevator, hooking a sharp turn to make it through in one try. Otherwise she'd have to back out and reposition herself, while ignoring the impatient looks she got from the less encumbered passengers. These same people looked strangely at her when she used the elevator ride to comb Max's hair with her fingers or to remove the sleep encrusted at the corners of Lily's eyes. Her neighbors didn't want to see the inner workings of her life this close up. But she tried not to care what they thought. She'd made it out of the apartment, and that alone was an accomplishment. The first time she ventured out with both kids, she had expected the doorman to applaud.

Her upstairs neighbor was inside the elevator and Nina cringed. Either out of loneliness or intrusiveness, this woman regularly penetrated the scrim of friendly anonymity that was the building's code of etiquette. Standing too close, talking too loudly, she liked to apprise Nina of all the things she was doing wrong.

"It's very damp out," the neighbor said, then turned to Max. "What do you think? Is your mommy smart to be taking you out in weather like this?"

Nina could point out Max's fireman raincoat and matching

hat, both bright yellow with the sheen of patent leather, which, in the throes of a fireman obsession, he wore every day. But her neighbor would find fault in whatever she said. She may as well say that Mommy is planning to take them outside naked, to dance in the rain.

She grasped Nina's arm. "Cherish every minute," she said. "It goes so fast."

Nina dawdled so she wouldn't have to walk out with her and listen to more. She checked her mailbox and read a sign that another upstairs neighbor was posting by the elevator. *Several items of my clothing were removed from the laundry room. If you took my garments by mistake, please return them immediately. If you took them intentionally, then I may not know WHO you are but I do know WHAT you are.* At the bottom he'd signed *Arthur Grayson, Apt. 14B.*

It was the third flyer he had posted this month. The previous two had complained of noise in the stairwells and of garbage cans whose lids weren't replaced securely. He was often around during the day, talking to the doorman and lingering on the front steps of the building. In her mind, she had come to think of him as Dog Man—both he and his dog were thin and tightly coiled, as though they were about to pounce, and their short black hair seemed cut from the same bolt of fabric. He'd lived here for a few years, but she tried her best to avoid both him and his dog because though Lily hadn't yet discovered fear, Max was terrified of dogs.

"I don't suppose you know anything about my missing laundry," he said as she tried to make it outside.

"I see you around, but I don't think we've officially met," she said, to ease the discomfort.

"I know who you are. I hear you in my apartment, every single day," Arthur said. Her irritation rose. Forget her attempt to be friendly. He was still Dog Man to her. She pic-

tured him and his dog wearing matching black capes as they
saved the building from domestic peril. He didn't stand idly
by when neighbors failed to replace the garbage can lids. Dog
Man passed himself off as an ordinary tenant, but really, he was
a force of civic neighborly beneficence.

Outside the day widened. The morning's springtime
dampness had given way to sunshine. Nina glanced at those
she passed. Had any of her neighbors woken to the sound of
screaming? Had anyone else been awake last night, watching,
as well? Even if they had, no one would admit it. They would
offer complaints and advice, but none would say, *I happened to
be up, I happened to look out.*

She grew up in New Jersey, in a house in a suburb where
it was so rare to walk that many of the streets didn't have sidewalks. It was a neighborhood where every lawn was well cared
for, every house sprawling and gracious. From the outside, her
parents' lives were equally pristine and immaculate. She and
her two older sisters had always been well behaved and studi-
ous. Her sisters, both married now with three kids apiece, lived
ten minutes away by car from their parents. They lauded Nina's
choice to stay in the city as valiant but one that was sure to fail.
"As soon as Lily starts walking," they assured her, "you'll be dy-
ing to move to the suburbs like everyone else." Whenever she
went back home to visit, she took the kids for walks around
her parents' neighborhood, longing for the city's spectacle of
people, the press of noise and light. It was why she resisted the
promise of backyards and closet space. She didn't want to live
in a place where the streets were empty, the adults walled inside
their houses, the kids fenced inside backyards.

Nina stopped the stroller in front of the construction site
on their block, which was Max's favorite form of entertain-
ment. It was wondrous, really: these sandy canyons opening up
all over the neighborhood, the diggers and backhoes trawling

across the dirt like slow desert creatures, their bladed mouths lowering to the ground to dig for food. They continued walking, the streets identifiable by their smell: the foul urinous tang of 100th Street, neutralized by the fresh bread of 99th, which vanished into the exhaust fumes at 98th. Upscale bakeries and cafés intermingled with rundown newsstands, bodegas, and SROs. Up ahead, a woman was handing out flyers protesting the neighborhood's lax zoning laws. And then, on the next corner, she saw her friend Wendy.

"Your kids look tired!" Wendy exclaimed as they approached, her four-year-old twins, Sophie and Harry, buckled into their stroller. "Are they sleeping any better?"

"Max is still up at least twice a night. And so is Lily, but never at the same time," Nina said.

"I feel so lucky that my kids are such great sleepers," Wendy said.

Nina grimaced as Max rattled off a series of demands. "Cheez-Its," he screamed. "Apple juice," he insisted as the pacifier fell from Lily's mouth. Nina couldn't hide the fact that she was dispensing such unhealthy snacks, but even though there were no signs of dirt on the pacifier, she pocketed it as if she were planning to take it home and run it through the autoclave.

"We finally made a decision," Wendy announced. "We're moving to Larchmont."

Nina was about to respond, but Wendy was already in cheerful forward march. "Our day is packed," she said. "We have a playdate and a coffee date, but we'll see you later, at Gymboree!" Wendy had once been a management consultant, but though she now was home full-time with her kids, she never seemed to share the regret Nina felt over leaving her job. In between exclamations of how delicious her kids were, Wendy only occasionally mentioned the work she had once done, as if referring to a past life. As far as she could tell, Wendy looked at her kids and their needs filled the lenses of her eyes.

Nina kept walking and didn't notice, until they were almost face-to-face, someone else she knew. A woman whose class in nineteenth-century American art Nina had taken years ago as an undergraduate at Columbia was coming toward her. At the last moment before she passed, Nina was about to say hello, but the woman drew back, surprised at the show of recognition. It wasn't the first time Professor Stein hadn't remembered her. Nina often passed her on the street and once, after introducing herself, told her how much she'd loved her class. She'd hoped to have a longer conversation, but her former professor had pretended to recognize her, then, afraid of being ensnared in conversation, had nodded politely and hurried away.

After ten blocks, Lily was quiet. After twenty, Max was drowsy. By the time they reached 79th Street and turned back uptown, Nina had accomplished her mission. The kids' heads bobbed and their eyes closed. She stopped walking. Until they awoke, Nina sat in Starbucks and read. Her children's dreams would smell of coffee.

"Didn't I tell you not to do that?" screamed an elderly woman sitting near her.

"Why do you have to be like this?" her husband screamed in return.

"You idiot!" she yelled, and swatted him with a napkin.

They'd forgotten they were in public, or else hoped people would take sides. Nina exchanged amused looks with the man at the next table. She'd seen him here before and he always looked familiar. The last time she saw him, he was immersed in a book titled *On Kissing, Tickling, and Being Bored,* and until she saw the subtitle—*Psychoanalytic Essays on the Unexamined Life*—it had sounded like a good description of motherhood.

"They must not want us to know how their fight ends," the man said, once the couple shuffled out, both stooped and, despite their argument, clutching each other's hands.

"If they scream in public, don't you think they want us to hear?" Nina asked.

He looked to be in his late fifties, tall with graying hair that swept across his forehead. He wore a pressed button-down shirt and dress pants and had an air of muted distinction that she found appealing. She'd never initiated a conversation though, not wanting to be one of the people who lurked all day, using a moment of eye contact as an excuse to talk. Nor, in case he turned out to be one of these overly loquacious strangers, did she want to be entrapped.

"I think we're neighbors," he said, and they introduced themselves.

"Where do you live?" she asked.

"298 Riverside."

"Then you're right. We live right across the street."

"I've seen you outside with your kids, in front of the building," he said with a smile.

"My son is obsessed with the construction. If it were up to him, we'd spend all day watching."

"You should hear what it sounds like in our apartment."

"Have you heard the woman who's always yelling at the construction workers? She makes more noise than they do. This morning, I almost expected her to start throwing things," Nina said.

He startled slightly. "I'll have to listen for her. It probably makes her feel better—it gives her the sense that she has control. It's funny, I never used to think I could get anything done in here, but I've discovered that I work better with noise."

"What do you do?" she asked.

"I'm a psychologist. And you?"

"I used to be a lawyer. I'm on what was supposed to be a three-month maternity leave but has turned into full-time leave."

"I have a daughter too, but she's a little older than your kids," he said.

"How old?" Nina asked.

"Twenty-eight."

"Where does she live?" Nina asked.

"Actually she's staying with us for a few weeks. She broke her ankle and lives in a fourth-floor walkup." He studied her kids' sleeping faces. "You know the saying: 'Little kids, little problems. Big kids, big problems.'"

His expression was wistful but worried too. If she'd caught it on videotape, she could have played it back and better deciphered it. But in front of him, Nina managed to hide her curiosity. Even when the city contracted, taking on the guise of small-town life, you had to maintain the illusion of anonymity. You couldn't say, "I wonder if it's you and your wife I watch every night. I wonder if it's your naked daughter I saw from my window." You couldn't ask what you most wanted to know.

C LAUDIA GAVE EMMA the space she needed. When her daughter was ready to talk, she would come to her as she always had. At her desk in the so-called maid's room, Claudia tried to lose herself in her work. She was accustomed to working while distracted. Emma was born while she was in graduate school, and as a result, her dissertation had taken nearly ten years to complete, an amount of time that might appear unimaginable from afar, yet each of those days had been filled with the seemingly infinite needs of her daughter. With Leon finishing his doctorate, she had been on her own, writing while Emma napped, sure that the sound of her ideas flowing was what woke her daughter.

Eventually she had received a teaching position, but despite the publication of a book about the history of American stained glass, she hadn't gotten tenure. After a few years on the job market, she had received a lectureship at Columbia, but this too hadn't worked out, and the disappointment had been hard to recover from. For years after, she had floated from college to college, holding various adjunct positions, always carrying with her the taste of failure. This year she had no position lined up, and in the absence of teaching, she had resumed work on a long-standing project, a book about the great American stained-glass maker John La Farge.

Usually the pleasure of her work was enough to block out

her other worries, but today when she managed to corral her thoughts, the incessant noise of construction set them loose. Eager to maintain her concentration, Claudia decided to leave the apartment and work at Georgia's, even though she planned to meet Emma and Leon there later. It was such an inviting place she was happy to go twice.

In the elevator were two mothers, their children in tow. One of them was talking about how the construction inevitably woke the kids from their naps, and when they glanced at her, she worried they'd heard her screaming. She felt a rush of shame, pelted suddenly by the possibility that the entire neighborhood had heard her.

Outside, the construction site was boarded in bright blue plywood on which someone had scrawled, in black letters, *Yuppie Condo.* Overhead a billboard proclaimed *The Celestial: Reaching New Heights of Luxury City Living,* with a rendering of the new building, a Richard Meier knockoff with glass walls. Despite the attempt at transparency, it would still be far taller than any building in the vicinity, casting shadows and blocking natural light. Though she normally liked glass exteriors, she had to agree with that scrawl of graffiti. The abundance of windows seemed not a function of design but a means of showmanship, not so the investment bankers who would live here could look out, but so envious passersby could see in.

As Claudia waited for the light to change, she noticed an acquaintance approaching her. The woman ran a neighborhood organization whose bimonthly newsletter was slipped under every apartment door and which most people threw away along with the menus for Chinese food that accumulated there.

"What do you know about the monstrosity being built outside my window?" Claudia asked, and told Barbara about the morning's noise, omitting her part in it.

"I could kick myself. We barely protested the demolition

of the brownstones that made way for that eyesore. And now another condo is going up in the same five-block radius. But this time I'm prepared to fight," Barbara said, and described her plans to call the head of the community board's Land Use Committee and implore them to schedule an emergency session. "It's a wake-up call. They're putting these buildings up as fast as they can, and it's a disaster waiting to happen. You should come to one of our meetings. Or what are you doing right now? We can have coffee and I'll tell you what's going on."

Claudia wrote Barbara's number on a scrap of paper she fished from her bag, even though she knew she wouldn't get involved. Though she'd sign a petition, she felt both admiration and embarrassment for those who manned tables and carried clipboards. She suspected that other needs were being filled.

She also decided against joining Barbara for a cup of coffee. Her worries about Emma occupied too prominent a place in her mind. She didn't want to appear standoffish, but she wasn't one to forge friendships through confession, nor would she talk about her work. Except for the one or two colleagues with whom she'd stayed in contact, her interest in the minutiae of window frames or leaded glass would make the uninitiated feel sorry they'd asked. This was true even for Leon and Emma, who joked that Claudia studied details most people didn't notice. People would rather ask about Leon's work, hoping to be entertained with stories of other people's craziness. But too principled to reveal anything, he told those who asked that despite popular perception, his was a profession not of grand drama but of small moments of insight.

Few people understood the pleasure she took in her own work. Like Leon, she too studied something as ever-shifting as a person's emotional map. When she stood in front of a stained-glass window, she saw not one great work but a myriad.

Because the light was always changing, it was futile to think that she could ever know any of John La Farge's pieces entirely. But with the prospect of discovery tantalizingly ahead, she kept trying to capture some elusive part.

Claudia found a table near the window of the café. If she worked well, the next few hours would be spent inside her book. It would be noon, then it would be three; the hours between would cease to exist.

She'd been working on the La Farge book for so long that even when she wasn't actively writing, the book was there, hiding behind a wall in her mind. She had stopped thinking she might ever find her way to the end. But she was happy to spend her life inside these pages, especially now when she was on the verge of a potential discovery. It had been so long since she'd published anything that most people in her field had probably forgotten her name altogether, but now she'd written an article for the *American Art Journal* making a bold claim. After years of meticulous research, she believed she had discovered the existence of a lost work of art, one last great La Farge window.

As she was arriving at that clearing in her mind, another pair of mothers and their kids entered the café and installed themselves at the next table. Unbuckled from their strollers, the kids circled Claudia's table. The mothers turned their enraptured gazes from their children's faces to check for equivalent reactions around them. When she was a young mother, such swooning hadn't been as central to the job description. Of course there were moments of joy, but her generation of mothers hadn't talked of parenting with the same language they used to describe falling in love.

"Can you say hi?" the mothers prompted, and one of the kids garbled an answer.

Claudia smiled, then turned back to her work. But she

couldn't dispense with the kids so easily. They began screaming for no apparent reason, running as if they were at the playground. Claudia felt sympathy for the mothers, but they were
untroubled by their children's behavior. These mothers saw
nothing, heard nothing, said nothing as their children raced
to the rear of the café, spewing crumbs, then back to the table
where they shoved cupcakes into their mouths. They made no
distinction between the café and their living rooms, between
the worlds of children and adults. She and Leon might have allowed Emma a freedom that would have been incomprehensi-
ble to her own mother, but even so, they would never have per-
mitted such public misbehavior, sanctioned by these mothers
who let their kids know, *Your every wish is my command.* It was
hard to believe this was the child-centered philosophy that she
and Leon had once embraced.

"Excuse me, but this isn't a playground," Claudia finally
said.

She glanced at those sitting nearby, hoping they would
smile approvingly at her willingness to take a stand, but no one
met her eye. She had intended to be only mildly rebuking, but
apparently she had sounded far harsher. She blushed and felt
the same shame as earlier, when she had been caught screaming
from her window.

"It's not a library either," said one of the mothers. Though
they continued to shoot Claudia annoyed looks, they made
grudging efforts to control their kids.

"Use your words. Use your inside voices," the mothers instructed.

"But when do we get to use our outside voices?" one of the
kids asked.

Finally, the mothers began to pack up, discussing in loud,
narrating voices that their next stop was Gymboree. The children attached themselves to the pastry case, sucking their lips

against the glass like catfish in a tank. It had been restocked with fresh cupcakes, and though the children pleaded for more, the mothers said no; they'd exceeded their daily allotment of refined sugar and artificial color. Though they were so intent on fulfilling their kids' every need, certain limits were apparently established and enforced. But where in their hierarchies of all things bad for their children did an extra cupcake fall? These young mothers had so many rules for their kids and yet none at all.

"Was everything okay?" asked the lavender-haired young woman behind the counter when, an hour later, Claudia returned her teacup and saucer. The girl's hair matched the icing on the cupcakes, which suddenly looked irresistible, like rare gemstones or ancient artifacts you could not only touch but consume.

"The tea was great but am I the only one bothered by the noise?" Claudia asked.

"No one can stand it. The other day I tripped over a stroller and everything went flying," said the purple-haired woman. "Why can't these moms keep their kids home until they're old enough to behave?"

"That would be a long time. But maybe they can use their so-called inside voices in the meantime," Claudia said.

Looking at her teacup, Claudia noticed for the first time that the same cabbage rose pattern had decorated a tea set in her mother's house. It was one of the few things in which her mother had taken pleasure, along with a collection of antique glass bottles that she'd lined up by her bedside window where she spent much of her day, entranced by the flicker of light against the blue and green glass.

If Claudia's father, an economics professor at a small college near North Easton, Massachusetts, hadn't died so young, if her mother's life hadn't been permeated by the feeling that she wasn't given enough, perhaps she would have been less embittered. With a precision that was remarkable, her mother had always known how to make Claudia feel bad. In displeasure, or maybe just bafflement, her mother regularly proclaimed her signature "I don't understand you." She certainly didn't understand Claudia's decision to go to graduate school in art history, a subject she considered a waste of time. She had no interest in hearing Claudia's descriptions of the works of art that had captivated her, some of which were a few blocks from their house. As a teenager, Claudia often walked past Unity Church, and one day she'd noticed the open door and taken in the two majestic stained-glass windows inside. With the afternoon light streaming through, setting every color on fire, the world was no longer as small and confining.

Any attempt to explain this to her mother was met with condemnation. Nor could her mother understand a daughter who was unwilling to put aside her ambitions when she, her mother, became increasingly sick. Claudia had moved to Boston to start graduate school, going home on weekends, then less frequently when her every visit was met with a barrage of recrimination. Even now, so many years later, Claudia avoided returning to her hometown. Once she met Leon, the estrangement from her mother hadn't mattered as much. With Leon, she thought she could create her family anew.

Three years later, when her mother died, she was already pregnant with Emma. She sold off what little there was but took the glass bottles, because she wanted to remember how, when the light shone through them, a smile had escaped her mother's pursed lips. Despite the ever-present disapproval, Claudia had always thought of her mother's love for beautiful things as an impetus for her own work.

As she held the teacup in her hand, Claudia felt her mother's presence anew. She had spent her whole life trying not to be like her. But now she recognized a surprising new version of herself, one who spoke the darker parts of her own mind, and she felt a fledgling rustle of understanding.

FTER A MONTH with little sleep, Jeremy's body refused to comply. His hands shook from too much coffee. His skin had a gray, sickly pallor. He paced the length of his office, then sat back at his desk. But it was no use. Pen in hand, Jeremy dozed, his dreams and documents spliced together. He awoke, placed numbered tabs on each exhibit and schedule, then fell asleep for so long that the motion sensor lights in his office switched off. In the dark, he awoke, clicked Print on his computer, briefly fell asleep, then hit Print again. Only when he saw the multiple copies waiting at the printer did he realize what he'd done. On the way back to his office, he moved slowly, worried he might fall over. If he did, the other lawyers would simply step over him. Someone would call maintenance to move him out of the way.

He was a fifth-year associate in the real estate department of a Manhattan law firm, and for over a year he had been working on the acquisition of two Upper West Side apartment buildings. The first building, deep into the construction phase, was across the street from his own apartment, though he was never home to witness its progress. The second building had suffered a series of delays, but after months spent doing due diligence in a windowless conference room surrounded by mountains of documents, he'd just finalized the purchase and sale agreement.

Jeremy fell asleep again, and this time he startled awake to the sound of the phone ringing, unsure whether a minute had passed or a month. When Richard's extension appeared on the phone display, Jeremy jumped. As a second-year associate, Jeremy had been assigned to work for Richard. Plucked from the ranks of junior associates who would inevitably be thinned out due to attrition or exhaustion, Jeremy believed the assurances that the long hours would yield their reward. Richard had promised to look out for him, shielding him from other partners intent on giving him new assignments when he was already swamped. Once, he clasped him on the shoulder and said that in Jeremy's dedication he saw a younger version of himself.

Two minutes later, Jeremy was sitting in Richard's office. At his desk, Richard was wearing a khaki field vest over his dress shirt, the same thing he'd worn earlier to a meeting with the client. Even in this era of business casual, it was odd, but Richard could show up in a matching safari hat and Jeremy wouldn't say a word. He wouldn't dare breach the wall between their work and their lives, even though he spent more nights with Richard than he did with his wife; he'd sat so often in his office during conference calls that he could mimic Richard's every facial expression: the half smile when he was willing to negotiate, the twitch in his cheek when they'd arrived at an impasse. He wouldn't have been surprised if he'd started to look like him as well.

Jeremy waited for him to say that he'd done a good job, but praise was in short supply. Richard demanded a document that Jeremy knew nothing about, and he stared in disbelief when Jeremy said so.

"Do you have any idea how much money is on the line? Do you know how impatient the client is?" Richard asked.

Richard had been acting strangely since hearing murmurings of neighborhood opposition to the second building, but Jeremy didn't expect to see him so rattled.

"I don't think you want to imagine the response when I tell the client that my associate fucked this up. Every delay costs them a few hundred thousand dollars a day," Richard fumed.

Jeremy stammered an explanation, hating how plaintive he sounded. Getting ahead was the same as trying to stay afloat. If he didn't work these hours, someone else gladly would. He and Nina had spent all their money on an apartment they couldn't afford, mortgaging themselves to his future earnings. They had long ago believed in an egalitarian marriage, though recently he'd overheard Nina say, only half joking, that they'd ended up with the kind of egalitarianism in which she did everything. "Don't undo anything," Nina warned him whenever she was rushing to get the kids out of the apartment, afraid that if she left him with the kids for a moment, time would move backward; the breakfast would come uncooked, the shoes off, the pajamas back on.

But that was only for now. In another year or two, Jeremy would be up for partner. If they could make it through these years, their lives would once again match their aspirations. Making partner, they had come to believe, was the portal to the rest of their lives—even if he was too tired to remember what they wanted that future to look like. He promised Richard he would correct the situation and left his office in shame. On the way back to his own office, Jeremy heard the tapping of other keyboards but didn't stop to say hello to any of his fellow associates. They'd all been yelled at by unhappy partners, but he preferred to bear the humiliation alone.

In his office, Jeremy stood at the window and gazed at the thicket of buildings, a view that had once bestowed a sense of grandeur upon his work. "Look at them," Richard had said when they first started working together and Jeremy had found him staring out a conference room window. "All these buildings are here because of people like you and me." It was the kind of thing his father might have said; sometimes he imagined those words extolling this profession had actually come from his father, that it was he who looked over the documents Jeremy drafted and nodded with pride.

Six years ago, his father had suffered a ruptured aneurism while at work. How terribly fitting, it had seemed to him then and now, that his father who had lived at work had died there too. At the time, Jeremy had been in his last year of law school. "You can do anything you want, after law school," his father used to joke, but of course it wasn't a joke. In his family, there was only one way. His father too had started off as an associate in a law firm whose offices Jeremy could see from a conference room window. When he hadn't made partner, they'd moved to Chicago where Jeremy's mother had grown up and where his father joined a small firm. Though his father acted as though the move had been his choice, Jeremy had always heard the disappointment at the path his career had taken.

Before law school, Jeremy had struggled to find things to talk to his father about; no matter how hard he tried, he felt a gaping distance. But when he'd gotten into NYU law school, his father's alma mater, he'd basked in the approval and hoped this would make up for all the other ways he was becoming less the person his father wanted. But when it came to his father, there had been endless ways to disappoint.

Jeremy's e-mail beeped, an angry missive from Richard. "I'm waiting," the subject read, followed by a message bearing only a single question mark. Servitude came easily to him, but a part of him wanted to hit Reply and fill the page with a barrage of question marks. Even in a state of exhaustion, he was usually able to put aside the question of why he was working so hard. No matter how late, he still felt the craving to be like the partners he'd envied since he was a summer associate, with their swaggering, expectant ways.

But tonight he was so tired that his eyes burned in their sockets. The room spun if he stood up too quickly. He couldn't free himself from the imprisonment of the day. That morning, descending into the subway, his eyes had darted, as they always did, to the people nearby, none of whom were looking anxiously around. Was he the only one who still worried about being stranded too far above ground or trapped too far below? So many years later, Jeremy still felt a quiet swell of panic upon entering his office in the Citicorp building. Its sloped peak was the tallest in its immediate vicinity, and as planes flew up the East River, visible from his window, he worried that his fear would guide them like a light stick toward his building. As a child beset with a nightly assortment of fears, he'd made bargains with God, trading obedience for protection. He had been raised in an Orthodox Jewish family, and though he no longer was observant, a part of him still believed that he could bargain his way to safety. One night, he'd lain awake in fear, and his father came into his room, sat beside him, and took out a prayer book. The words his father pointed to were ones he knew well: *The Lord is my light, whom shall I fear.* He'd said the psalm, but what really comforted him was his father next to him, and the wish that he would stay there the whole night through.

His father had often talked of those who left Orthodoxy in anger, forging fiery trails of rebellion as they wandered foolishly, recklessly from the path. Now Jeremy was among them. For months after he'd stopped wearing a yarmulke, he had expected to put his hand to his head and feel the small crocheted circle there. For far longer he was sure that its imprint was still discernible in his hair. He hid each trespass, censoring what he said to his parents. Long ago, he had imagined himself angrily, bravely demanding his right to be his own person, while other times he imagined timidly sneaking the words in as a casual aside at the end of a conversation. All these would-be scenarios

took place at far-off future dates, but his father had died before
Jeremy could tell him, before he allowed himself to wonder if
his father already knew.

When the subway had come, Jeremy had pushed his way
into the crowded car. He could not think about the press of
fear, not now. If he forced those feelings into increasingly
smaller spaces inside himself, perhaps one day they would dis-
appear altogether. At 96th Street, the passengers rushed across
the platform to the express train, which miraculously waited.
He'd transferred to the Shuttle, then got on the downtown
6 train. A seat opened, and Jeremy squeezed himself into the
valley between two people. With exhaustion the most effective
salve against fear, Jeremy closed his eyes.

After a few minutes or an hour, he'd awoken. An empty car.
A black tunnel. A screech of wheels. The car was turning, and
out the window he saw a sign for City Hall station. He had
missed his stop. Or was on the wrong train. Or survived an
emergency by sleeping through.

As the train curved through the tunnel and quieted, Jeremy had pressed his face to the window to catch sight of a station he hadn't known existed. It was eerily deserted, yet even in
its neglected state, the station's one-time grandeur was evident.
The ceilings were vaulted and arched, lit with skylights held in
place by ornate wrought-iron canes. A grand staircase, just visible from the train window, led to the street level. The walls
were decorated with bursts of red and green tile that had darkened with age but still revealed their intricate handiwork.

With Jeremy's face against the glass, the train had sped up
and reentered the dark tunnel. Intent on seeing what was rap-
idly disappearing from view, he'd craned his neck backward for
one last glimpse, and as the subway hurtled forward, a passageway had opened inside him, a vista to somewhere else.

WITH AN HOUR until he was supposed to meet his family, Leon walked toward home. By the end of the day, he was used up. After he'd stepped inside so many people's lives, his own family felt farther away and the prospect of meeting them made him weary. His emotional saturation made him wonder why everyone didn't shut themselves away from the tangle of need, from the inevitable frictions of life among people.

His mind was still on his last appointment of the day, a woman whom he didn't particularly look forward to seeing, having to hear each week of her fear of losing her temper with her kids. From the outside, she appeared poised and calm as she diligently recounted her interactions with her twins. It had taken a few sessions to notice that she always sat with her arms tightly folded across her chest, as if holding herself together, and that her nails were digging into her skin. She expended so much effort to sound happy and was so tightly controlled that he couldn't help but imagine the moment in which the pressure reached such a level that she erupted before his eyes. Until that happened, any admission of a negative feeling felt like a victory painfully extracted.

As he'd prepared to leave his apartment that morning, Leon had already been thinking about her and the various patients he would see that day. He had padded across the living room and had almost made it out the front door without waking his daughter. But when Emma awoke, she had caught him off-guard, searching his face for an answer to a question she hadn't posed. Underneath her confident exterior, he glimpsed a scared child. He stepped back into the living room but gave himself away by glancing at his watch. At the wounded look on Emma's face, he realized this was a mistake, one he wouldn't have made at work. His patients never liked to feel that they were taking up his time, even though they were paying for it, and because of this, he kept his clock on the bookshelf behind where they sat so he could unobtrusively keep track.

He had waited for Emma to say what was on her mind, but all she offered was the pain in her ankle. Of all the things she might have said, this was the least complicated, and in his hurry to leave, Leon hadn't wanted to consider the possibility that it was anything more. But when he said goodbye, he could see that he had failed her. "It is a pleasure to be hidden, but a disaster not to be found," he thought, from the work of the child psychologist D. W. Winnicott. It was true, and not just of children playing hide-and-seek.

Until Emma had come home, he and Claudia had passed their nights reading on the couch, turning pages as a form of conversation. But every night was now spent in hushed conference, Claudia picking apart Emma's words to assemble an explanation of what was really wrong. Even if he had the patience for the discussion, he couldn't muster the same concern. From a young age, Emma had not been the kind of child you worried about. He took great satisfaction in his daughter's self-sufficiency, a trait she had inherited from him as surely as her dark curls and heart-shaped mouth were from Claudia. They had been subjected to the usual jokes about therapists' kids being screwed up, but he'd always laughed off those comments because Emma, with her ebullient confidence, her ease of accomplishment, had so clearly emerged unscathed.

After leaving the apartment, he had sat in his car which was as old as Emma, a Volvo wagon, boxy and white, with 250,000 miles on the odometer. It had begun its life as a family car, with toys and crumbs buried under the seats, but now it was his private ship. He was in control of the music and the climate. The doors could be locked. People who walked by might see him, but no one would knock.

He'd watched the people who passed: The old man shepherded by his female attendant, then the children on tricycles, metal poles attached to the backs for the mothers to push when the kids grew tired. Next came the two dogs who hated one another. The small gray terrier wearing a bejeweled blue collar was seemingly of a different species from the black Great Dane. The little dog was fearless, barking incessantly, as though no one had informed him of the impotence of his high-pitched yap. The owners were well matched to their dogs. A petite woman with cropped gray hair and bright blue glasses, exuding the same nervous energy as her dog. A tall, pompous, dark-haired man with excessively straight posture and an air of proprietary combativeness. If Leon were to guess, he'd say that the man drew his fierceness from the dog. Was that true for all pet owners? he wondered. On the leash or in the cage, was some real or imagined aspect of ourselves made manifest?

His fellow parkers began stepping out of their cars as though given word that they'd docked on dry land. He too emerged from his car, now allowed to park in the spot he'd been holding all morning. Instead of moving forward into his day, he was still thinking about the look on Emma's face. Though he feigned being in a hurry, he'd had enough time before his first patient to go back and ask her what she'd really wanted. He wasn't proud of this aspect of himself, but there it was, true and unchangeable: At work, he had the capacity to give endlessly. At home, he was impatient before he'd even begun. Instead of going to talk to Emma, he'd gone to Starbucks. Though he'd once chafed at the idea of paying three dollars for a cup of coffee, now he gladly paid for the luxury of sitting undisturbed. Was this the secret to the chain's success? No one wanted to be home.

Now, at the end of his day, Leon walked back uptown, the streets crowded, people's worshipful faces upturned toward the sun. For a few blocks, he was behind a woman in jeans, pushing a stroller laden with bags. As Leon drew closer, he recognized her. She was the young mother—Nina, he recalled, was her name—whom he'd met earlier that day in Starbucks. He'd spoken to her only because he'd become aware that she snuck glances at what he was reading, and he felt a prickle of pleasure at her interest.

When she stopped at a Don't Walk sign, he had a few seconds to decide whether to acknowledge her. Better, perhaps, to leave unexamined those moments of strangerly connection, to allow them to dangle without taking on a fixed meaning. But it didn't matter what he decided. As though she knew him far better than she did, she turned and smiled as he approached.

"Leon, right?" she said.

"Are you following me, or am I following you?" he asked.

"Both," she said.

He fell into step beside her. They were going in the same direction, and like him, she was a fast walker. The first time he met her, the children were sleeping. Now they were babbling, snacking, spilling. Both kids had inherited her straight, dark hair, pretty blue eyes, and round face with its innocent, unguarded expression. Once again, he noticed her unexpected curiosity, as though she was waiting for him to say something. It wasn't unlike the look Emma had given him that morning, but somehow with this woman, it was intriguing rather than exhausting.

"Are you heading home?" she asked.

"I'm meeting my wife and daughter at that new café at Broadway. Have you been in yet?"

"The cakes look tempting, but my kids are too noisy," Nina said.

"The whole city is noisy," Leon said, and thought about their earlier conversation when he'd lied about not having heard the woman screaming. At the sound of Claudia's voice, he'd rushed into the bedroom thinking she was hurt but had stopped in the doorway, shocked, as before his eyes, his even-tempered wife had come unleashed. It was one thing for him to see Claudia this way, but disturbing to realize that of course others heard her as well. She would be mortified if anyone knew that she was behind that screaming voice, yet he was propelled, inexplicably, by the need to say more.

"My wife is the one screaming at the construction workers," Leon confessed.

She took in what he'd told her, as surprised as he was by the revelation.

"Why does the noise bother her so much?" she asked.

"I don't know," he admitted. "To be honest, it didn't occur to me to ask her."

They walked quickly. Leon had no need to look at the signs to know which block they were on. The Victoria's Secret on 85th Street jarred with his inner map, and for those who'd lived here long enough, the storefront with the pink-and-white-striped awning and lingerie-clad mannequins would always be Broadway Farm. All those who lived here crafted their own internal rendering of the city based on how long they'd been here. He too carried his own version of the neighborhood—he'd grown up on the West Side and remembered when it had boasted one of the city's highest crime rates. His parents had lived with an ever-present worry that he would be mugged, and had they been alive, they would have relished the upscale stores and safe parks. Like him, they wouldn't have bemoaned the neighborhood's transformation. He could never summon the indignation of those who'd once gathered outside Victoria's Secret to protest, with equal vigor, the skimpiness of the attire and the lack of a good neighborhood grocery store. Skeptical of their motivation, he wished their placards conveyed not the slogans written in bright, bold letters, but the quieter internal ones, such as *Afraid of Change,* or *Need Outlet for My Anger.*

"How long have you lived in the city?" Leon asked Nina.

"Since college. My main criterion for picking a school was that it had to be in New York."

"I take it you like it here?"

"I do. I want to stay here but my husband has had enough. He doesn't know where he wants to move, as long as it's far away."

On the corner of Broadway and 100th, they stopped in front of a small brick building. Signs plastered on the window of the dollar store on the ground level announced, in big red letters, *LOST OUR LEASE.*

"It's going to be another luxury apartment building," Nina told him.

"How do you know?"

"Jeremy, my husband, is a real estate lawyer, and he's been working on the deal nonstop," Nina said, and Leon noticed that all the while, she had been stealing glances at him, her gaze lingering a little too long. Like him, she was an observer, though he doubted that for her it was a means of avoiding engagement. On the contrary, her watchfulness seemed like a prelude to something more.

Her interest ignited his own. Perhaps she thought her curiosity was well hidden; so intent on watching other people, she forgot they were doing the same to her. He had the surprising urge to call Claudia and say he would be unable to meet her and Emma after all. Instead of being recruited into a family conversation, he wanted to ask this woman whom he barely knew if she wanted to walk until they reached the edge of the city, then walk some more. There was little risk: he could easily return to the state of not knowing her. Strangers were blank canvases, and there was an inexhaustible supply of them.

Overhead a sign was displayed on the building, courtesy of the Royalton Company. *Building the New West Side,* it read, next to a picture of a smiling little girl holding the hands of her young well-heeled parents, striding happily into their towering new home. He could decry what these flashy façades represented and bemoan their assault on the character of the neighborhood. Yet as he stared up, he surprised himself once again. He wanted each colossus to rise proudly in their midst. With their glass and steel, their unabashed presence, they would shatter the inertia that suddenly felt suffocating, in his own life and all around.

HER PARENTS' APARTMENT triggered a Pavlovian urge to eat. As soon as her mother went out, Emma went into the kitchen where, supported by her crutches, she stood in front of the refrigerator, fighting the impulse to consume everything in sight. She was probably not supposed to feel such pleasure in eating her way through their fridge, just as she was probably not supposed to feel so relieved to be sleeping in her old bedroom as though she were still a child.

Every morning since she'd been home, her mother had brought her breakfast in bed. She made her grilled cheese sandwiches for lunch, the same as she'd done whenever Emma had stayed home sick from school, the day spreading out before her with a seemingly endless number of hours to fill as she wished.

Emma had urged her mother to turn her former bedroom into an office, instead of squeezing herself into the tiny maid's room, but her mother wouldn't hear of it. As a result, her bedroom remained untouched. On the walls were the black-and-white photographs she'd taken in college and developed herself. There were copies of her high school literary magazine which she'd edited and to which she'd contributed numerous poems that now made her laugh with embarrassment. On her bulletin board were a slew of tacked-up awards. She had starred in a high school play, won a school science award; she had spearheaded a fundraising project to buy goats for villages in India. The room was a trophy case to her early achievements.

In the past, she had flitted from one passion to another; she might not have known what she wanted to do, but she hadn't worried about it. The world was filled with possibilities, especially when you had parents who trusted every decision you made and were willing to support you through any adventure. Newly out of college, she had backpacked through Europe for six months. When she came home, she took acting classes, then dropped out because what she really wanted to be was an art therapist. Her parents never said anything directly but eventually she felt their impatience. In search of what she really wanted to do, she'd once marveled at how her mother could study one artist for so many years and never get bored. "It feels new every day. I always come away with something unexpected," she had said, and Emma had never forgotten it. Her own interest in French was one of the few things that had lasted. In college, she had fallen in love with French history and literature, but more than either of these, it was the language itself she wanted to live inside. Her parents had treated their areas of interest as sacred subjects; when they spoke about their work, they possessed languages of their own. Now she would have her own language and world, one as robust, as all-consuming, as theirs.

After a few more false starts and abandoned plans, she had started her graduate program with great enthusiasm, studying late-nineteenth-century French women writers and writing her dissertation about the period between George Sand and Colette, looking at several relatively unknown women who were considered part of the burgeoning *littérature féminine.* Their increased visibility had prompted a rash of outrage by the male literary establishment, who likened them to hysterics and prostitutes. The fear of the female body was ever-present, but Emma wanted to study another fear, the fear of the female mind.

On the desk beside her, the books were waiting; there had once been a time when she would have viewed a broken ankle as an opportunity to get work done. But her inability to concentrate had persisted. Instead of reading, she ate one container of soup, two servings of pasta, three helpings of salad, but she was still hungry. Foraging through her parents' kitchen cabinets, Emma found a bakery box, from the café where she was later meeting her parents. Inside the box, four purple cupcakes were decorated with tiny flowers. The only things missing were the candles and a rousing chorus of "Happy Birthday." She knew she should probably save two for her parents, but the cupcakes were already a few days old and looked like they'd been forgotten. It was sad to eat such pretty creations alone and all at once, but even when the sweetness became corrosive, Emma didn't stop. Perhaps sugar was the best medicine of all, because with each bite, she minded less that Steven was gone, that she hated being in school, that she had no idea what to do with her life.

She first met Steven at a café near Columbia. He had been hunched over a laptop but looked occasionally in her direction as she talked to a group of fellow students in French. She had always been told that she talked too loudly, but when she was excited it was hard to hold back. At first she was flattered by his attention, wondering if he mistook her for a native speaker. She spoke louder until she finally realized that he was simply hoping she'd be quiet. His eyes were as dark as his hair, and his stare was remote and hard to read. She was always drawn to the ones who tucked themselves away and, in doing so, invited you to come in pursuit.

In preparation for her orals, she was supposed to be reading, or at least skimming, six hundred books in nine months. It was hard to sit still for such long periods of time, and to make it easier, she started spending her time in the café where there was the possibility of human contact. She glanced at Steven when he wasn't looking, then stealthily looked away when she thought he was about to look up at her. The few times she got caught, there was no choice but to smile.

A few weeks later, they had both been on campus late in the evening, though a blizzard had been predicted. He was teaching in the Columbia MFA program and she had been holed up all day in the library. They ran into each other as the snow was falling, the streets emptied of both people and cars, and he had followed her lead in walking in the middle of Broadway. To fill the silence, she'd talked about her dissertation topic and her classes and her fellow students and the time she'd spent in France. He had listened at first but then playfully put his hand over her mouth. If anyone else had done this to her, she would have been outraged. But they stood with their eyes locked, their hair, their coats, dusted with snow. She willed herself not to look away until he brought his lips to hers and kissed her.

She grew accustomed to his quiet moods and to how he retreated when he was in need of space. Waiting for the moment when he would turn to her, she learned to hover silently at the edges as he slowly doled out pieces of himself. With past boyfriends, she'd simultaneously wanted them and wanted to be free of them, but she never got tired of being with Steven. She could chase him forever and never quite catch him.

They had been dating for two years when Steven broached the subject of marriage. Until now, she hadn't been sure what she wanted, but her life was finally taking shape. She moved into his apartment where the two of them worked side by side, he on his novel, she on her dissertation. It was just as she'd imagined her parents' lives when they were newly married. In her mind, they had managed seamlessly the task of being both together and apart.

If she had what she wanted, why, one day, had she awoken and been unable to get anything done? One week off turned into another and she still couldn't return to her work. Instead of reading or writing, she decided that no one could live in an apartment with peeling white walls and so little color. She spent hours at the hardware store, plucking paint swatches from the display, enthralled with the range of possibilities as laid out by Benjamin Moore: Symphony Blue, Turquoise Haze, Harbor Fog, Sapphireberry, Billowy Down. Not caring if she dripped onto the floor, Emma plunged in, taking pleasure in the tangible work of her hand. This was her true calling. Instead of finishing her dissertation, she would paint houses professionally, matching moods to swatches. Her walls would take on the quality of the gemstone rings she'd worn as a kid that were said to change color according to your mood.

When every wall in their apartment was covered in Atlantis Blue, she biked through Central Park and baked bread and made gnocchi from scratch. She attempted, unsuccessfully, to make her own jam and pickle vegetables. She tried to talk to Steven but he couldn't understand the part of her that was incapable of sitting still when he was proudly proclaiming that he was almost done with his book. A hard spot of envy grew inside her. Maybe if she knew more about his book she wouldn't feel this way, but the secrecy shrouding his work was as important as the work itself.

She put off a meeting with her adviser as long as she could, but by the end of the semester, having run out of excuses, she hastily threw together a few pages which she submitted in advance of their meeting, in the hope that, if looked at in the right way, they might resemble the very preliminary outline of a very rough draft of a first chapter. She was used to being able to talk her way through any situation, but she was sure this would be the moment in which she was revealed as an imposter. Instead, she watched in silence as he rifled through her pages and nodded with satisfaction. "Excellent work. You're off to a very promising start," he said.

She felt relief, but what did it mean that her adviser was pretending to have read something she was pretending to have written? The writers she studied were flinging conventions aside, living boldly. She didn't want to write about these renegade women; she wanted to be them.

When it was time to meet her parents, Emma went outside for the first time in two days and squinted at the brightness. The light wasn't unusually blinding but she had been inside for too long.

From each person Emma passed, she received kind looks or expressions of sympathy. Her neighbors and the doormen didn't hold back from asking what was wrong, a question that was usually off-limits. This was true any time she left the apartment—was one small excuse all people needed in order to start talking? To anyone who asked about the broken ankle, she explained that she was running late at night and had known, the second she fell, that the bone was broken. She described the way Steven had helped her up and had first assumed she was overreacting, despite the immensity of the pain. She knew she was giving too much information to strangers, but they were willing to listen, so why not tell of the six-hour wait in the emergency room where Steven brought her, annoyed at having to be there for so long? Finally, she told him to go home, which he did, leaving her to wait alone on one of the orange plastic chairs where people sat in silence, the stench of vomit doing battle with the hospital antiseptic. All patients would be seen in order of need, and unless she threw in a chest pain or coughed up blood, she'd quietly sit for hours. When it was finally her turn, a doctor drew a curtain around her and pressed on her foot. "Where does it hurt?" he'd asked, a question that struck her as the most beautiful in the world.

At the café her mother was reading, and Emma waited in the doorway until she looked up.

"Dad's coming. He must be running late with one of his patients," Claudia said as Emma sat down.

"He's always running late."

"That's not true," Claudia protested, looking her over. "Doesn't it feel better to get out? It's good to see you dressed."

Emma shrugged. Her mother was on the verge of asking again what was really wrong, but she was saved by the arrival of her father, who slid into the chair next to her.

"I hope you ordered me a cupcake," he said.

"We did, but I ate it," Emma said.

He looked her over as well, a feeling of inspection to which she was becoming accustomed. She wasn't sure what she'd expected earlier, yet she was still annoyed at how easily he'd walked away.

"I'm not used to seeing you awake. I thought you'd become nocturnal," he said, oblivious.

The cupcakes arrived, but after a single bite, her parents glanced at each other.

"I realize I haven't asked you why you were out running so late at night," Claudia said, and at the knowing look on her mother's face, Emma recalled the central tenet of her childhood: *You shall talk about how you feel.* Until recently, she'd never had reason to hold so much back. But once this restlessness and indecision had taken hold of her, she had only presented her life as she wished it was. As a child, she had been bolstered by her parents' pride in her accomplishments, but now they were additional voices to which she had to answer.

No matter what she did, both her parents always had the casual expectation of her success.

"Running at night is the best way. You're not sure where you're going and you have to trust your feet to find the way. And I'm so busy with my dissertation that I never want to take a break until late," Emma said, and realized that lying was the right decision. Her mother's words might be inviting her to tell, but the fearful look in her eyes was imploring her not to spoil who she imagined Emma to be.

"I used to be the same way. Do you remember when I was writing my dissertation?" Leon said. "We had a tiny apartment in Harvard Square and we managed to squeeze two desks into the bedroom, which worked as long as we didn't both need to get up at the same time."

Emma forced a smile, though it was an anecdote he told so often that she felt as if she'd actually been in that apartment with them. "If you think you worked hard, you should see Steven. He'd work all night if I didn't make him take a break," she said.

"When did you start running? I'm surprised you never mentioned it," Claudia said.

"I need to be outside more," Emma said, and stabbed the remaining cupcake with a fork.

Before Steven left, they had both stayed at her parents' apartment, in the trundle bed in her old bedroom like two kids having a sleepover. Steven tried to be deferential, offering to bring her drinks or dinner, anything he could easily supply. He touched her gingerly, finally recognizing that other parts were broken as well. For so long she'd wanted him to see how lost she felt, but now she said as little to him as possible, in order to maintain the pretense that she was alone in a room. There was no point saying how she felt—he only wanted to see a small sanctioned part of her; the rest of her had to stay hidden from view. In their relationship, there was no room for the thrashing uncertain parts of herself.

Instead of talking to him, she spent her time in front of the living room windows. In the apartment she and Steven shared, their window faced a brick wall, but here, she liked that people could see her. Instead of imagining how other people spent their time, she liked to think about the various lives they might conjure for her, as though she could step inside whatever fantasies they created on her behalf. Pressing her face to the window, her hands up against the glass, she thought she saw a face staring from an opposite window, maybe someone waiting with cupped hands to catch her were she to attempt escape.

"Why won't you talk to me?" Steven had asked plaintively, but she didn't relent. Let him try in vain to get her to open up. She couldn't help but smile at having used her silence to pierce his detachment—access by any means possible. "Emma," he'd pleaded, "look at me," but she trained her gaze out the window. He came up behind her and his body asked a question of her, insisted that she offer an answer. She resisted, but only briefly. She allowed herself to be led back to the couch, allowed him to take her crutches and lay them on the floor. She lay back on the couch, Steven on top of her. Usually she liked the crush of his body upon her, pinning her down, her wrists encircled by his hands, making her feel that she couldn't go anywhere even if she tried. He was so close to her, yet had no idea that tears ran down her cheeks. He kissed her without noticing that she was curled up inside herself. As he took off her pants, she opened her eyes to see his eyes narrowed in concentration, the same as he looked when he was deeply absorbed in his work.

She pushed aside the voices that named all that wasn't right between them; she stopped thinking about the strangeness of being undressed in her parents' living room, stopped minding that a panoply of windows lay in full view. She stopped feeling the pain in her ankle. Thinking of that face across the way, and the other night watchers surely out there as well, she wriggled out from underneath and went astride him. It no longer mattered that even Steven's most intense gaze was incapable of seeing down to the part of her that wanted to flee. Only a small fraction of her was trapped here with Steven. The rest of her was illuminated in the night sky. A city of eyes watched her, a city of hands was upon her body, every touch magnified, multiplied.

THE WORLD WAS recast in primary colors. All hard surfaces were covered with foam. Children bounded from mat to mat, crawled through tunnels, and disappeared inside a maze of passageways.

In a tone of ecstatic jollity, Mike, the Gymboree instructor, was singing "Wheels on the Bus." The mothers sang along, their hands going up and down, open and shut, swish, swish, swish. Mike referred to them collectively as "the mommies" and probably made fun of them the second his bubble wand was put away. Like Steve from *Blue's Clues,* like the inimitable Mr. Rogers himself, he was a rare male visitor to their land. At the end of the day, he rode out as freely as he'd arrived.

"'The mommies on the bus say I love you, I love you, I love you,'" Mike sang, and Nina laughed. Not even the mommies on the bus were allowed to *shh, shh, shh* anymore.

"Do you think Mike has ever been on a bus with a crying kid?" Nina said to her friend Wendy and to the other mothers sitting next to them.

"The kids love Mike," said Wendy as her twins, Sophie and Harry, banged together red rhythm sticks.

It was best to just sing along. The children played with balls and scarves, the mothers monitoring the kids' interactions like UN peacekeepers, determining whether intervention was needed. When Sophie stopped banging the sticks and slid one up her nose, Wendy grabbed her hand. From her diaper bag she pulled a small plastic bottle.

"Purell, anyone?" Wendy offered, and all around her, mothers obligingly rubbed some between their hands.

When Circle Time ended, the kids moved on to the mats and jungle gym. "Be careful," Wendy called to Harry as he climbed. "I'm worried he isn't up for this today," Wendy explained. "Usually the kids sleep a solid twelve hours—they actually like going to sleep—but I don't think Harry got in his full sleep last night. He dozed in our bed while I was reading to him and I had to wake him to bring him back to his bed."

"Why didn't you leave him in your bed?" Nina asked as she nursed Lily, who still expected that at the sound of her cry, a nipple would magically appear in her mouth.

"You sound like my husband—he thinks anyone can get a kid to sleep. He has no idea how complicated it is. I'm doing Weissbluth, and he says that anytime a child sleeps somewhere besides his own bed, it doesn't count as sleep. It's not the good kind," Wendy said, waving to Sophie and giving a smile intended to telegraph confidence that *You can do it! I like the way you're climbing up there, all by yourself!!*

While the other kids returned their musical instruments to the basket, Max refused to surrender his tambourine. He rustled against Nina's leg, and she tried to read his face, which could register a grownup's range of feelings, even if he didn't yet know how to name them.

When Mike tried to convince him to put away the tambourine, Max ran to the far reaches of the room. Preparing to give chase, Nina kissed Lily's fuzz-dusting of hair and put her on the mat, momentarily grateful for her immobility. Though she still complied with the role of easygoing second child, surely the tantrums were encoded inside her, sleeper cells waiting for the right moment to emerge.

"Max, sweetie, it's going to be fun, okay? Remember how much fun you had on the slide?" Nina said to Max, who was now wearing the tambourine on his head, a crown of defiance that if pulled any lower would need to be surgically removed.

"Gymbo doesn't want you to be sad," Mike tried, holding his puppeted hand in Max's face.

Max lay down and began to scream and kick. The shoes came off, then the socks. As he was splayed on the floor, thrashing so furiously that he seemed to be made entirely of limbs, all the mothers stared at her. She was the pariah of Gymboree.

But Max was only getting started. Still to come, the furious striptease of T-shirt and pants, down to his Buzz Lightyear pull-up, which, after a moment's pause, came off and landed with a thud. So much for her attempt to hide the fact that Max was resisting her civilizing efforts. She'd long ago passed the stage of elimination communication and had failed countless times at potty-training-in-a-day. Now that you had to attach yourself to a particular parenting ideology, she had no choice but to embrace the new and improved Brazelton, who endorsed these extra-large pull-ups. She'd convinced Max to wear underwear for a few hours each day as "practice," but it was mere ornamentation.

The other kids weren't embarrassed to rubberneck. "He's naked! I see his penis!" they screamed. With bright cheery voices, their mothers shepherded them away, while from the corners of their eyes they watched as Nina attempted to quiet a hysterical kid, without raising her voice, without lifting a hand. *Who is the mommiest of them all?* they asked in the reflections of each other's eyes.

The red illuminated Exit signs hanging at either end of the room beckoned. If she bolted, she could add this to the secret chronicles of maternal failure: The time Max vomited as she was about to go to work, so she quickly bathed him, changed his clothes, juiced him up with Tylenol, then took him to school. The time he heard her swear, and to wrest his promise that he wouldn't repeat the word in public, she allowed him to say the word in front of her, so that in especially tender moments, he leaned close, his apple juice breath warm on her cheek, and whispered *shit* softly in her ear.

"Are you sure he doesn't want to hug Gymbo?" Mike asked, as Max writhed at her legs, as Wendy and the other moms smiled combinations of pity and pleasure.

"No," Max screamed, the same no that resounded inside her body and that she tried to swallow back down.

"*No,*" Max screamed again. "*No, no, no.*"

"One kiss for Gymbo?" Mike asked.

Nina tried to make the right words emerge. "Fuck Gymbo," she said instead.

Max narrated the way home: A mailbox, a bus, a pigeon. A pay phone, a taxi, a subway station. They passed a woman and Max loudly asked, "Why is that lady so fat?" They passed a man on crutches, and Max asked, "Why does that man only have one leg?" Nina explained that Steve was a real person but Blue was an imaginary dog. Mermaids were imaginary but dragonflies were real. Max's world was one where the real effortlessly intermingled with the pretend. As amazing as it was that her body could form another body, what truly stunned her was that she could birth a separate consciousness.

Along the way, they were joined by a menagerie of Max's imaginary friends, his favorite of whom was Maurice, who had x-ray vision and sometimes was invisible, not just imaginary. She had been amused by the emergence of these characters, Max's conversation suddenly containing references to people she didn't know. A mother she knew made birthday parties for each of her child's imaginary friends and set places for them at the dinner table, acting as though she too could see them. But Nina had decided to leave Maurice for Max alone.

"Mommy? Does Hop know his name is Hop?" Max asked.

The animal in question was all too real, hatched in the fish tank in his nursery school classroom and now living as their summer guest in a small glass bowl on what used to be her desk. Max had named him Hop, in anticipation, though at the moment he was still in the nebulous territory between tadpole and frog.

As Max talked, Nina realized that coming toward her was the crazy woman whom, through a coincidental confluence of schedules, she saw nearly every day. Today she was wearing a sequined blue beret, a loosely knit white sweater with a red bra underneath, and a floor-length pink satiny skirt that, in a previous life, was probably the inner lining to another skirt. On her feet she wore white lace-trimmed bobby socks and black patent leather Mary Janes; from the knees down, she was a little girl dressed for a birthday party. Usually Nina tried to look away, but today's outfit was so outlandish that Nina couldn't help but stare.

Spotting the set of pay phones nearby, Max ran toward them, grabbing one of the dangling receivers. "Maurice?" he screamed into it.

The woman stopped walking and approached him. "Hello, beautiful," she said.

Max smiled and for a moment, they all stood still, as if someone had located the city's Pause button. Inspired by Max, Nina broke the rule prohibiting eye contact and smiled with what she thought was sympathy.

The woman's expression grew wild. "I always see you staring at me, you asshole, you crazy bitch," the woman hissed at her and spit.

Drawing back in fear, Nina glanced first at Lily, who was

sleeping blithely in the stroller, then looked around, wondering who else had heard. Ignoring Max's repeated questions of "Why did she say that to you? What did you do to her?" Nina buckled him into his spot in the stroller and left a message for Jeremy, wanting to tell him about their day which took place not miles but continents apart from his. She wasn't surprised that he was unavailable. He rarely answered when she called, and when he did, she felt like she was taking him from his work. Her anger at him reared. If by some miracle Jeremy had been the one at Gymboree, he wouldn't have needed to know how to handle Max. His presence alone—a daddy on the bus!—would have earned universal acclaim.

Rather than go home to another lonely stretch of evening, in which she would wait in vain for her husband to come home, Nina kept walking until she reached Georgia's, where displayed in the window were the three-tiered cakes that looked like the fanciful illustrations in a picture book. A new sign was hanging on the door, the words written in bright red Magic Marker: *Children of All Ages Are Reminded to Use Their Inside Voices.* Would mothers of loud children be chastened, she wondered, or would they bring the whole nursery school in to stage a protest?

As she'd hoped, Leon was still inside with his daughter and wife, their faces bisected by the white grids of the windows. She looked more closely and saw that she had been right. His daughter was the one she'd seen in the window. Leon and his wife were the couple whose quiet contentment she'd watched and envied.

But now that image came apart. In the daylight, their expressions didn't match what she'd envisioned. The wife, whose back was to Nina, was talking but no one was listening. She reached for her daughter, who pulled her hand away. Instead of appearing bold and unabashed, the daughter looked small and uncertain. If Leon noticed the tension in the exchange, he showed little reaction. Glancing at his watch, at his phone, at the people next to them, he seemed so distant he may as well have been sitting at a different table.

From the privacy of her apartment, Nina felt entitled to watch: flip off the lights and they were hers. Outside, in public, people would wonder why she was standing here for so long. But curiosity trumped self-consciousness. She needed to know why Leon had told her that his wife was the one screaming. She needed to match the wife's face to the enraged voice, needed to look at their daughter's eyes and see if that glimmer of freedom was still evident.

Nina busied herself with the kids, dispensing snacks, wiping imaginary crumbs from their cheeks. It took patience and luck. A passing bus backfired, Max screamed, and the wife turned around. Through the window, Nina recognized her former professor, Claudia Stein. It was no longer a stranger she'd been watching but someone she knew.

GHOST STATIONS WERE in existence throughout the city, ten of them in all, sealed off but intact. The old 91st Street station, once a stop on the 1 train, was fleetingly visible from the window of a passing train. The tiles of the Worth Street station could be briefly, faintly seen. But City Hall, the station that Jeremy had caught sight of the week before, was the most majestic of all.

Designed by George Heins and Christopher Grant La Farge, it was used until 1945, when the trains became too long to fit into the circular station. Though it was closed to the public, it continued to serve as the turnaround for the 6 train, the vaulted ceilings and intricate tile work a testament to the grandeur that once was.

Instead of drafting the documents Richard needed, Jeremy spent the week reading about this former crown jewel of the IRT. The management of the firm had blocked many non-work-related sites, but not even the most demanding of partners would think to block the website of a man who drew the subway in immaculate detail, every inch of station correct, every tile of mosaic in place. Instead of paying attention on a conference call, Jeremy found an article about brakemen who hid old train cars in unused tunnels so they wouldn't be scrapped. He found a support group for so-called foamers who rode in the front cars of the subway, their faces pressed to the window for the best view of the tracks.

He read the blogs of urban explorers in Portland and Boston and New York who traveled through underground drainpipes and subway tracks in search of infrastructural treasures. On one blog he came across, an underground explorer who called himself Magellan claimed that he and his band of explorers donned black trench coats and sunglasses to navigate abandoned New York City subway stations and scale the walls of condemned buildings, planting black flags once they'd reached their destinations.

At first this account sounded little different from the other blogs, but he startled at the bio Magellan had posted. When he wasn't leading his clandestine group on surreptitious missions to the hidden parts of the city, he worked a mindless job in a New York City skyscraper, which had inspired him to begin his explorations. On the blog, Magellan recounted the story of the structural defect in his office building which, upon being discovered in the 1970s, required workers to stabilize the skyscraper, secretly installing metal rods in each of the offices and adding a massive weight to the roof. Magellan claimed to have bought a hardhat at a costume shop and sneaked onto the rooftop to see the contraption on which their lives depended.

Recognizing the building as his own—everyone who worked in the Citicorp building knew this disturbing fact but tried to forget it—Jeremy e-mailed Magellan and skeptically asked how he'd made it past the security offices housed on the top floor. Magellan was probably a fifteen-year-old in Idaho with Internet access and an overactive imagination, but even so, Jeremy kept reading his blog, hoping it was true. He became newly curious about his coworkers; each person he passed in the hall harbored a similar longing to be somewhere else.

"Do you know when he's going to be back?" Jeremy asked

Richard's secretary when he finally finished drafting the first of numerous documents that were so urgently needed.

"He used to tell me everywhere he was going," the secretary said. "Now I have no idea what he's up to. Every afternoon, he puts that vest on and runs out of here as though his life depended on it."

In his mind Richard was also donning a trench coat, holding out the black flag. But it was impossible to believe — Richard was probably at the dentist, getting a root canal. Even so, Jeremy felt newly free. He told his own secretary he had a meeting and he left the office. Richard liked to tell stories of the irresponsible associates he'd encountered in the course of his career: the one who went on vacation in the middle of a major deal and never once checked his voice mail, the one who left a closing unfinished because her cat was sick. If Jeremy was caught, future associates would hear about the lawyer who had an urgent need to learn about an abandoned subway station. They would hear about someone who had seen a fleeting image from a train window and was consumed with a desire to stand inside that sealed space.

Jeremy escaped into a day that was warm and bright. Except for a few blocks at either end of his commute, it was rare for him to be outside. Squinting from the excess of visual stimulation, he jumped at the sight of a police car, as if an unsanctioned afternoon off was an actual crime. In front of the New York Public Library, he pulled out the *Michelin Guide to New York City* that Nina had bought him long ago, which they were still waiting to use. If he really were a tourist, he'd walk around the building, studying every detail. He'd ride by his office on the upper deck of a red sightseeing bus; the partners at his firm would spot him among the camera-wielding tourists, and for the moment before the bus turned the corner, they'd wonder, *Don't we know him?*

In accordance with the library's rules, Jeremy turned off his BlackBerry but wished they'd confiscate it at the door. In the main reading room, he searched for "City Hall Station." He brought call numbers and titles to the librarian, who sent his request in a pneumatic tube to the miles of stacks underground, in what used to be the underground water system of the Croton Aqueduct, another relic Magellan claimed to have explored.

In front of him, call numbers flashed across the screen like the ticker of the stock market. As he waited for his books, he glanced at the people around him, to see what they were so fervently studying. A man across from him took frantic notes in a tiny notebook as he read. Jeremy tried to meet his eye, but the man noticed nothing around him. The woman sitting next to him had a pile of books on her lap. On the spine of one of the books, he caught the name La Farge.

She noticed him staring and looked up in surprise. "Are you studying La Farge?" she asked.

"Actually, I'm interested in City Hall station," he said.

"Oh, then you're interested in Christopher Grant La Farge. I thought you were interested in his father, John La Farge," she said. "John La Farge was a brilliant stained-glass artist," she explained, and described the artist's use of imperfect glass in whose unpredictable lines and fractures he saw immense beauty. He embedded jewels along the borders, creating a dappled, rough texture that to her mind was superior to Tiffany's smoother, more perfect surfaces.

"La Farge was also a mural painter and textile designer, though he was a lawyer by training. His father was dead-set against it, but eventually he ran off to Paris to paint. John was notoriously difficult but he knew his own mind." He listened as she told him how John had had tensions with his father but had helped his own son launch his career. "If you want to understand the work of Christopher Grant, you should begin by researching the influence his father had upon him."

He was lost in her words until, for a moment, his mind found its way back. He would get caught being away from the office. Richard would demand to know his whereabouts. The firm would send search parties.

"I'm taking up your time," she apologized.

"Actually, I don't have anywhere I need to be."

"I assume you're a grad student?" she asked.

"I'm at Columbia. I'm studying with Marc Shultz," he said, pulling out a name he'd come across online.

"I used to teach at Columbia. I do nineteenth-century American decorative arts. Marc is wonderful. I know him well. What's your name? I've wanted to call Marc anyway. I'll tell him I ran into you."

"Maurice," he said quickly.

Seeing the call numbers of the books he'd requested flash across the librarian's screen, he stood up. Before he walked away, the woman grabbed his arm, though she seemed as startled by her gesture as he was.

"I don't know if you'd be interested, but this is something I wrote about John La Farge. It was just accepted by the *American Art Journal* for their fall issue," she said, and handed him a manuscript copy of her article. He thanked her and put it in his bag for later, then took the pile of books from the librarian.

He began to read. In the pages of a book called *New York Underground,* the city expanded. The Croton Aqueduct. The labyrinths beneath Grand Central. The steam pipes and atomic tunnels beneath Columbia. The unused Amtrak tunnels under Riverside Park.

Not even in his mind could Jeremy stay away for long. The

impetus to check his BlackBerry was instinctive. Outside the library and once again reachable, his dread descended. He had one message from Nina, four from Richard. He'd call Nina later, but Richard couldn't be put off so easily. Afraid that the sounds of the street would give him away, Jeremy waited to call Richard until he'd snuck back into his office.

"Where were you?" Richard demanded when Jeremy reached him. "You can't be out of touch like this. The client has been waiting all afternoon. The neighborhood activists convinced the local community board that there's support to block the project. There's an emergency meeting of the Land Use Committee tomorrow. The client's already in a hurry, and now these reactionary groups with no sense of financial realities are determined to create a series of roadblocks."

It was a speech Jeremy had heard countless times, and until now he had agreed without thinking about it. But the words remade themselves. Richard was speaking a language he'd ceased to understand.

"Some of these old buildings really should be landmarked. They're beautiful," Jeremy said.

Richard laughed, though it sounded more like he was choking. "No one has touched this building in forty years. Are we supposed to save it just for the sake of saving it?" he asked, and rattled off a list of what needed to be done. "I don't know what's going on with you, Jeremy, but your heart isn't in your work."

Jeremy was afraid to say anything, except to promise that he would get started right away. He followed Richard's instructions but did the bare minimum, producing the kind of sloppy work he'd always derided in other lawyers. He'd once worked so slavishly, paying attention to every last detail, in order to see another Royalton building fill in the skyline, to reap millions for clients who didn't know his name. All those nights of never coming home when he said he would, of forgetting he was anything other than his work. If the deal fell apart, all he'd feel was relief.

He printed out extra copies of the documents he had drafted and put them in his briefcase, not yet sure what he was planning to do with them. Taking newfound pleasure in defiance, Jeremy read Claudia Stein's article about John La Farge's work for Cornelius Vanderbilt II's mansion, which had once stood on the corner of 58th Street and Fifth Avenue. Cornelius died unexpectedly in 1899, and in 1926, with commercial buildings encroaching all around, his wife sold it to make way for what would eventually become Bergdorf Goodman. Knowing what the house and its art meant to her husband, she tried to preserve many of the great works contained inside, dividing them among museums and family residences.

Many of La Farge's murals and windows were moved either to museums in the city or to the Breakers, the Vanderbilts' summer home in Newport, Rhode Island. But not everything could be accounted for, and while most scholars believed that any missing works were of little consequence, Claudia Stein had become convinced that there had once existed inside that mansion a stained-glass window as important as any others La Farge had made.

Jeremy kept reading, no longer caring how late it was. She had identified several cartoon paintings that were studies for figures that didn't correspond to any La Farge creation that existed. In his studio records, she found expenditures for orders of glass billed to the Vanderbilt family that didn't correspond to any known project. She detailed an interview with a Vanderbilt descendant who remembered a striking window in the house with a blue background unlike any he'd ever seen. A relative's photo album produced a grainy image in which, she claimed, the outline of an unidentified window appeared faintly in the background.

When Jeremy next looked out the window, he imagined stained-glass windows unveiled from behind walls, and dark subway tunnels giving way to unexpected bursts of light.

NINA SPENT THE night in front of the computer, Googling the neighbors. She learned that Leon specialized in anxiety disorders. She found Claudia's book from ten years before about the history of American stained glass. She entered Emma's name too and found listings for the French language classes she'd taught and two conference papers she'd presented.

Since recognizing Claudia, Nina had been overcome with the urge to talk to Leon. She took the kids on evening runs to the grocery store, hoping she'd run into him on their block. Twice, she saw him sitting in his car while she was outside with the kids, and after that, she timed their walks to coincide with his mornings in the car. She stood in front of the construction site, waiting for him to pass. When she saw him on the street, she always stopped to talk, and he too was willing to linger. She had to remind herself that she didn't know him as well as she imagined, but even if he detected the longing in her expression, he wouldn't know how to interpret it. He wouldn't know what she saw out her window. He wouldn't know that she'd recognized his wife.

At home, in front of the window, she was a hunter lying in wait for some flash of movement, some rustling of life. Instead of offering solace, the view from her window made her lonelier. If only she could summon an emergency babysitter, or leave two sleeping kids by themselves for an hour—anything to be outside. As though they'd been alerted to her watchful presence, the last few nights had passed without her seeing Claudia or Leon. The only one she saw was Emma. The television, whose existence had been hidden inside a wood armoire, now glowed blue for much of the night. But finally, one night, the lights came on and Claudia and Leon took their places on the couch. Their books were open, but this was no longer a vision of shared solitude. Instead of seeing contentment, she saw only loneliness. Instead of imagining quiet murmured conversations, she saw a clipped, tense silence.

She reached for the pair of Fisher-Price binoculars her mother had given Max, part of the Outdoor Adventure set that had arrived following their last visit to her parents' house when Max looked nervously at the grass and asked if he was allowed to walk on it. As the faces across the way sharpened, so did the feeling that she was doing something wrong. But she tried to push away her guilt; if this was a crime, surely it was one without consequence or repercussion.

At the sound of Jeremy's key in the door, Nina put down the binoculars. She couldn't turn the lights on quickly enough, however, and when he came upon her sitting in the dark, binoculars next to her on the couch, he laughed.

"Stargazing?" he asked.

He was looking expectantly at her, as though arriving home at only eleven o'clock at night was a feat to be celebrated. She kissed him hello, but her mind was far from her body. She was glad she hadn't told him about her growing interest in the neighbors. Her day was filled with details, few of which he would care about, but this omission felt like a secret. Jeremy didn't have to say anything for her to read his thought: *So this is what happens when you spend your day with children.* Max had his world of make-believe. Now she had hers. If she thought

about what she'd done all day, there were no large accomplishments, nothing she could point to except the fulfillment of a
hundred different needs.

He took the binoculars. "Very high-tech. Does Max know
you're borrowing these?"

"How was work?" she asked.

"You don't want to know," he said.

"What took so long?" she asked, and he bristled. He didn't
have to say anything for her to know his response. It wasn't his
fault he worked so late, not his fault he could never come home.
With these excuses, he thought that he escaped her blame, but
now she realized that he left behind something more corrosive. She wished she could change the way she had started to
view him, but there was no way to avoid seeing his weakness.
He would always work these long hours, believing he had no
choice. He saw himself as powerless to make any change, powerless inside his own life.

"Are our neighbors up to anything exciting?" he asked.

"Nothing unusual."

"So why are you watching them?" he asked.

"I like to think about other people's lives," she said, and
pointed to the quiet scene of Leon and Claudia still reading
on the couch, long after so many other squares had darkened
or closed off. "Look—they keep the same hours you do. We
should have them over for a midnight snack."

"Hold up a sign and invite them," he said, spreading his
documents out on the table. It was hard to believe she too had
once worked these long hours, in an earlier century of their
marriage. It was hard to believe that they had once been mere
study partners, then friends. In their first year of law school,
neither of them was sure why exactly they were there, but
they both worked slavishly, lulled by the expectation that after
three years they would know what they were going to be. One

night, amid a pile of outlines and hand-scrawled notes, he had reached for her and kissed her. The notes lay crushed underneath their bodies, the next day's criminal law lecture forgotten for the moment. They happily stayed awake all night, lying side by side in bed, whispering to one another, *Tell me everything.* All semester, when they looked at the crumpled pages, they had smiled at what had been kindled between them. Even years later, when they both brought home stacks of legal documents, their lives overrun with paper, they had joked about wanting to crush those pages beneath them.

That memory was so distant now that it was a story told about two strangers. They were no longer a married couple but the co-owners of a daycare center. Their lives before kids were as fantastical, or at least as inaccessible, as life on other planets. There was no time to even entertain themselves, as they once had, by concocting a thousand and one ways in which their lives could be different. "We sell our apartment," one of them would begin. "And buy an RV." "And move to the country." "Or strap the kids to our backs and travel through Europe." "Open a small-town practice together." "Sell everything we own and go live in your parents' basement," they would say before they fell asleep and woke up the next morning to the way it had always been.

Watching fueled her restlessness. She wanted not just bodies laid bare but minds. With so many existing forms of surveillance, surely someone could invent a means of seeing inside people's heads. Online, she entered Claudia's and Leon's names in combination, as if this might turn up what she wanted to know, the search engine powerful enough to access not just posted words but private thoughts. You should be able to Google your neighbors and hear conversations that took place behind closed doors. Google your friends and uncover their varieties of unhappiness. Google your husband and find an explanation for why, on the phone or in rare moments together, he sounded more distant than usual; add in the words *our marriage* and see a description of who you were going to become.

Only before going to sleep did Nina remember to check on Hop, the pet Max had already started to lose interest in. Unable to recall the last time she'd fed him, Nina steeled herself to the possibility that she'd killed him.

Not only was Hop alive, he was thriving. In the absence of attention, Hop had taken the final leap. Finally more frog than tadpole, he had emerged from the water and stood on the rock, calmly taking in his surroundings. It was almost midnight, but Nina tiptoed into Max's room.

Breaking the cardinal rule of their existence, Nina woke a sleeping child. Max opened his eyes, confused, then thrilled. In the living room, they all looked into the bowl, Jeremy taking a break from his work, Max leaning in so close that his breathing fogged the glass.

"How did Hop know how to become a frog?" Max asked them.

"That's just what they do," Jeremy explained.

"It's how their bodies work," Nina said. In her son's eyes, a look of pure wonder, the world on the cusp of breaking wide open.

In the morning, Nina took the kids to the neighborhood pet store where the man behind the counter packaged six insects in a small cardboard box with holes punched in the top.

"These should last you a week. But you're going to need to feed the crickets too," he said.

While Nina worried about the prospect of housing an entire food chain, Lily waved to the fish and Max eyed the snakes, deciding which animal he wanted next. There was no need to trek to the Central Park Zoo when they could wander through a store in which chameleons, lizards, and turtles were stacked in glass tanks. At night, when the lights were turned off, the store was aglow with eyes. Taped to the back of the tanks were pictures of tropical escapes, the same lush fantasies that hung in the window of the travel agency next door. But only the geckos were fooled by these backdrops, their arms and legs suctioned to the back of their tanks, stunned to come up against glass.

While they gazed at the animals, Wendy came into the store to order five hundred goldfish for Hippo Park's summer carnival which she had volunteered to organize. Still embarrassed by the Gymboree tantrum, Nina pretended not to see her and tried to walk out. But there was no escape; the kids caught sight of each other and Harry threw his arms around Max, suddenly long-lost friends. Together, they pressed their faces to the tank of baby gerbils in a bald, red, wriggling heap.

"They have to separate the daddies because they might eat the babies," Wendy explained matter-of-factly.

"Do the mommies ever eat the babies?" Sophie asked.

"The mommies! Of course not," Wendy said as the kids moved on to the rats, exclaiming over them as though they were exotic creatures never before seen in the city.

"Can we get one?" Sophie asked.

"I'm so glad to see you taking such an interest in animals, Sophie," Wendy said, and turned to Nina. "Normally I have a no-screen-time policy, but I decided to make an exception for *National Geographic* DVDs."

"Please?" Sophie begged.

"You have a goldfish, honey," Wendy said.

"I'm sick of Swimmy," Sophie said.

"What do you have?" Wendy asked Nina as they walked out together.

"We have a frog. Or at least now we do. Max brought home

one of the class tadpoles," Nina said. Frog trumped fish. She's exposing her child to nature, bolstering his sense of competency. She's willing to feed live crickets to live frogs, all for the sake of her child.

"Can you believe that sign?" Wendy said when they'd walked farther uptown and passed Georgia's. "When I saw it a few days ago, I thought it had to be a joke. It's not really my problem, I know. In a few months I won't even be living in the city. But it's the principle that matters. I'm not going to let them get away with this. I'm going to call the owner and—"

"That bitch," Sophie said.

Wendy's face turned as pink as Sophie's wardrobe. "What did you say?"

"You said, 'That bitch hates kids.'"

"No one hates kids, honey," Wendy soothed. "You must have misheard me. And I certainly don't remember using that word, but it does sound like that's what you heard, doesn't it?" Wendy turned to Nina. "They're upset that they were yelled at by a stranger a few weeks ago." She turned back to the kids. "Were you scared? Do you want to talk about it again?" Wendy said.

Kids could say what they wanted, but the mothers were supposed to speak softly and have eternal patience. They talked to their kids this way, Nina realized, not because they wanted to respect their needs, but because they were terrified. The truth they took such great pains to cover: the kids were in charge.

"Do you ever get angry at them?" Nina asked.

Wendy looked up in surprise. "Of course not. They're delicious," she said as Sophie tugged on her arm, and Wendy gave that same joyous gaze, that same indulgent smile. Underneath perfect, Nina realized, she would only find more perfect.

• • •

"We're just going in for a minute," Nina said to Max and Lily once Wendy and her kids walked away and she realized that Leon was inside the café, reading.

Offering a prayer to the God of Tantrums, she navigated the double stroller into the café. Leon looked up at her with surprise, but it was apparent from his face that he was glad to see her.

"You just missed the old couple who scream at each other in public," he said, sitting at the same table where she'd seen him and his family a few weeks before.

"They upgraded from Starbucks?"

"They started fighting as soon as they sat down. It's hard to follow the argument, because they start up so quietly. Next time I should ask them to speak up."

"Ask for some background information," Nina said.

"Give me a list. I'll go up to them and say, 'You know that woman with the two kids? Here's what she wants to know.'"

He invited her to sit, and she did, surprised to feel so comfortable with him when her other friendships had been whittled down to those people whose kids were close in age to hers. Until now, she'd thought of men his age only as fathers, not friends.

A half-eaten cupcake sat on Leon's plate. At every table in the café, adults were eating cupcakes. Only one table was without food, and there, with a woman, was her neighbor Dog Man, though because he was neither in the lobby of their building nor with the dog, it took her a moment to recognize him.

"You're staring," Leon said.

"He lives in my building," she said.

"You know who she is, don't you?" Leon said. "She's the owner of the café."

"He likes to complain," Nina said. "He hangs angry signs all over our lobby."

"Whatever it is, they're taking it very seriously. Neither of them looks happy," he said.

"Believe me, he's thrilled to have a complaint," she said.

"You should sit closer," Leon teased, and though Nina laughed, she felt a flicker of guilt. It was one thing to spy on strangers, but he had started to feel like a friend. When she talked to Leon, she couldn't erase the picture of him sitting across from his wife, nor could she forget the image of his daughter and her boyfriend entwined on the couch.

"Are you okay?" Leon asked.

"Do I look something other than tired?"

He cocked his head, studying her face. "I'd say wistful," he decided. "Come on, what do you mommies say? 'Use your words.'"

She could say something about Jeremy or the kids—pull something from the growing stockpile of discontent or from one of the neighboring piles of joy. She could confess that she was tired, not because the kids were still up several times each night, but because it didn't matter where Jeremy's body was when his mind was increasingly at work. What she felt most fully of him was his absence. No matter what beliefs she and Jeremy had long ago set out with, she was in this alone.

"I know your wife," Nina said, trying for casual, but something more complicated broke into her voice.

"Really. How?"

"I went to Columbia. I took her class."

"How did you know she's my wife?" he said.

"I saw you here a few weeks ago. I was walking past."

"Was she a good teacher?"

"I loved her," Nina confessed.

"I don't suppose she seemed like the type of person to be screaming out the window. I probably shouldn't have told you that," he admitted.

"Don't worry, I don't think she has any idea who I am. I see her around the neighborhood, but she never remembers me."

"She's terrible with faces. And she's very preoccupied these days. She's not teaching anymore and is spending a lot of her time at the library because she can't concentrate at home. Emma's cast is coming off next week, but Claudia is convinced that it's more than just the ankle, and she's probably right. She usually is when it comes to Emma."

"What do you think it is?" she asked.

He lowered his voice. "I don't know. I try, but after all my years as a parent, the truth is, I really have no idea," he said, and this time, she heard not just friendly banter between parents but the darker undertones as well. She stopped seeing him through the frame of a window or the crosshairs of her mind's imaginary lens and instead saw him as he sat before her. On his face was a sadness and vulnerability she hadn't seen before. At the corners of his eyes, wrinkles of worry and fatigue that made him look older. At their epicenter, pools of discontent.

"I want to go home," Max said.

From his inflection Nina could gauge how much time remained before a meltdown. She promised they would go in one minute. She would buy cupcakes on the way out. She rummaged through the diaper bag. Every pretzel bought ten seconds. A package of goldfish crackers, five gorgeous minutes.

"Are you interested in stained glass? Is that why you took Claudia's class?" Leon asked.

"It was a nineteenth-century survey class. I majored in art history and at the time I was considering going to graduate school. I wanted to be like her. She used to have so much passion in her voice when she lectured. I even went to talk to her once, hoping she would encourage me," she said.

"And did she?" Leon asked.

"I asked a lot of questions but was too shy to say more. She probably saw countless students like me who weren't sure what to do with their lives. Even if she had encouraged me, I probably wouldn't have pursued it. I decided to go to law school because I was sure that I'd graduate and always know exactly what I was doing. But on maternity leave, I started to question why I was a lawyer in the first place. When I gave notice, all I had to do was explain my decision in terms of the kids. I didn't have to admit how little I liked my job. I'm supposed to claim that I'm fulfilled by being home, but the truth is, I'd be working if I liked what I was doing."

"Are you still interested in art?" Leon asked.

"It's been so long since I thought about it. I don't know what I'm interested in anymore," Nina said.

Inside his pocket, his cell phone rang, but he made no move to answer it. Nina made halfhearted motions to pack up, but she lingered. The tingling in her body took her by surprise—since Lily was born, her body belonged primarily to the kids. Lily lunged at the sight of her nipples; Max liked to fall asleep lying atop her. Her most titillating fantasy was of a bed in which she slept undisturbed.

"If you ever want to rekindle your interest, Claudia has a great library. I'm sure she'd be happy to have you come over and borrow a book," Leon said, and scribbled his cell phone number on a napkin.

She looked around, worried that her feelings had been evident. She should ask herself what she was doing. She should retreat to a safer place instead of standing on the edge of something she wasn't willing to name. And yet, a voice inside her, one she hardly knew existed, pushed aside her impulse for caution.

"When?" she asked.

N THE READING room of the New York Public Library, Claudia waited for Maurice. Several times her eyes played tricks on her—every man who entered the room was, for a moment, the one she was waiting for.

In vain, Claudia tried to reassemble an image of Maurice. She remembered the dark hair and glasses, but his facial features had blurred. When she met him, she'd thought of him as close in age to Emma. But now he was nearer to her age, more distinguished, more sure of himself. When she first felt Maurice's eyes on her, she had worried that she was supposed to know him, but if he'd been her student, she'd never remember his name. She could recall every detail of a work of art, but names and faces slipped irretrievably from her mind. She had been baffled by his apparent interest, then flattered. Though her impulse was to pretend to be unaware that he was watching her, she had forced herself to meet his eye.

Waiting for him to say something, she had followed his gaze to the pages on her lap and understood. It was not her but John La Farge he was curious about. But rather than being disappointed, Claudia had been even more intrigued. The possibility of a shared interest was as tantalizing as if it were her face that had captivated him. To discover in someone a mutual love for a subject was as alluring as any other kind of love.

If she were to see him again, she would get his number,

ask if he wanted to meet for a cup of coffee, to discuss the La Farges, his and hers. She and Maurice would pore over pictures and descriptions. She would describe how the abundance of color and the play of light in these windows had long ago captivated her, and confess her desire to establish the existence of one more La Farge window. Though it was unlikely she'd be able to locate the actual window, it was enough to prove that after all the windows La Farge had completed, he had the vision and drive to create one last great work.

Claudia had shown Leon her article when it was accepted for publication, but as far as she knew, it lay buried in his piles of unread newspapers and journals, an oversight she tried not to take personally. There was no point raising the issue, no point protesting the givens of their life. It was easier to talk about Emma, who had become agile on her crutches and was out most nights with friends.

"The cast is coming off next week," she'd reminded Leon as she sat in her customary place next to him on the couch.

"I know. I was thinking about going with her to the doctor," Leon had said. "I thought it would be nice for her to have company."

"We could all go. We can make it a celebration," Claudia had suggested, but then reconsidered. "Actually, you should take her by yourself. You should have some time alone with her."

When he readily agreed, she felt envious, though for years she'd wanted Leon to be more present for Emma. "You're her father. Can you at least try?" she had asked him countless times, to no avail. She and Emma had grown accustomed to his absence—even when he was right beside them, he had an air of impatience and distraction. When she first met Leon, they'd both understood the desire to surround themselves with their work. The sight of him immersed in reading, his mouth slightly open as he bent over a book, enabled her to sink more fully inside her own work; in some alternate sphere, their respective subjects interacted with one another, his people living inside her buildings, enchanted by her windows.

But as his career flourished and hers floundered, as she was drawn deeper into the vortex of family life and he farther from it, she alone had discovered the impossibility of living for work alone. He still spent his nights at his desk, hardly noticing that she was no longer at hers. Any notion of being engaged in a silent conversation had faded. No longer expecting more from Leon, she had stopped asking about his work, having realized that he had little need to talk. She had stopped trying to discuss her own work as well. It was better to say nothing than to have your excitement met with indifference; better not to talk than to find you were talking to yourself.

In the library the next day, she checked Columbia's departmental website. She Googled Maurice's name and subject matter, hoping that even with such scant information she might find mention of a talk he'd given or a paper he'd published. She searched for his dissertation topic, using every combination she could think of, but she found no trace of him. Claudia e-mailed the former colleague with whom Maurice was studying, under the guise of telling him about her article. In her last sentence, in as casual a tone as she could manage, she wrote that she'd happened to meet a promising student of his. She was embarrassed at her persistence, sure that her intentions, murky as they were even to her, were apparent.

A day later, her colleague sent back congratulations but said there must have been some mistake. He had no student named Maurice, not now or anytime that he could remember.

This man, this Maurice, had such a presence in her mind, and yet, as far as she could tell, he didn't actually exist.

N HIS CAR with Emma, Leon didn't know what to say. On the ride to the doctor, Emma had chattered to him with nervous energy, but now, on the way home, apparently it was his turn. The silence felt like proof of his failure. If Claudia were riding in the back seat, she would certainly see it that way. She liked to accuse him of not sufficiently trying—with Emma, but most of all with her. For most of his married life, he had been assaulted with the word *try*, a forked weapon always sharpened and ready.

As he stole helpless glances at her, Emma slumped in her seat and studied passing cabs. She rolled down the window and changed the radio station, which apparently she still considered her prerogative to do.

"So," he said, "do you think you're ready for four flights of stairs?"

"It's only been six weeks. Are you trying to get rid of me already?" she asked.

"This was a short-term lease, remember. Valid only as long as your ankle was broken. When is Steven coming back?"

"In a few more weeks, but even then, I'm not sure I'm going to be ready to go home," she admitted.

"I'm assuming this isn't because of your ankle," he said.

"Dad. Shouldn't that be obvious to you by now?"

He startled, surprised at her directness. He had always assumed that Claudia and Emma were so close that there was little need for him. But how wrong he was to think he'd get away
so easily. In family life, there were surely no bystanders.

"I thought that the last thing you needed was for us to force
you to talk before you were ready. I assumed you needed your
space," he said.

"No, that's what you needed," she said. They were already
close to home and Leon circled the block, in search of parking.

"See, I gave up my parking spot for you. That has to count
for something, doesn't it?" he said.

"That's true love."

"I'm sorry if I haven't made this evident enough, but I hope
you know that you can tell me anything."

His voice was strangled with discomfort, but the right
words had emerged nonetheless. He found a spot and pulled
in. When he looked directly at her, she began to cry. Making
him promise he wouldn't tell anyone, she confided that she'd
barely touched her dissertation in months. She told him about
the night she broke her ankle, how she and Steven had been at
home, he working at the desk in their bedroom while she paced
the living room, no longer able to maintain the pretense that
everything was fine.

"Steven was staring at me like he had no idea who I was,
but I didn't care. Nothing mattered, just this need to run. It
was almost midnight but I ran from our apartment to Riverside
Park, with Steven following me. I know it sounds crazy, but I
thought that if I could run faster, this would be the moment
that changed everything. I thought I could outrun not just Steven but myself," Emma said, as he waited in silence, afraid that
if he made a sound, she would stop talking.

"Near the entrance to the park, my flip-flop caught between
the cobblestones and my ankle twisted. I thought I would have

time to catch myself. Or that Steven would steady me. Or that I would land on the grass and end up with nothing more than a pair of skinned knees. But when I heard the cracking sound, it wasn't only pain I felt. There was this overwhelming relief, like some sort of decision had been made on my behalf."

Emma faltered. "I keep trying to convince myself that the problem is just school, but I know it's Steven too. I keep hearing these voices telling me it's not too late, I can still back out, I can still run."

He took in her words. A month ago, he would have said that Emma and Steven were fine. Emma looked happy, which at the time seemed sufficient though now was so little. She was in no hurry to leave the car, and it brought to mind a memory of her he'd long forgotten. On family vacations, she'd liked to climb into the way-back of the station wagon, where she'd lie down unbelted as they drove late into the night, her sleep punctuated by the lights of passing cars, safe in the knowledge that when they arrived at their destination, she would be carried inside, to bed.

"What does Steven have to say about all of this?" he asked.

"I haven't told him. I'm just so glad he's gone. For the first time in months, I feel like I can breathe," she said, and in an instant, his arms were around her. It had been ages since he'd held her like this, and he worried his tentativeness was evident, as though a hug were a contortionist's most challenging feat.

They got out of the car and walked down West End. On the corner of 102nd, a woman was collecting signatures. She had a card table stacked with flyers in shades of fluorescent green and yellow, words in bold and all caps, every sentence erupting in exclamation marks. **SAVE OUR NEIGHBORHOOD!!! NO MORE DEVELOPMENT!!!!**

He and Emma watched as another woman approached the table and read the flyers. She was wearing orange cowboy boots and a yellow lace dress that, despite the summer heat, was partially covered with a green wool sweater.

"We have a chance to stop this development. The community board is on our side, and we're prepared to fight," said the woman behind the table, and smiled encouragingly. "Would you like to sign?" she asked hopefully, even though this oddly dressed woman was probably a resident of the San Souci, the neighborhood SRO whose presence various community activists had protested to no avail.

"You'll sign, won't you?" she called as Leon and Emma walked past. She watched him, awaiting recognition.

"We've met before. I'm Barbara, I'm friends with Claudia," she said. "And you must be her daughter," she said to Emma.

Leon feigned recognition, but not quickly enough because he saw the flicker of hurt on her face, wanting more than a signature.

"I like the new buildings," he said.

She narrowed her eyes in distaste, yet her mouth revealed an inadvertent smile; having been ignored all day, she was ready for a debate. "Are you aware of the damage done to the quality of life by these monstrosities?"

"I am," he said. "But what can I do? I like them anyway."

Glaring at him, Barbara gathered a handful of flyers. "I would assume your wife doesn't feel the same way. Can you give these to her? I've been trying to get her involved."

"She's been busy," Leon said with an apologetic shrug.

"We're all busy. But someone needs to stop this," Barbara chided him as she began to pack up the table.

Leon gladly ended the conversation with Barbara, whom he now recognized as the owner of one of the warring dogs he watched from his car. That morning, as the dogs circled and barked, the owners had avoided looking at one another. When intervention was finally required, the owners yanked back on the leashes, and the dogs were momentarily suspended in mid-air, wet, red mouths open, tongues hanging. Leon couldn't tell whether the people or the dogs had initiated the bad feelings, but they all shouldered them equally now.

Continuing down the block, he looped his arm through Emma's to steady her, afraid she might re-injure herself. Once he had a patient so overwhelmed by caring for both her young children and her ailing parents that she happened to break her arm three times in one year, accidents each of them, although he'd of course wondered.

"I don't want you to say anything to Mom," Emma said.

"I don't know if I can keep this from her," Leon said.

"Pretend I'm one of your patients with the right to confidentiality."

"I'll have to bill you," he joked.

They laughed, though Leon remained unsettled. If Emma really were his patient, he'd know better what to say. In the midst of a recent session, his tightly controlled patient had interrupted her discourse on what her twins had eaten that day to tell him how much she hoped to run into him in the neighborhood. At first he had felt his customary impatience toward her, but he softened, his sympathy expanding. She was so embarrassed at her confession, as though she'd come up with the most outlandish fantasy ever uttered in this room. "And what would that feel like?" he'd asked her. "What would it mean for you to see me in that way?" As he listened to her wish, and understood the need to have more than she'd been given, he'd thought of Emma, his hand almost reaching for his phone. Upon arriving home that day, he'd offered to accompany her to the doctor because he had been struck by a fear. All these years, had he placed himself in an approximation of the therapist's role, willing only to discuss needs but never gratify them? When he'd offered to drive Emma, she had looked at him with surprise. It was such a small gesture, yet her gratitude made it appear that he'd promised something far larger.

Leon stopped walking and looked searchingly at Emma. She gripped his hand, mistaking the pained look on his face for sympathy. But there was no escape from the truth: today's small effort notwithstanding, his experience of fatherhood was never something to which he'd given sufficient thought. It existed closer to the margins of his life than at its center.

"I still don't know what to do," Emma said.

"I know. Neither do I," Leon said, and wished he could give Emma what she wanted. If only he could ask her explicitly, "What do you need me to do?"

They continued walking, and at the construction site on their corner, Leon paused, glad to have an excuse to lighten the mood. In a matter of weeks, the site had progressed from a razed ground of rubble to a completed foundation. In a few more months, the steel frame of the building would be completed. In a year, the interiors would be in place. At least in this one spot, there was no indecision, no inaction.

"There's one of Mom's former students. I'll introduce you," he said, noticing Nina standing in front of the construction site. She was holding Lily while Max peeked through an opening in the plywood barrier.

"You really are out here all the time," Leon said as Max picked up in the middle of an agitated conversation with an imaginary friend who was apparently suffering from a host of phobias.

"Maurice is invisible and he has x-ray vision, but he's still afraid of the city," Max said to Emma.

"This friend of yours is smart. If it were up to me, I'd tell him to pack his bags and move to the country," Emma said. As Max launched into an account of Maurice's day, Leon studied Emma's smiling face as she asked Max about the continued

adventures of Maurice. His daughter was a quick-change artist. No one would know that a few minutes before, she'd been
crying in his arms. Her voice grew more animated, and he was
reminded of the child she'd once been. She'd yet to shed some
wide-eyed hopefulness, some inner playfulness. Now that she
was encountering the pains of adulthood, she would lose those
qualities, which was probably for the best—it was the only way
to survive the sadness inevitably awaiting her.

"Maurice isn't usually this friendly to strangers," Nina said.
"He must like you."

"They're cute kids," Emma said. "And anyone whose imaginary friend has x-ray vision is someone I want to hang out
with."

"Emma used to be the most highly sought-after babysitter
in the building. Once I found her in our apartment with the
kids she was baby-sitting for, as well as a group of friends that
they'd picked up along the way. They were all sitting on the living room floor, mesmerized by a story Emma was telling—and
it was pretty clear she was just making it up as she went along,"
Leon said.

"If you ever need a babysitter, you should call me," Emma
said to Nina, and Leon looked at her in surprise.

Emma shrugged. "I'm not doing anything right now. It'll
be good for me. And in a few weeks, I'll be steadier on both
feet and be able to keep up with Maurice."

As they spoke, the woman with the disheveled hair and mismatched clothes drew closer to them. In an effort to be polite
and treat her like everyone else, the adults ignored her. Only
Max waved and looked mystified when she failed to respond.

"She's lived in the neighborhood for years," Leon said when
she was out of earshot.

"How do you know?" Nina asked.

"I used to see her around, and once she came up to me and

started talking. It was easier to listen than find a way to extri-
cate myself. That was a long time ago, though, and she was in
much better shape. She has schizophrenia and is probably not
taking her meds."

"He likes to diagnose people," Emma said. "It's an occupa-
tional hazard."

"I'll have to be careful," said Nina.

"Don't worry, I only diagnose strangers. It's much safer,"
Leon said.

"You don't remember who she is?" Nina asked.

"That's right, you're interested in these things. You want to
know everything about everyone," he said, and Nina blushed,
which sparked inside him an inexplicable happiness.

Emma glanced at him, ready to go home, but he pretended
not to notice. No sooner had he resolved to be more fully present than he began to seek a way out. He couldn't help himself.
He was stirred by the way Nina's eyes once again rested on him
a moment too long. Regardless of her intention, it was both
baffling and alluring. He'd started talking to Nina because she
was a stranger, with no claims on his time. But if you kept talking to strangers, he realized, eventually they became friends.

R ICHARD CAME INTO Jeremy's office and closed the door, a sure sign of trouble. Upset that the permits hadn't come through yet, he wanted to confirm that Jeremy had filed everything properly. With his heart pounding, Jeremy assured him that he had. Having fallen hopelessly behind, there was no choice but to lie to Richard and await the next set of commands.

"I promised the client that there were no grounds to stop the building, but even so, I want you to go back over all the diligence. Look over every scrap of paper. We don't want any surprises," Richard instructed, then said he would again be away for a few days. Jeremy didn't bother to ask Richard where he would be because any question would be treated as an intrusion.

Jeremy used to believe there would be an end in sight, but a few weeks before, he'd been in Richard's office when the head of the firm called to ask Richard to work on a new deal. Already swamped, Richard had pleaded to get out of it, but to no avail. There was never an end; the rest of their working lives would be measured out in billable hours. At least his father had the Sabbath; in the last few minutes before sundown, he'd walk into the house, emptying his pocket of his wallet, his keys, his cell phone. The world was divided by this impenetrable line. The phone and fax machine might ring, but for that one day, he belonged solely to them. Now Jeremy had no mandated break. It was one of the few things about Orthodoxy that Jeremy regretted giving up, the chance to become unreachable.

The firm was unusually empty that night, and since face time was useless with no one to see it, Jeremy went home, wondering if he might catch one of the kids still up. He had sworn to himself that his kids wouldn't try to keep themselves awake, as he had, in order to hear their father arrive home from work. Yet every choice he'd made led him away from that promise. To Lily he was a voice on the phone saying good night, step three in the five-part bedtime routine. She probably mistook his voice for one of the talking toys. If he ever came home early, Max was confused, then had five stories to tell him, three toys to show him, two games he wanted to play. It would take hours to do everything Max had in mind and require impossibly empty days with nowhere they needed to be.

When he got home, the kids were asleep, but Nina was in her usual spot on the couch.

"How are your neighbors tonight? Are they up to anything exciting?" he asked.

"I've stopped watching them," she said.

He spread his documents out on the table, and Nina looked over his shoulder at them.

"There's unexpected opposition and the client is flipping out," he said.

"Do they have any legal basis?" she asked.

"Not as far as we know, but I'm a little behind," he admitted.

"What does Richard think?"

"He's nervous, but every time I talk to him, he's either rushing out of the office or distracted."

"Did you ask him what's wrong?"

"Yes, I took his hand and told him that if anything was bothering him, he could talk to me."

"Really. What do you think it is?"

"Midlife crisis? Who knows," he said.

This was the moment when he should tell her about his glimpse of City Hall station, followed by the outings to the library. But having become so accustomed to lying to Richard, he found it easy to do the same with Nina. It was the same way he had been with his father, pretending to be Orthodox. If he had told his father that he no longer believed, his father would have felt betrayed. If he were to describe to Nina his outings to the library, she'd add up the hours when he could have been home. From everyone, he was stealing time, defying expectations, but what of his own life belonged to him? There was no room to consider what he really wanted. He had always imagined that when he no longer thought of himself as Orthodox, he would feel only freedom, but of course it wasn't so simple. The world was supposedly wide open, but he had found other ways to close himself in.

When Nina gave up and went to bed, Jeremy stayed at the table, intermittently dozing. He fought the urge to join Nina, or to ask her to wait up. When it grew light, Jeremy went to the window and picked up the binoculars Nina had left on the windowsill. Apparently she was still watching after all. At first he'd enjoyed her interest in their neighbors' lives; he'd always felt like one part of her hovered dreamily overhead, but close enough that he could still pull her back. Lately, though, she'd seemed out of reach and he'd started to wonder what the neighbors' lives really meant to her. He held back from asking because he wasn't sure he wanted to know. At the end of the day, in the perpetual middles of the night, he had no energy for long, open-ended conversation. He would surely fall asleep if he attempted any such discussion; there was no room in his day, equally no room in his mind, for anything more.

"Jeremy," Nina called, having woken up from the sound of his pacing, from the tapping of his pen, from the emptiness on his side of the bed. In a state that could no longer be called asleep but didn't yet qualify as awake, she stumbled into the living room.

"What time is it?" Jeremy asked.

"Late," she said.

Leaving his work on the table, he groggily stood up to hug Nina. He held on to her as though she had arrived in the living room on a rescue mission. He allowed himself to be led to bed, where under their blankets, Jeremy's hand found her thigh. "Are you too tired?" They were always too tired. They were destroyed, ruined, wrecked; they were exhausted, they were sapped, they were crazed. Even so, small, tentative feelings of desire peeked out. Her body made a compelling case to forgo the extra sleep, or, in Jeremy's mind, the equivalent of four units of billable time. But desire was no match for fatigue. He kissed her, she curled toward him, they fell asleep.

At his desk the next day, Jeremy studied the environmental issues, the neighborhood opposition, the historic possibilities. There were no easements, no reason to believe that construction would cause structural damage to neighboring buildings. From boxes of building department documents Jeremy pulled stacks of paper detailing the construction done since the building was built in 1897 as a townhouse and later subsumed into a larger structure. In 1963, an adjacent building was backed up to it with a party wall.

Rereading these documents, Jeremy slowed down. The building inspector had made more copious notes than was customary. In a hand-scrawled comment at the end of the last page, he had recorded that on the building's south façade, all the windows had been covered when the new building was attached. One of those, he recorded, was a stained-glass window which had been boarded up front and back before the new building was connected.

Jeremy took a lap around the office. From his desk he retrieved Claudia Stein's article and read it again, wondering if he'd fallen into a delirium brought on by sitting in one spot for too long. But if this was a dream, he'd rather stay inside it than return to the pseudo-wakefulness to which he'd been subjected for months.

In this state, more potent than the best caffeine, Jeremy's mind was newly alive with the possibility that somewhere inside the building his client had acquired, sheetrocked behind walls, sealed off by later construction, Claudia Stein's stained-glass window was embedded, lost and waiting to be rediscovered.

A RE YOU SURE you want to do this?" Nina asked when Emma called and said she was interested in baby-sitting. What did it say about her, Nina wondered, that she was suspicious of an adult who wanted to spend time with children?

Until now, she had been reluctant to hire a babysitter; if she was going to give up her job in order to be home with the kids, she wanted to actually be with them. Instead of rushing out as soon as Emma arrived, Nina was tempted to stay and talk. Emma was barely in the door, and already she was talking to the kids and laughing. Nina tried to reconcile this woman with the figure she'd seen out the window, a memory she'd replayed again and again in her mind and that now seemed as hazy as a dream. Standing before her, Emma laughed easily and seemed at ease with the kids, but in her eyes there was a hesitance that made her seem far more delicate, as though her outer cheer were simply a role she had been assigned.

"So why baby-sitting?" Nina asked.

"I'm taking some time off, from school, from my fiancé, basically from my whole life. My poor parents—they thought I knew exactly what I was doing, and now I'm taking everything apart. I guess it's never too late to have a huge meltdown, is it," Emma said, trying for lighthearted, but the pain in her voice was evident. "You probably don't want to hear this. I'm sure you have places to go," Emma said.

"No, please, I want to know," Nina said, envying the idea of every day wide open, Emma's whole life, in fact, wide open.

"When I first broke my ankle, all I wanted to do was come home. I thought that I would be able to put everything back in place. But I'm learning that the idea of home is better than actually being home," Emma said. "You can't go home again, right? I love my parents but they're the kind of people who are content with things exactly as they are. I used to refer to them as brains on a stick. I used to think I could be like them, but I'm not so sure anymore."

"Do you know what you want to do instead?" Nina asked.

"Anything but sit in a library all day. I hate my dissertation —I can't stand the thought of writing one more word. If I even open one of my books, all I think of is what I'd rather be doing instead," Emma said.

"Can you talk to your mother about it?" Nina said.

"I wish. She was thrilled when I first told her I was getting a PhD. You'd think that it was her own dream that had come true."

"What about your father?" Nina asked.

"I never used to talk to him about anything. He was always the kind of person you could joke around with, but I always had the feeling that I had a limited amount of time. But now it's easier with him—I don't know if he's changed or I have, but I can tell him more," Emma said, only realizing belatedly that Max had stopped playing and was listening to every word. Nina glanced down at him, and Emma sensed her hesitance.

"You know my parents so I probably shouldn't be telling you this," Emma said.

"I only know them from the neighborhood. I haven't really talked to your mother since I was her student. Even then, I didn't know her very well. You look so much like her, you know."

"People always tell me that. I used to look at pictures of her when she was young and think that she was me," Emma said.

"I want to do laundry," Max interrupted. He had come over to where they were standing and instead of minding that his mother was going out, he was gazing at Emma with interest.

"Are you sure you wouldn't rather go to the park?" Nina asked and explained that the laundry room had become Max's favorite place to play. Loading the machines and waiting for the clothes to be washed was his new hobby.

"Why not let him do laundry, if that's what he likes?" Emma said.

"It's such a beautiful day outside. Don't you think he should be at the park?" Nina said.

Emma laughed. "He'll have the rest of his life to feel like there's something else he should be doing."

"Fine. Do laundry," Nina relented.

Three hours was as vast as a day. She could be like Emma and do as she wished: sit in the park, ingest a whole novel, see a movie, wander through the Met. Time alone was the most endangered of species. She'd forgotten that she could leave the house with less than half an hour's worth of preparations, that she could walk the streets without narrating every car, bus, dog she passed.

Nina was standing on the corner, still deciding what to do, when a silver Honda Odyssey pulled up alongside her.

"Hop in," Wendy said, from inside. "It's my maiden voyage. I'm supposed to be practicing my driving. We just bought the car. I'm officially a soccer mom."

Nina got into the car, even though driving around Manhattan in a minivan wasn't how she'd envisioned spending her free time.

"Where are your kids?" Wendy asked as she pulled the car out among the line of oncoming cars, cringing when she was met with the honking of horns.

"They're doing laundry with the babysitter. Max is obsessed with the laundry room."

"I didn't know you had a babysitter," Wendy said.

"She's a family friend. And it's just for a few hours," said Nina.

"It's so beautiful out. Shouldn't they be at the park?" Wendy said.

"If Max loves laundry, why not let him do it?" Nina said.

"Maybe that's why your kids aren't sleeping well. I always make sure to get Sophie and Harry outside for a few hours. Otherwise they have too much energy at the end of the day."

Her voice was confident but her body gave her away. Wendy gripped the steering wheel tightly, as though she were driving at the edge of a dangerous mountain road. Her eyes were glued on the rearview mirror, trying to anticipate everyone's next move.

"Are you okay?" Nina asked.

"Of course I am. Why, do I not look okay?"

"Are you excited about moving?" Nina asked.

"Of course I am. We bought a beautiful house, with a huge backyard. When they're older the kids are going to be able to walk to school."

Such a pleasant picture. So why did Nina want to press against it until it oozed something darker?

"Why are you looking at me like that?" Wendy asked. "I'm fine."

Instead of sitting here, Nina wished she had stayed home to play with Emma and the kids. Or else she wished she were inside a fantastically messy apartment where a play group was in full swing, the kids playing on their own, the moms on couches in the next room. Instead of assaulting one another with their tales of delight, they played a game of Truth where everyone was brutally honest and no one felt ashamed afterward.

"You're always fine," Nina said. "No matter what the kids do, you're fine. You leave a fabulous job and you're fine."

"And what about you? You act like you're always fine too," Wendy said.

"Is that what you think? Because actually, no. I'm not fine," Nina admitted. "Do you ever walk around your apartment imagining all the ways you could escape? Do you survive hours in the playground by concocting alternate versions of your life? Have you ever squeezed their arms too hard, leaving the half-moon indentation of your fingernails, then when they accused you of hurting them, pretended it was an accident? Have you ever put them to bed angry, then felt so bad you purposely woke them up so you could do the night over again?"

She hadn't meant to say all this—she hadn't even known she felt all this—but there was no denying the pleasure in speaking her mind. Wendy was staring at her as though she had gone crazy, but her face took on a starker expression than Nina had seen before. Gone was the beatific smile. Gone the scripted lines that the kids were always delicious and she wouldn't miss this for the world, and there was nowhere she'd rather be, and yes, it did go so fast.

"Fine. Do you want to know what I really think? Do you know what it feels like to pour all of myself into the kids, to love them so much and want to give them every single thing they need, and yet even then, to worry that no matter how hard I try, it's not enough? Do you know what it feels like to so badly want everything to be perfect but to worry all the time that I'm going to ruin it by getting angry at them?"

After all the time they had spent together, maybe they were actually friends. "I think we all need to lose it once in a while. Maybe it would be good for them," Nina said.

"I never used to feel like I could lose control. In college, I played varsity ice hockey. Can you believe that? I was completely in control of my every move. Sometimes I try to get myself into the same zone I was in before a game, visualize myself flying across the ice, seeing only the other goal."

"Do you still skate?" Nina asked.

Wendy shook her head. "Not since the twins were born. It's like that person doesn't exist. I thought that if we moved I would feel more in control. But I keep having this nightmare that I'm driving carpool and instead of dropping the kids off, I get on the highway and keep driving until the squad cars are chasing me OJ style, and all the headlines say 'Soccer Mom Goes Crazy. Refuses to Get Out of Minivan.'"

Nina laughed. "Should I even ask how your nightmare ends?"

"According to my husband, it's going to be much easier once we move. But I always thought we'd stay in the city. The only place I said I'd move to was Australia. Do you read your kids the Alexander books? Whenever I'm having a terrible, horrible, no-good, very bad day, that's what I whisper to myself over and over—just the word *Australia*."

"When do you want to go?" Nina joked.

Wendy laughed too, though she looked like she was on the verge of tears. "Do you want to know the other crazy thing? For years, I thought soccer moms played soccer."

F INDING HER FATHER alone in the apartment, Emma circled, gauging his mood before attempting to talk. When Emma gave an especially exaggerated sigh, Leon put down his book.

"Steven is coming home today," she said.

"Is that a good thing?" he said.

"I don't know," Emma admitted. "He's been gone for almost two months and I still can't figure out what I should do. I can't even remember why I'm getting married in the first place."

"So why are you getting married?" he asked.

How could she put into words the rush of emotion that used to come over her when she was with Steven, the feeling that in his presence, she had grabbed on to something deeper and truer than was available elsewhere? Someone else might compliment her, but it meant little; the same words from Steven, so whittled down to the bare-bones truth, carried her for weeks. He pulled her toward him, into their bed, or on the floor, or up against the wall, and stared her down. "You understand me," he whispered in her ear, words that she assumed were an emotional palindrome, equally true when read in reverse.

He had proposed to her on the beach in Montauk, the same week that a hurricane was brewing off South Carolina. The storm was far off, yet the waves in Montauk crested so high that no one dared to venture in. But she had stood at the edge as the water slammed against the shore. Despite the danger, she'd felt sure that if she walked into the waves, she would be buoyant, then emerge dry and unscathed.

"At the time, it seemed so clear to me that this was what I wanted to do. When we got engaged, I wasn't even nervous. I was so sure of how happy I was," she said.

"So what changed?" he asked, and checked his watch, as she was about to describe how every decision she'd ever made was now assaulted by a barrage of questions that tore into her. There was no part of her left whole and intact. She swallowed back her words, feeling embarrassed to have taken up too much of his time. How quickly his attention faded when she was still in need of so much more. *I'm sorry but we're out of time,* she imagined him saying at fifty-minute intervals to her as well as to his patients, about whom she'd always been curious, their need for him seemingly more pressing and valid. But unlike her, they came to him with their problems. In order to get the same attention, she had to earn it with accomplishment. He was proudest of her when she needed the least.

"Are you happy?" she said, turning on him.

"It depends on how you define happiness," he said.

"Come on, Dad. What am I supposed to do with that?"

"I'm not sure what you want me to say." His expression shifted, something inside him breaking open, and for a moment he looked as lost as she felt. "I wish I had all the answers, but I really don't know," he said. "All these years, what I've wanted most was to be left alone. Is that happy? You tell me."

What strange hole in the wall had she passed through? She was used to her father, dispassionate and calm. Before she could ask him anything else, he pulled out a notepad and ordered her thoughts into columns of pros and cons. He listed for her all the reasons to stay with Steven, lined up next to all the reasons to leave. All the reasons to finish her dissertation. All the reasons to find something else to do. When she was a teenager, he'd occasionally made these lists for her when she was wrestling with a decision. Those were moments she had wanted to stretch out, adding reason upon reason, all so that he would continue talking to her. She'd never felt as organized, as listened to, as when the contents of her mind were written down with her father's pen, in neat block letters that conveyed such sure-handed authority and were so eminently readable, unlike her own scrawl that was sometimes illegible even to herself.

The door opened and Claudia walked in. Both Leon and Emma jumped as though they'd been doing something wrong.

"Come sit with us," Leon invited Claudia as Emma put the list in her pocket and stood up to leave.

"No, it's fine. I don't want to disturb you. You look like you're involved in something," Claudia said. Though she acted unbothered, Emma caught sight of pained resentment, and she understood that the hurt expression on her mother's face wasn't directed at her but at her father.

Despite her parents' pretense of normalcy, Emma was newly aware of the tension. As close as she and her mother supposedly were, she knew little of her inner life. She had managed not to know that her mother had one at all. Apparently she hadn't passed the stage when it was impossible to imagine her mother as an independent being. Never had her mother confided in her anything about her marriage; rarely had she heard her parents fighting. Whatever more complicated dynamics existed between them took place quietly behind closed doors, if at all. Rather than think of their relationship as having its own oscillations, Emma preferred them to be entirely fixed and unchanging. She would always be moving while they remained firmly in place, markers from whom she could always measure her own movement.

But now there was no denying that flash of pain across her mother's face, no way to pretend she had not seen the way her mother's eyes clouded and she drew more deeply into herself. Emma recognized on her face a loneliness she should have seen long ago. She was pulled momentarily from her own life into an unexpected view of someone else's. As she understood her own nearsightedness, her mother changed shape in her mind.

Baby-sitting was a way to exchange her family for another. It was a chance not to think about her own life. With the kids, she didn't have to worry about what she would say to Steven when she saw him later in the day. She didn't have to be anyone other than who she was. She could talk as loudly as she wanted; there was always something to laugh about and there was no-where they needed to be. Max could spend hours describing the further adventures of Maurice; they could take thirty minutes to walk a single block. As soon as she walked in the door, Max launched himself in her direction and started telling her how Maurice had recently relocated from the laundry room to the Central Park Zoo.

"Do you know, when I was a teenager, my friend and I once snuck into the Central Park Zoo at night?" she said. "Someone told my friend how to do it, and one night she told me to meet her after my parents were asleep. It was going to be our secret adventure and I couldn't tell anyone, not even my parents."

"Did you tell anyone?" asked Max.

"I didn't," Emma said, as she noticed that Nina too was listening to her story. Wanting to impress her—to appear as someone who knew what she was doing—she scooped Max up and carried him to the couch.

"I was afraid, but I decided to do it anyway. I watched the clock as I lay in my bed, and when it was ten o'clock, I tiptoed out of my room, still in my pajamas."

"Did your parents wake up?" whispered Max.

"They didn't, and when I got downstairs, my friend was waiting for me in her pajamas. 'Run!' she said, so we ran until we reached the zoo. It was closed, of course, but my friend knew how to climb over a fence, and as scared as we were, we climbed up. We jumped over to the other side and were alone in the zoo. We could see because it was a full moon, and I couldn't believe it. Late at night, when no one is around, the zoo changes and it's not really a zoo anymore. The animals aren't asleep like they always are during the day, or bored, roaming the cages. They're free to roar and run and growl."

The story she told him had at least a kernel of truth — she used to sneak out at night with friends and sprint in large groups in the park, around the lake, through the Great Meadow, thrilled to be out late. She embellished the story as she talked, letting it become as fantastical as it had felt in her mind when she looked back at that person reveling in the freedom of being outside.

"One day I'll tell you where the secret entrance is. We can go there together. You should come too, Nina," she said.

Nina laughed. "Maybe I will."

"The next full moon," Emma said as Nina stood up to leave.

Alone with the kids, Emma began to plan what to do that day. In the few weeks that she had been baby-sitting, she had taken them on bus tours of the city because Max was afraid of the train. She'd sat on the floor and strung plastic beads, while cradling Lily in her arms. While Lily rewarded her gaze with a startlingly beautiful smile, Max had bedecked her with necklaces and bracelets. When every free surface was decorated with

Max's creations, he played Candy Land against Maurice, because he said it wasn't a game grownups knew how to play.

Today Max wanted to play dress up, an activity she'd loved
as a child and still did, this chance to transform at least the
outer parts of herself. Max wore a lion costume and Emma had
a silver cape tied around her neck when they ventured to the
laundry room. While Emma bounced Lily in her lap, reciting to her the French nursery rhymes she'd had to memorize in
college, Max sat in his chair in front of the washing machine,
awaiting the climactic moment when the red light changed
from Soak to Rinse.

Emma helped herself to some of the Veggie Booty Nina
had packed in a diaper bag containing enough supplies to sus-
tain them were they to be trapped in the basement for weeks.
Around Nina she was probably supposed to put on a professional front, but she felt Nina's interest, which opened her up.
It was hard to believe she was only a few years younger than
Nina; she tried to imagine herself in Nina's life, but the fact
that she had these kids made her seem light-years away, closer
to her mother's age than her own. She wouldn't want to be her,
not exactly, but it had to be nice to feel that so much of your
life was fixed in place. It had to be nice not to want to upend
everything you had.

While they waited for the washing machine to finish, Max
rested his hand on Emma's arm, lightly grazing her skin. Max
put his imaginary friends on pause when the washing machine
rumbled and rested. A dryer stopped, and Emma unloaded its
contents onto a folding table and put in their laundry. As they
scooted their chairs over to watch the second act, a man entered the laundry room and walked over to the dryer, drawing
back in affront at the sight of the bright colors inside.

"Who touched my clothes?" he demanded, staring at Max
and Lily as though their very presence was an offense.

"I believe that would be us," Emma said, and smiled.

"Perhaps you're not aware of the rules around here, but you're supposed to wait twenty minutes before removing someone's laundry."

"Do you want us to rewash your clothes? Max would love that—anything to be down here longer," Emma said. Until now, she had forgotten they were still in costume, and she expected that the man might at least crack a smile at their get-ups.

"You don't even live here, do you?" the man said through gritted teeth. His expression was still angry, but even so, his gaze flickered across her body.

He wasn't unattractive and in his ornery, spindly way reminded her of Steven. Emma waited for him to say more, or at least check her out again, but apparently she couldn't compete with the allure of his laundry. The more intently he ignored her, the louder she spoke to Max, which made him more intent on ignoring her. And the more he ignored her, the more attractive he became in her eyes. *This, Max,* she wanted to say, *is a game that only grownups know how to play.*

She couldn't figure out why she cared, yet she felt a twinge of disappointment when he piled the clothes into his basket and left the room without looking back at her. When their own laundry dried, a man's dark sock was clinging to a pair of race-car pajamas. Max surveyed it ominously. They could post a sign alerting the entire building to what they'd found, or ask the doorman which apartment this man lived in and knock on his door.

Suddenly fed up with her compulsion to go in chase of those who were the most elusive, Emma handed the sock to Max. "I think this is Maurice's. He must have dropped it on his way out."

• • •

Emma went from the kids to Steven. He'd called to say he was home, annoyed that she hadn't been waiting for him with a homemade dinner and outstretched arms. Explaining that she'd had to baby-sit longer than expected, she suggested they meet at the 82nd Street Barnes & Noble. She'd claimed that the stairs in their building were still hard, and though the lie felt hollow, Steven had reluctantly agreed.

With an hour until Steven arrived, Emma browsed the self-help aisle at whose contents she'd always rolled her eyes. Now she would read every book if one of them listed ten ways to tell your fiancé that you weren't sure you wanted to get married after all. "I've adopted two kids since you left," she could tell Steven. "I've left you for a three-year-old."

When their meeting time arrived, she went to look for Steven. As she was descending on the escalator, Steven turned. For a second, his face looked unfamiliar, but that quickly passed. Except for the goatee he'd grown, he looked like the person with whom she'd once fallen in love.

"No cast," he said, and they surveyed each other, newly shy.

"Good as new," she said, and couldn't help but smile. He'd grown skinnier while he was away, or else she was just bigger in comparison, but even so, she had the urge to be tucked entirely inside his arms.

"Why don't we walk a little," Emma suggested. "I'm fine as long as we don't go too fast."

Each block they arrived at was going to be the one where she told him how she was feeling. By the time they reached 86th Street. Surely by 90th Street. But the blocks passed too quickly. The words wouldn't come. They fell into step, holding hands, and it was possible to believe that nothing was wrong. If she tried hard enough, she could push away her doubts and force her love from its hiding spot.

Steven made initial efforts to slow his pace to hers, but after a few minutes, she struggled to keep up. As they walked, he talked about his wood-paneled writing room with a view of hills, lake, and sky. With nothing to do but write, he'd pretended that the rest of his life didn't exist, or if it did, it was on the other side of impassable hills.

Emma listened, but the particular loneliness she felt in Steven's presence returned. No matter how close he drew to her, he could see only himself. This time, though, she thought not of her feelings but of the look on her mother's face as she'd rushed from the apartment earlier that day. She had longed for her parents' contentment, but what of their relationship had she really replicated?

"I think I need a time-out," Emma said finally, on the corner of 96th and Broadway.

"From walking?" he asked.

"From us."

"What are you talking about?"

"We need to talk," she said, her voice suddenly hoarse. She wished she'd brought the list her father had made, so she could hand it to Steven with all the authority of a note to a teacher explaining an absence.

"I don't want to finish my dissertation. I don't want to be in school anymore. I don't know if I want to get married."

His disbelief changed to alarm. "I just came home. Why are you ruining it?"

"Do you remember that I ran? I kept waiting for you to ask me what was wrong," Emma said.

"Of course I asked you," he said.

"You asked about my ankle. Didn't you wonder what was really wrong?"

"What did you expect me to think? You were running down the street like a crazy person."

"You didn't want to know. Did you notice that I wasn't doing any work? Did you notice how unhappy I was?" she said.

"Of course I did. But what was I supposed to say? How was I supposed to fix whatever was wrong?" Steven asked.

"You were at least supposed to try," she said, still wanting to believe that it was impossible you could feel this bad, yet be left so alone. Was it a leftover childhood expectation that someone would always come running if you called out in distress in the middle of the night?

The light turned, and with his hand on the small of her back, Steven steered her to the median in the middle of Broadway where they sat on a bench.

"What is it you want to do instead?" he asked, his voice becoming stony.

"I don't know," she said.

"What don't you know?"

She struggled to find words, her mind empty, her mouth dry. "Everything," she said.

The light changed, and people began crossing the street, staring at her as she started to cry. A woman in black patent leather Mary Janes and a rumpled maroon taffeta dress speckled with rhinestones sat next to them on the bench, oblivious to the scene upon which she was intruding.

"Great, the march of the crazy people," Steven said.

But Emma felt sympathy for the woman whom she recognized as the schizophrenic her father had pointed out. At the time, she'd felt a strange envy, a twinge of yearning to have her own malady be so easily diagnosed. Emma locked eyes with her. At least this woman didn't have to maintain a pretense of normalcy; everyone who looked at her knew instantly that something was wrong.

"I like your dress," Emma said, and reached for her hand.

Shocked to have been touched, the woman stared at Emma yet made no move to pull away. Her nails were painted electric blue and were bitten down to the skin. Her hand, though, was surprisingly soft, as though one small part of her had been shielded from the forces that had made her face so ragged.

People continued to stare at their mismatched summit on the median, but by the next block, both she and this woman would pass from their minds, one small spectacle in a day already crowded with spectacle. You could position yourself in full view, but sooner or later you discovered that it was simply your own need reflected back. How many people had arrived at this realization; yet that was no comfort when you came upon it as well. She could lay herself bare before every person on Broadway. She could cling to the wish that others would solve her problems, that help in one form or another was on the way. Was this the great realization of adulthood, the iron bar that stood firmly across its doorway? It didn't matter what other people said or did. She alone could decide what she wanted. Only she could save herself.

J EREMY SKIPPED OUT of work and went to the Met. In the American Wing courtyard, he gazed at John La Farge's *Welcome* window. In luminous color, encrusted with jewels of glass, an angelic-looking woman was depicted pulling back a curtain, bidding him to enter. How many people, and how many hours, had it taken to make such a creation? Even those craftsmen in the back rooms whose contributions were anonymous—had they been aware of the grandeur they were creating?

The light rushed in, and the exuberance and defiance of the colors reminded him of the story Claudia Stein had told him about the tension between John La Farge and his father. Had the son tried to lecture himself about the requirements of duty and responsibility? Had he eventually come to the realization that he had no choice; in the pages of his law books, had he seen only the glimmers of color? In Paris, where the son had gone to study, had a world opened up? Upon his return, had the son taken his father into his studio and declared, "This is what I want to do"?

There were other La Farge windows in Manhattan, mostly in churches, and on subsequent mornings, Jeremy went to visit them. How far he'd traveled from his former self, that he now spent his workday visiting churches.

At the Church of the Incarnation in midtown, a caretaker

noticed him as he walked in and Jeremy jumped, half expecting to be told that he didn't belong here. He worried he might turn and see Richard, here to collect his wayward associate. But it wasn't only Richard he feared. Jeremy felt his father's presence more viscerally here in this church than he did anywhere else. He remembered something that he hadn't thought of in years. When he used to visit his father's office, his favorite activity had been not to gaze out the windows at the view of downtown Chicago, but to open the bottom drawer of his father's desk. There he kept supplies for his own hobby, building miniatures of boats, cars, and monuments. Jeremy used to carefully pick up the X-Acto knives and small squares of balsa wood, his father showing him with great pride what he'd built, his eyes lit with a sparkle his son rarely saw.

Inside the church, the sounds of traffic grew faint, and the bustle of the city vanished as it had at the library. In a red velvet pew, a man sat with his head bowed, also seeking refuge from some part of his life. The walls were lined with stained-glass windows, by Tiffany and William Morris, but Jeremy walked past those to the one by La Farge, which depicted a vintner looking down over his translucently bright purple grapes and the cherubic faces of young children. In the noon light, this window was the brightest; even without locating it in the pamphlet he'd picked up at the entrance, Jeremy immediately knew it was the one.

The window reminded him of a favorite phrase of his father's: "My father planted for me, now I plant for my children." Before, Jeremy had heard in these words only a sense of endless duty, but staring at the window, he also saw the glint of love. The language of work was their chosen dialect, but in all their conversations, he'd never once thought to ask his father if he liked what he did. Now, when it was too late, their relationship would be preserved as it had been then. Only in his mind, in his wishful fantasies, could it take on new forms.

The story Claudia Stein told him was probably more complicated than he had initially believed. John La Farge was a grown man when he'd gone to law school, a grown man when he'd run away in order to do what he wanted. Maybe his father had tried to prevent him from doing what he wanted, but surely his own internal conflict stood in the way as well. Perhaps the tether on his own father's love had been longer than he'd realized. It was easy to blame it on his father, easy to blame it on his work: the entire world, a waiting repository for blame. In the center of himself, everything was dangling, unfixed, unformed. He had gone to college, to law school; he had married, had two children of his own—cocooning himself in all the things he was supposed to be—yet he had never grown past the larval stage of his own becoming.

Jeremy continued his treasure hunt to places he'd walked past but never noticed. When was the last time he'd stopped to look up? Only gaping tourists made such blunders. Metal plaques marked buildings of historical significance that only people on specialized tours stopped to read. Stone-carved wreaths and family crests decorated the buildings as gargoyle sentries watched over the streets. At the glistening gold entrance of the Fred F. French Building at Fifth Avenue and 45th Street, Jeremy craned his neck to see the colorful terra cotta along the building's exterior. He walked uptown to a building near Columbus Circle called Alwyn Court, whose façade was covered in lavish flowers, vines, mythical animals, grotesque human faces. If he stayed long enough, would swarms of people stop alongside him, to see what marvel he had spotted? But rather than join him, passersby regarded him with suspicion, everyone more likely to see danger than beauty.

Back in his office, Jeremy prepared an amendment to his original due diligence memo in which he'd wrongly claimed there were no foreseeable historical issues that could derail the proposed construction. Instead of filing the permits as Richard had ordered, Jeremy slaved over the new amendment. When he needed a break, he stood at the window. Traffic was slowing, the lights in other buildings shutting off, but Jeremy wasn't tired. He wandered into the partners' empty offices. In Richard's office, he found a pair of binoculars on the desk, not Fisher-Price but an expensive pair of Swarovski. Wondering what use Richard had for them, he picked them up, tempted to bring them home for Nina as a consolation prize.

The amendment grew longer than the original document. Jeremy added footnotes, pictures, and a bibliography, not sure if he was writing a legal memo or a college term paper. But after hearing Richard say that his heart wasn't in his work, Jeremy wanted to create something, however small, in which its beating was audible.

With fifty hours of billable time amassed, he sent the document to the word-processing center downstairs and dozed at his desk. When the document was ready, Jeremy went downstairs where the night shift was in full swing, in the area of the firm that Richard derisively referred to as steerage. The woman in charge directed Jeremy to Jon, a tall, skinny man with a long blond ponytail.

When Jeremy gave him the file name, Jon sprang to life and eagerly shook his hand.

"It's great. Really great. If you want my opinion, I think it's definitely possible. There's stuff buried in this city you wouldn't believe."

Taped to the side of Jon's computer was a small black flag, displayed in plain sight but invisible to most people. Jeremy had been down here countless times but never once wondered why it was there.

After his initial hopeful weeks, he'd stopped checking out

each person in the building, having resigned himself to the fact that Magellan was nothing but a fanciful creation. But now Jeremy felt as though he were standing at the entrance to a previously unexplored realm, stepping through a wall in his building into an urban forest tangled with underground pipes and tunnels.

"Magellan?" Jeremy asked.

The proofreader glanced at his coworkers, making sure they were bent over their documents. "This is it," he said. "My headquarters."

The document Jon handed him was still warm from the printer. Thirty well-researched pages about the possible existence of a stained-glass window in a site where the Royalton Company wanted to build multimillion-dollar luxury condominiums. His eager, optimistic sentences, the photocopied color pictures attached. He could already anticipate Richard's furious, bewildered response. No one knew for sure that the window existed. And even if it did, no one would allow it to derail a deal.

Jeremy started to leave but turned back, wanting to grab hold of Magellan. "I was just wondering. Have you ever been to the old City Hall station?" he asked.

"City Hall," Jon said, and laughed fondly, as if Jeremy inquired about a long-lost friend. "That's our next conquest. In a month the MTA is going to service the tracks of the 6 train and that's our chance. We're going to make an attempt. You should come with us."

Jeremy laughed as well. Even if he had time to sneak into underground spaces with eccentric members of the staff, he was afraid. And yet he surprised himself by asking, "When?"

THIS TIME THE sign was all bold, all caps. YOU MUST WAIT 20 MINUTES BEFORE REMOVING LAUNDRY FROM THE MA-CHINES. THIS RULE IS IN EFFECT EVEN IF THE LAUNDRY APPEARS DRY. IF YOU DISCOVER THAT YOU ARE IN POSSESSION OF CLOTHING NOT YOUR OWN, YOU ARE REQUIRED TO NOTIFY THE BUILDING STAFF IMMEDIATELY.

Arthur printed out multiple copies, then tore them up. His neighbors would no more heed this sign than any of the others. No matter what he did, the garbage can lids were never placed on tightly, the noise in the stairwell never ceased, nor was his laundry ever returned. The sock he was now missing had probably been stolen by the costumed woman in the laundry room, but there were others who would do him harm. He'd once seen a Roman Polanski movie about a group of neighbors who conspired to drive a new tenant crazy so they could have his apartment. He didn't want to wallow in paranoia—surely that woman in the laundry room was just trying to annoy him —but it was hard not to wonder if conspiracies indeed lurked behind shaded windows.

Churchill bounded over, ready to go outside. Now that it was just the two of them, their needs had synchronized. More than ever, he couldn't imagine his life without Churchill. When he'd started his own Internet security company and begun working from home, he hadn't known that his wife was on the verge of leaving and that he would be alone day and night. He hadn't known that, in her absence, he would miss the rhythms of an office. Even when he had complained, as he occasionally did, about those who typed or talked too loudly, those sounds had delineated his day.

On their way out, Arthur grabbed a bunch of signs and slid them under his neighbors' doors, where there was a better chance they'd be seen. After doing so, he and Churchill walked toward Broadway, trying to ignore the stench of garbage that overtook the streets.

As always, he set out believing that this was the time they would take a different route, but once again he ended up in front of the café, which was crowded as always. Even he had to admit, the cakes displayed in the window did look wondrous, with flowers that cascaded precipitously off the tiered, deliberately uneven surfaces, their beauty like their maker, haphazard, almost accidental.

It wasn't a quality he would have expected to be captivated by. He'd met Georgia at a six-week seminar for people who wanted to open small businesses. She always arrived late, with an air of disorderly upheaval. Her ginger hair was flyaway, her clothes loose and flowing, her scarves of a fabric so textured it was hard not to want to touch them. Sometimes her shirts were smudged with food and icing; once she'd arrived with a faint streak of blue frosting on her cheek. Some might have considered her heavy, but he loved the delectable curves of her body. The freckles that dotted her face and arms were speckles of cinnamon.

Initially he told himself that he was awaiting her late arrival just to see how much noise she would make as she climbed over people sitting in rows, offering apologies along with an endearing smile. No matter where he sat, she always ended up a seat or two from him, a fact that he turned over in his head, trying to parse her intentions. If it was impossible to arrive on time, it would make sense, of course, to arrange to have an aisle seat saved for her, but he couldn't bring himself to suggest it, too enraptured by how she burst into the classroom with such unbridled exuberance.

On the whiteboard, their instructor detailed how to project expenses and calculate loans. Georgia looked confused as she tried to copy everything into a notebook whose every surface was covered with heart-shaped doodles. "I can help you with your business plan, if you want," he'd said to her one day as she was trying to stuff her papers into her bag. It was, quite possibly, the bravest thing he'd ever said. His words might be as unadorned as any ever spoken. Yet hiding inside them were other words that confessed that he couldn't stop thinking about her, words that made professions in language so flowery, so heartfelt, that they rivaled the love songs of the most romantic of poets.

For a year after that, Arthur had put aside his own professional aspirations and worked on Georgia's business plan. By the time she secured initial financing, they were engaged. When she signed the lease, they had been married for almost a year. She spent months trying to come up with the perfect name for her café, but it was he who suggested that she call it simply, perfectly, Georgia's.

How quickly your whole world could come undone. How little control you had over the most intimate parts of your life. One night she had come home smelling of caramel and buttercream and sat at the edge of the bed. "I don't know if I love you the way I thought I did," she had said. He had stayed silent, perfectly still. If he gave no sign of having heard, it was possible this wasn't happening. Instead of thinking about what she was saying, he remembered the first time they had been alone. She had taken his hand and pressed it to her face, then took his other hand and placed it on her waist, on her breast, atop her beating heart. He felt the inviting call of her body and marveled with gratitude that she wanted him. As he lay atop her, his face to hers, his thin chest to the abundance of hers, he tried to see himself through her eyes. The discovery of her was equally a discovery of himself.

Now there was no escape from Georgia's presence: the red sign in front of the café was indelible in his mind. He wouldn't make this mistake again, opening himself to the havoc of people who trampled you with their rampant unleashed selves. He sealed off the part of himself that was capable of feeling love. To console himself, he cataloged Georgia's faults, the clothes she dropped on the floor, the dishes she left in each room. Even so, he was unable to remove two cups she'd left in what had once been their shared apartment, one on the dresser, the other on the windowsill. They were dusty and dirty now, but he kept them, a monument to her one-time presence in his life.

Until a few weeks before, he'd planned to never enter Georgia's. But if he couldn't have her love, at least he could have a confrontation. He had gone into the café and asked to speak to her. They sat down at a table, and Georgia had waited for an explanation of why he was there. At his silence, Georgia had pleaded with him. "You have to let go." But all he could do was stare, dumbfounded, at this woman who was once his wife. Because he was supposed to let go of what, his heart?

The memory pained him and he pulled himself away from the windows of the café. Trying to expunge Georgia from his mind, he and Churchill went to the dog run in Riverside Park. As soon as Arthur removed the leash, Churchill began to run, suddenly desperate for freedom, though when he was on leash, the confinement didn't appear to bother him. Churchill bounded from one end of the dog run to the other. Not until he almost crashed into the fence did he turn and run in the opposite direction.

On the way home from the park, he and Churchill passed the gym where a sign announced a sale on memberships. Arthur had often thought about stopping in, tempted by the prospect of the lap pool, though it probably wouldn't be the right temperature nor would the chemical balance be sufficiently monitored. But remembering Churchill's joy in bounding back and forth, Arthur pushed those reasons aside, and after dropping the dog at home, he took a tour, then surprised himself by buying a yearlong membership.

SOMEONE HAD ACTUALLY listened to her complaint. When Claudia thanked the young woman behind the counter at Georgia's for hanging the sign banning noisy children, she told her that one group of customers loved it, while another was incensed. Each time Claudia came in, she updated her on the neighborhood battle the sign had provoked.

"Don't let them sway you," Claudia said, and smiled at the young woman whose hair was now peacock blue.

"We've been flooded with e-mails. I'm hanging them all on the wall. Most are in favor, except for a few moms who are pissed off. I heard they're even talking of boycotting. I say, go ahead."

One of the posted e-mails caught Claudia's eye. "I can only assume that those of you who cannot tolerate the sounds of children laughing have not been blessed with being a mother."

Since the sign had been posted, Claudia had hoped to run into these mothers, to see their response to someone who had dared to say no to their kids when they, enthralled by love or beset by weakness, were only able to say yes. But now that several weeks had passed quietly, the urge for confrontation had dissipated. There were no noisy children in the café. The whole city in fact was quieter now that it was August, and so many people were away.

Claudia worked. The hours passed, uninterrupted, the pages unfurling inside her head. When she looked up, she wasn't sure how much time had elapsed. Only the view out the window oriented her. She watched the passersby, then startled in recognition as Leon and Emma walked by with the hunched, hushed air of confidants. When she knocked on the window, they looked up as though she'd purposely ambushed them.

Theoretically she should have been happy to see Leon and Emma's newfound closeness, but she felt slighted that it had come at her expense. "Obviously it's fine if Emma is confiding in you instead of me. I'm just wondering what's going on," she had told Leon a few nights before. She didn't know what she'd expected him to say, but his silence had outraged her.

"She's not a patient of yours, Leon. Please tell me. I have a right to know."

"It's nice spending time with her, but trust me. I don't know any more than you do," he'd said finally.

She had believed him, because why at this late date would Emma turn to him? Though she should have been sorry that Emma was uncomfortable confiding in either of them, she'd felt, to her shame, only relief.

When Emma and Leon came into Georgia's, the relaxed smile on Emma's face faded; she looked like a child made to say hello to a long-forgotten relative. Claudia's resentment deepened. There had always been strange comfort in feeling that Leon had little time for either of them.

"You're walking well. Your ankle must be better," Claudia said to Emma when she and Leon agreed to sit down for lunch. She'd never known Emma to pass up a free meal, certainly not now when it was impossible to keep enough food in the house. Emma had always been thin, though now she existed in a constant state of ingestion. The weight she had put on was evident, but Claudia wouldn't dare mention it. The body that was once in her domain was now off-limits.

"I was thinking we should make plans to help you move back home. I imagine you're ready to get back to your life," Claudia said.

"Am I in your way?" Emma asked.

"Of course not. I love having you home. But surely you don't intend to live with us forever. And surely you don't plan to make baby-sitting your full-time career."

"I like baby-sitting," Emma said. "I can't remember the last time I had this much fun."

"So why did you go to college and graduate school?" Claudia asked, trying to sound lighthearted.

"It's more complicated than that," Emma said, and looked at Leon, a coded transaction passing between them.

"Please, Emma. Is it too much to ask for the truth?" Claudia said.

Emma finally met her gaze. "I know you don't want to hear this, but I'm thinking about dropping out of school. I don't want to write my dissertation. And I don't know if I want to get married."

Claudia was silent. Was this some kind of belated adolescent crisis? Was even a happy, well-adjusted child an exquisitely crafted time bomb that, at any moment, could go off in your hands?

She glanced at Leon, who was staring into his coffee. She was accustomed to his ability to bear any news with only the slightest trace of outward reaction, but when she met Leon's eye, she realized that despite what he'd told her, Emma had already confided in him. Fathers got away with their absence. Never so parsed or scrutinized, they got credit just for showing up. Where was her own father in her memories? He had died when she was ten, but even when he was the quiet figure behind the pages of a newspaper, the half-asleep shadow in the comfortable corner chair, she had loved him boundlessly.

"Every relationship has difficulties. Don't you think you and Steven can work this out? And you're doing so well with your dissertation, but if you feel stuck, you could take some time off. I'm sure you can defer your fellowship for a year," Claudia said.

"I've already taken time off. What do you think I've been doing for the last six months?"

"Why didn't you tell me?" Claudia asked. "I could have helped you find your way through it."

"All you wanted to hear was that I was fine," Emma said too loudly, inviting the gaze of curious onlookers.

Claudia recoiled in embarrassment at how they must sound, a family drama, splayed in public. Even if the people sitting nearby didn't look up, they were still taking in every word. But their sympathy, she realized, was exactly what Emma wanted. All those listening in would hear the oldest story of all, the mother who had wronged her daughter. They would hear nothing of all she had wanted to give Emma.

"I don't understand," Claudia said.

"I know you don't. That's always been the problem," Emma said, her face pink with anger as she stood up and pushed her way through the tables.

"You knew," Claudia accused Leon.

"It wasn't mine to tell," he said. He glanced toward the door where Emma was making a quick exit.

Claudia shook her head. She didn't know what to do. "Go with her," she said, and with only a glance in her direction, he followed Emma, leaving Claudia alone with the startled faces around her. She slammed down her teacup, which once again had the same pattern as those stored in her mother's breakfront. Had the blue-haired girl behind the counter reserved the cup especially for her?

How foolish to imagine that she could create a family that would soothe the pain of the past; how foolhardy to believe that she and Emma could avoid the distorted lenses through which mothers and daughters saw one another. When Emma was born, she'd felt the chance to redo what had gone wrong with her own mother. In her daughter's dark hair and round, dimpled face, she had seen a mirror image of herself. She had rocked Emma to the promise that she would never be the mother who looked her daughter up and down on a fault-finding mission. She would be the mother who—how simple it once seemed!—gave her daughter everything she needed. She had no idea that one day she too would wind up on the other end of an angry gaze.

THE LAWS OF probability, briefly suspended, were back in effect. It had been almost two weeks since Nina had run into Leon, and she looked for him on every corner, expecting him to turn up in the unlikeliest of places, pushing through the crowds at the Children's Museum, walking through the gate of Hippo Park. After a few more days without crossing paths, Nina called Leon on his cell phone, tentatively mentioning the long-ago promise of a borrowed book.

"I was just thinking that I haven't run into you in a while. Where are you now?" Leon asked.

"Broadway and 98th."

"I'm a few blocks from there. A patient canceled and I have an unexpected free hour. I was going to walk to the boat basin," Leon said.

"I've never been there."

"How is it possible you've never been to the boat basin?" he said, and she heard the smile in his voice. She laughed; she could write a dissertation comparing the merits of each playground in Riverside Park, but the boat basin remained on the list of places she had yet to take the kids.

"I almost didn't recognize you without your kids," he said as she approached.

"They're with Emma. They love her, and so do I," Nina

said, and told him how each time Emma came over, she was excited about the day she had planned. Even doing laundry or going to the park was made out to be such an adventure that she wanted to join them. Nina liked to tell herself that Emma could be so enthusiastic because she got to go home at the end of the day, but she knew it was more than that. When she relayed the kids' antics, Nina felt how quickly Emma had fallen in love with her kids. It probably filled some other need inside her, but that was fine; it filled their needs as well.

As she walked next to Leon, the streets seemed newly strung with currents of attraction. The kids slipped from her mind. There was nothing but time, free and open. Shyness fell away; so did effort. On every street corner, at every passing, people looked each other up and down, invisible threads of energy connecting eyes to hips, eyes to chests, eyes to eyes. She initially checked out everyone approaching her for fear someone might recognize her, but she pushed the worry from her mind. What was there to see? she reassured herself; she was having a conversation, he was her friend. Even if someone saw her, who would linger long enough to notice the ways in which she leaned ever so slightly toward him or held a smile a second too long? What kind of security camera, mounted overhead, could catch something so imperceptible?

They walked under the highway overpass and along the promenade, surrounded on both sides by Rollerbladers and bikers. They walked down to the river and onto the pier. A few feet away, seagulls swooped down. On the pier, a man was fishing beside a sign that instructed No Fishing. By the river, Nina's senses were heightened. The sounds of traffic were replaced with the caws of seagulls. For once, Manhattan actually seemed like an island.

"Are you taking any vacation?" Leon asked.

"We were supposed to go away next week, but Jeremy had an emergency at work. I probably should be angry, but mostly, I'm just no longer surprised," Nina said.

"There's always something to fight about, isn't there? Claudia and I are going to Cape Cod for the last two weeks of August. There's a beach I go to every morning—I pretend to Claudia that I'm doing work but the truth is, I just want to be by myself. On the beach, you can't see anyone for miles. You actually forget anyone could walk by. Behind the beach are huge dunes that make you feel like the area is impassable. I'd be perfectly content to sit there all day."

They leaned forward into the pier's wooden railings, the breeze providing relief from the heat. Kids screamed nearby, but they weren't hers so she didn't care. She wanted to speak and listen at the same time; she wanted to stand here until everyone else had gone home. She would tell him everything Emma had said, then have him fill in the conversations with Claudia that she'd watched from her window, to confide whether their quiet nights were signs of closeness or distance. She would ply him with more questions, numbered and in chronological order, some of which would require the equivalent of essays, each answer peeling away another layer until there was nothing of him she could not see.

"I still have to lend you a book," Leon said as his arm grazed hers, the faintest of touches, yet her whole body was electrified. Though they pretended nothing had happened, she was sure that, at that moment, for both of them, it was the only thing in the world that had.

"One of these days, I'll actually have time to read," Nina said, but the lightness of her tone didn't match the intensity on her face, or the way in which her entire body had turned inside out. Her body's swell was so pronounced that surely it was evident to Leon; her heart was beating so furiously that it had to be audible to everyone who passed. And in that moment, she wouldn't even mind. No one could find her, no one would know who she was. All she wanted was to give in to the great gasp of desire, to the feeling of freedom unencumbered.

"Do you know that our windows face each other? I see you from my living room," she confessed.

A small noise, somewhere between a gasp and a laugh, escaped Leon's throat. Looking at her with half-lowered eyelids, he asked: "What can you see?"

WHENEVER JEREMY SAW Magellan in the hallways of the firm, he tried to avoid him. Richard was already looking at him suspiciously, and he didn't need to be seen hanging out with members of the staff. Ever since Jeremy handed in his book report about La Farge, Richard had given him small, easy assignments and watched him carefully. Maybe Richard had seen this before: the associate who cracks up or burns out. For all Jeremy knew, the firm had an underground office with round-the-clock staff whose job it was to punish those who no longer cared.

Magellan kept him updated about the plans for their upcoming mission, and each time, Jeremy told him that if he had free time, he should be home with his kids. Magellan stared at him as though he'd offered the most bizarre of excuses, but then, he probably lived in an apartment with an ever-shifting cast of roommates, spending his nights sprawled on a futon where he ate cereal for dinner and watched hours of TV.

Oblivious to Jeremy's attempt to avoid him, Magellan smiled mysteriously, willing to play along with the conceit that there were spies around every corner. He reminded Jeremy of the college classmates who'd played Assassin through the hallways of their dorms, so intent on their missions that they forgot where they were.

While Jeremy was getting a cup of coffee, Magellan suddenly appeared. "It's not enough to read about a ghost station. You have to see it for yourself," he whispered in Jeremy's ear.

Jeremy looked away, trying not to be lured deeper into the fantasy. "Aren't you afraid?" Jeremy asked Magellan when he next saw him in the hallway.

Magellan looked as though he had been waiting for this question. "When we were climbing up the girders of the Brooklyn Bridge, I was scared out of my mind. I had to turn back. It took me three attempts before I made it up there. When we were in the Croton Aqueduct, the tunnel narrowed out of nowhere and one of the guys I was with literally shit his pants. But the best expeditions are when we're petrified and we go anyway."

On Magellan's websites, there had been no mention of these moments of doubt. He'd described only the view from the top of the bridge and posted a picture of himself and a group of people at the entrance to the Croton Aqueduct in an inner tube, a six-pack of beer in hand, ready to merrily set sail. But Jeremy wished he had added a description of his fear; he'd rather read the version in which Magellan and his band of intrepid explorers had almost, almost, turned back.

Jeremy stopped thinking of this as a voyage of the imagination. With his admission of fear, Magellan started to seem real.

N LATE AUGUST, with all the therapists away, the city's problems flowed, untreated. But Wendy wasn't entirely on her own. Dr. Davison was a presence in her day, a voice to summon when she was about to erupt in swirling, swarming rage. She'd grown up with a mother who was a screamer and she knew how that felt. Around her kids, she needed to maintain calm, yet nowhere else did she feel so on the verge of losing control.

Over the past weeks, she had become aware of her feelings for Dr. Davison. She looked forward to each session, taking great care in getting dressed. She started seeing him walking ahead of her on the street; her heart soared with anticipation only to crash-land in disappointment when she realized that it was not in fact him. She was envious of his daughter and wife, whom he'd once mentioned in an offhand way. They had unlimited access to him.

After their last session before his vacation, she'd actually passed Dr. Davison on the street. She had pretended not to see him, and only when he was out of her line of vision had she turned around in regret and followed him to what she guessed was his building. She was embarrassed to be someone who did this, yet she needed to see him outside the confines of his office, to know that their connection existed beyond that private space.

In his absence, she looked for ways to keep herself busy. She reorganized the kids' closets. She continued her efforts to protest the sign that still hung in Georgia's window. She called a friend who freelanced for a small local paper and told her about the sign. Over the listserv of the nursery school, she sent an impassioned note about the rights of children.

Finally, she got a response, far better than she'd imagined. A reporter for the *New York Times* Metro section contacted her and asked to interview her. After putting the kids in front of the latest *National Geographic* movie, Wendy laid out her points which the reporter dutifully recorded. The words flowed from her. Not since leaving her job had she felt such purpose; not since then had anyone taken so seriously what she said.

"It's really an issue of how we define public space," Wendy said, and explained that it wasn't the sign itself she disagreed with—certainly she had the responsibility to control her children—but she had been stunned by the hatred on the other patrons' faces. People took over cafés with their laptops; they talked loudly of anything that came to mind. Everything was tolerated except the noise of children.

When she got off the phone, Wendy went to check on the kids, who sat spellbound by the screen. To celebrate the fact that her publicity efforts had succeeded, she decided to make cupcakes that would outrival the cakes at Georgia's. In her mind, she rehearsed the cheerful, busy version of the day she would describe for her husband. He had been skeptical that she would be happy at home all day, but with these cupcakes, with outings to the zoo and the Met, with a refrigerator door adorned with art projects, she had more than proven him wrong.

She let the kids watch the rest of the movie, and as they learned about the wonders of nature, she replicated those animals in fondant and buttercream. If she were here with other moms, they would exclaim over her creations, yet privately attribute the cupcakes to excessive competitiveness, to maternal one-upmanship. They wouldn't think about the satisfaction she derived from matching the image on the table to the one in her mind. They wouldn't know her pleasure at seeing the work of her hand.

She was almost done when she heard screams from the living room. "What happened, what's wrong?" Wendy asked as she rushed in.

"Promise you'll save me," Sophie sobbed as Harry described the scene they'd watched, where the mommy eagle stood by while one baby pecked the other to death.

"No, sweetie, that's not true. I'm sure you must have misunderstood," Wendy reassured them.

She sent them to the bathroom to wash their hands, and while they were out of the room, she replayed the scene in which the narrator calmly explained that the African black eagle, like the mother panda and the mother penguin, allowed for the natural selection of her young. She watched the scene to the end, transfixed by the carnage. In equal parts, she wanted to rush in to save that baby eagle, and wanted to sit back and watch nature run its hungry course.

When her kids came back into the room, Wendy smiled brightly and turned off the movie, stashing it on a high shelf where no one could reach. She put on another movie, this one a cartoon of smiling fuzzy baby animals where no one was mean and no one got hurt, and she finished icing the cupcakes.

"Come see what I made for you," she said, wanting to erase the predatory images from their minds.

Vanilla-iced polar bears, with miniature chocolate chips for eyes. Chocolate monkeys, orange lions, yellow birds, white and pink bunny rabbits, an entire forest coming to life in their kitchen.

"You made these?" the kids asked in awe.

It was as though she'd shown them the Grand Canyon and said she was the one who'd created it. As the kids sat and ate, she wished she could grab hold of this moment, decorate it with glitter, and display it on her fridge. She wanted to preserve it whole inside the leather-bound scrapbooks of their lives. In those pages they would see the documentation of her perfect love. They would know, one day, how badly she had wanted them and how close she had come to losing them.

On the day she reached thirty weeks of her pregnancy, a few hours passed without her feeling the babies kick. She drank cold water, prodded her stomach, and willed the babies to kick, but there was no response. Another twenty minutes passed. Relax! Relax! She called her husband, who tried to reassure her that this was nothing. In front of him, she tried to swallow the rising, spiraling, incapacitating fear. He expected to see her calm and in control, and she wanted to remain this way, always intact. Only to her doctor could she confess the terrible fear, and only his commanding voice instantly soothed her. It was impossible to believe that in his presence anything could go wrong. The mere sight of him in his scrubs made her feel that she was safe.

Finally, when she could stand it no longer, she called her doctor and this time he told her to come to the labor and delivery floor. Everything's fine, the nurses assured her. Relax! Except this time, they couldn't find either heartbeat. Relax! Her doctor quickly turned on the sonogram machine where, on the screen, one of the normally pulsing white comets was faintly moving. Everyone began talking at once. Her stretcher careened through the hospital corridor into the operating room where someone jammed a needle into her back. She was lifted, tugged, torn open; her body ceased to belong to her.

From the blue-gray sheets draped over her body one baby emerged, then another, as if they'd been birthed from the sea,

from the expanse of a rainy-day sky. Wendy didn't see her children until they were hooked up to respirators, lying in a row
of incubators filled with babies so small they seemed closer to
rodents than humans. On bright signs their names were written, as if these words might carry them to safety. Harry Alexander. Sophie Elizabeth. Their heads were disproportionately
large, and their skin still so translucent that the blue veins that
ran the length of their chests were visible. The cartilage of their
ears had yet to form, and they were folded down like unneeded
flaps of skin. Each weighed little more than two pounds, and
they were the most beautiful things she'd ever seen.

As her babies were hooked up to ventilators, to feed-
ing tubes, she sat by their side. Slowly, slowly, her babies
grew larger. The ventilators were removed and they began to
breathe on their own, first Sophie, then Harry. She suctioned
her breasts with the hospital-grade Medela pump, filling speci-
men containers intended for urine with enough milk to line
her freezer. Soon both of their IVs were disconnected; both her
children had passed out of the port of danger. Only then did
the resident who was on call the night they were born tell her
how, when they lifted the babies out of her body, they had been
startlingly blue. "You came this close," he said, pinching his
fingers almost imperceptibly apart.

The resident had meant to reassure her, but he had unwit-
tingly increased her fear. What if she hadn't gone to the hospital when she did? They took the babies home twelve weeks after
they were born. Stepping through the double doors of the hospital, Wendy had waited for a nurse to call them back. Buck-
ling their car seats into a taxi for their first views of the world
outside, she waited for an alarm to sound. Only once the hospital grew smaller in the rearview mirror had she realized that
these babies actually belonged to them. No more monitors, no
more IVs. Their lives were in her hands alone.

EON AND CLAUDIA'S apartment was larger than Nina had realized, the hallways extending farther back, rooms opening into other rooms whose windows she couldn't see. What she'd only glimpsed took on definite shape and form. What had been impossible to see now lay before her.

The rooms were spacious, with an abundance of light. Nothing was cluttered or out of place. On the walls were black-and-white photographs of Emma as a kid, matted and framed. The beige damask curtains were drawn back as usual. But mostly, the apartment housed books. They lined every room, on ceiling-high, built-in shelves. The only interruption to all these books was the windows. There were books and walls, and then, all of a sudden, there were grass and trees, there were other buildings, there was a park, a river, a sky.

It had been a few weeks since Nina had seen Leon. Even if he hadn't told her of their plans to be away, she would have known because their windows had been dark. Nina too had escaped the city. Tired of being alone every night with the kids, she'd taken them to her parents' house for a week where they played in the backyard. At night, Nina went outside and looked at the houses beyond the fence. From here it was hard to know what really went on in people's lives. If she looked out her parents' windows, she might know whom she was watching, but there would be less to see. She'd have to traipse past the backyard wonderlands of plastic toys, entangle herself in their bushes, if she wanted to catch a glimpse.

But there were other things to look at. When she tipped her head back, she saw, to her surprise, not the insides of apartments but the smattering of stars. When she was a teenager, her family had taken a trip to the Grand Canyon and they'd stayed after dark to hear a park ranger explain the constellations; for the first time, she'd seen the Milky Way, so bright and alive she couldn't believe she'd never seen it before. Now, having lived in the city for so long, she'd forgotten that such wonders existed. For the first time, she hadn't longed for the city's people and light. Under the solitude of a night sky, under these less imposing lights, she tried to seek refuge not just from other people but from the surround sound of her own self.

Upon coming home, she thought about telling Jeremy how she'd felt but didn't know how to explain her restlessness. To talk about it would supposedly make it better, but she knew there lurked another danger as well: she would talk and he wouldn't understand. After a few nights home alone with the kids, she was once again looking out her window, binoculars in hand. Even if she didn't see Leon, she felt the sensation of contact. She called him when she realized he was back in town, once again using the book she was going to borrow as her excuse. Now they stood in front of his living room windows, which offered the best view of her own.

There, across the way, were the baskets of colorful plastic toys on the windowsill. If she looked closely, would she see herself inside her own apartment, busy with the kids; could she wave, one part of herself bidding hello to the other? A part of her wanted to run home, grab the kids, send Emma home, and close the door, to keep herself inside her glass-domed world which suddenly felt fragile.

"That's where we live," she said to Leon.

"I know," Leon said. "The other day, I was looking out my window and I happened to see a woman dancing in her apartment. At first it looked like she was alone, but then I realized that she was with her children. I couldn't see the look on her face, but on the kids' faces, it was pure joy."

He hadn't seen the less idyllic moments that preceded this, or the even less idyllic ones that followed, but he had seen that one. "Let's dance," Max had said, and she'd scooped up Lily, taken Max's hand, and they'd spun around. In a matter of minutes, someone would inevitably scream, hit, or cry, but until then, she'd wanted to hold on to the happiness on their faces.

"What else have you seen?" Nina asked.

"I'll never tell," Leon joked.

"Then neither will I," she said, and the feeling between them fluttered, with no way to grab hold of it.

"Claudia's right," Nina said, becoming aware of the sounds of construction. "It is much noisier here. Our apartment isn't nearly this bad."

"We're much closer. Come, I'll show you something."

Nina followed Leon to Claudia's office, where he pointed to the construction workers out the window, a few feet away, on cages of metal scaffolding. If they opened the window, she could touch them.

"You should bring your kids over. It's better than having a view of the Macy's parade," Leon said.

"Doesn't it bother you?"

"I don't like the noise but I don't mind the construction workers. I pretend they're not there. Do you think they care what's going on in here?"

On Claudia's desk was a small stack of books and a manuscript held together with a rubber band. Pens were laid out like surgical instruments. Tacked up on a bulletin board was an article bearing Claudia's name, and on the wall above her desk

were Post-it notes arranged in rows of varying heights, a jag-
ged skyline of ideas. Along the windowsill were the glass bottles
she'd seen in Claudia's office long ago. They were bright blue or
green, some small enough to cradle in the palm of a hand, others tall and thin, closer to wine bottles or vases.

Nina couldn't keep her hands to herself. She touched the
pile of typed pages and one of the glass bottles. She felt a stir
of longing for her job. She might not have loved the work, but
she missed the feeling of escape on Monday mornings when
she'd arrived at her office. She missed knowing she was good
at what she did. If she'd pushed past these demanding years,
something more fulfilling might have awaited her in the future.
The problem that once had no name now had many names
but still no solution. Already the kids seemed older. After numerous attempts, she'd finally stopped nursing Lily. With the
end of summer, Max had started back at nursery school; in a
few years Lily would be doing the same. And then what? Life
is long, the advice givers would say, offering cheerful remind-
ers that she could indeed have it all, just not at the same time.
True, perhaps, on both counts, but it meant little now, standing in Claudia's office.

"What's Claudia working on?" Nina asked.

"A book about John La Farge," Leon said. "Don't worry,
most people haven't heard of him. He was a nineteenth-century
stained-glass maker. Even I don't know much more than that."

"Does she let you read it?"

"We have very different interests. And she doesn't want anyone to read it in an unfinished state. Lately she's convinced herself that she's going to unearth a long-lost window, but I can't
help wondering what she's really looking for. I wouldn't say
this to her, but I don't think she wants to finish the book. She
wouldn't know what to do without it."

"How did you and Claudia meet?" Nina asked.

"It's a funny story, but Claudia hates it. She gets mad at me whenever I tell it—she thinks it makes us both look bad. We were both in school in Boston and had lots of friends in common, so we ran into each other from time to time. Or so she claims. I never remembered meeting her. When our friends introduced us at a party, I thought I was meeting her for the first time. As you well know, she's terrible with faces, but apparently I'm just as bad."

"Was she interested in you from the start?" she asked.

"Yes, but it took a lot to get her to admit that. She was offended that I hadn't remembered her. What about you and your husband? I hope you have a happier story."

"We met in law school. We were on *Law Review* together. We were both hard-working and ambitious. We used to pull all-nighters together, footnoting. It's very romantic."

"You were on *Law Review*? Very impressive."

"It feels like a lifetime ago. If you had told me then that I wouldn't be working, I'd have laughed."

"Welcome to adulthood. What you thought it was going to be like has nothing to do with anything," he said, and turned away. "We should probably go. Claudia is very protective of her office. Emma and I used to joke that she'd instinctively know if one of us ever ventured in to borrow a pen or use her printer. I shouldn't complain. I feel the same way about my car. If Claudia or Emma were ever to use it, I'd feel like they were invading my inner universe."

His discomfort initiated hers, and Nina followed him back to the living room where they stood next to the windows, between the shelves of books. She saw Claudia's name on the book about the history of stained glass which she'd come across online. When she flipped to the back cover, she saw a photograph of Claudia, although it was taken so long ago that she resembled Emma more than herself.

"Do you ever close the curtains?" she asked.

"Why? Are you afraid we're watching you now?"

"I was just wondering."

"Tell me, really. What have you seen?" he asked.

"I used to love seeing you and Claudia on the couch. Once I saw you dancing and I kept watching to see if you were ever going to do it again."

"You must really have us under constant surveillance."

"Why don't I see you on the couch anymore?" Nina asked.

"We've been busy. With Emma here, there have been few free moments."

"She told me she was moving back in with Steven, at least for now."

"She is, in theory. I'm not sure whether I should consider this a victory, but I convinced her to give it another chance before she makes any decisions. I've been spending so much time talking to her, giving advice as if I really know what's best. Who knows? Maybe my advice was self-interested. Maybe all I wanted was to have quiet nights again."

"I used to imagine what you and Claudia were saying to each other," Nina said.

"I wonder why you're so interested in watching us," he said.

"Every night, when I was home alone, I saw the two of you and you looked so content."

"And what about you? How content were you?" he asked.

"Are you going to teach me about the concept of projection?" she asked.

"Isn't that what every good voyeur learns? Things aren't always what they seem."

"So how are they really?" she asked.

"Aren't you curious," he said.

"And aren't you evasive," she said, and couldn't hold back a smile.

"You too," he said, matching her smile. "What are you hiding from? What if you didn't look into other people's lives?"

"What would I do instead?" she asked.

They looked at each other and waited. One moment passed. Then another, and neither of them spoke. He lightly touched her arm, a small gesture that ricocheted through her body. His voice was suddenly softer, almost unrecognizable.

"That depends on what you want," he said.

She was emptied of words. She was not the kind of person who would ever do this, and yet. She was not someone who had ever contemplated leaving the path laid out for her. Having marveled at stories about people who with one great move, one rash act, dynamited their lives, she'd always thought they were of a different breed from her. But she understood them better now. They too had told themselves that they were entitled to their thoughts, the estates inside their heads places where they were allowed to roam. They too wandered off their prescribed paths, taking small, barely noticeable steps, not looking back until they were too far gone.

She studied his hand, the air between them so thick it was hard to breathe. She was not doing this and yet her hand was grazing his, permission and invitation at once. Exquisitely aware of her body, every inch of physical presence, her fingers interlaced with his.

She should turn back. She should bolt right now. She should, she should. But she wanted to slay whatever came after those words. Her body came free from her mind, then his arms were around her, and he was kissing her. His hands roamed her body, entangled in her hair, down her legs. She was not doing this, yet her shirt was coming off, then his was as well. Her bare skin against his, her hands came to life as well, traveling his chest, his back, his face.

She had thought she could step closer to the edge and pull

herself back. She had thought that she could live safely inside the confines of her mind. But if this was so, why was she pulling him down onto the couch? This should be the moment when she remembered who she really was. She should feel the unstoppable urge to return home, to where she was supposed to be. Her own apartment was suddenly far away; she could no longer see into the distant life taking place inside that small square.

Only this moment, only this now. The wrestling, doubting, yearning part of herself would not stay hidden any longer. Leon's face was just above her, his chest upon her. She felt the shock of a new body. This other person whom she had watched from afar, whom she had constructed in her mind, was not behind a pane of glass but here, in life.

THE POTENTIAL FOR quiet had returned, yet all they did was talk about Emma. Even in her absence, she overtook their nights.

"Do you know what's really going on between her and Steven? Do you know why she wants to drop out of school? Do you think she even knows why herself?" Claudia asked as she and Leon sat on the couch.

"Why are you so convinced it's the wrong decision?" Leon asked.

"I'm just trying to understand. She won't tell me anything."

"Maybe she'll be happier," he offered.

Claudia chafed at his words. Was happiness the currency in which work, in which life for that matter, was to be measured? It was a concept so abstract that it was irrelevant, the province of wishful, impossible fantasy. She remembered something La Farge had said when he completed one of his North Easton masterpieces: "I have finished the Ames window and have suffered much for it." She had always assumed that Emma knew what it was to be in love with an idea. She thought Emma understood that the frustration was inseparable from the pleasure.

"She's still undecided. All we can do is let her figure this out on her own," Leon said.

"That's what you always say," Claudia said, as Leon got off the couch and looked out the window. She had no idea what he was looking at, no idea what would draw his attention. Studying his face, she couldn't stand what she saw. Though she didn't know its source, she knew him well enough to see it. A new glint in his eye. A smile on his face while he was lost in thought. The unforgivable signs of his own private happiness.

Leaving Leon in the living room, Claudia went to her office. All those years in which she'd given up so much in order to be available. All those years in which she'd taken such pleasure in the fact that she and Emma were so similar. To look at her daughter was to see not a separate entity but a part of herself reflected back. She couldn't help but take Emma's plan to drop out of school personally. She saw it as a rejection not just of what she had wanted for her daughter but of who she was.

There was no one to share this with, so she did what Leon had so easily done: closed the door to her office and banished her family from her mind. She was reminded of something she'd long known to be true but came back to her now with the force of revelation: you always needed a place to claim as your own, and her work was the sole thing she had, as surely as if it were a small cabin in a quiet woods.

At her desk, Claudia read and ate a piece of cake she'd brought from Georgia's. In the privacy of her office, she consumed it without stopping. She hadn't wanted to sit in the café, not after she'd walked in that morning and saw a *Times* article taped to the front door.

The article, on the front page of the Metro section, was titled "In Neighborhood Café, a Clash About Noisy Children." There were two pictures accompanying the article, one of a mother, her mouth open in conversation with her kids, the other of Claudia bent over her laptop. "Is there no place in this city where quiet still exists?" Claudia was quoted as saying, and the article gave her name and identified her as an art historian who frequented the café.

When a reporter had approached her one day as she was working there, she had still wanted to lash out at those mothers. But now she no longer felt like shushing anyone. If she could call that reporter back, she would tell her how it felt to have a daughter treat you as though you'd done everything wrong. If she had one more chance to talk with those mothers, she would warn them that one day they would look at their children and wonder who they really were.

The only consolation was her newly published article. Though there wasn't the bright light of fame that other areas of research might attract—no one would ever stop her on the street to say they'd read her piece—she was no longer working entirely in the shadows. She received notes from several former colleagues and was invited to speak at the Society of Architectural Historians' annual meeting, at a session on new discoveries in Victorian decorative arts. A graduate student in Texas e-mailed her about his work on the relationship between La Farge and the sculptor Augustus Saint-Gaudens.

She checked her e-mail, wanting more e-mails, more response. She Googled Maurice again, searching for him in vain. It wasn't too much, was it, to long for someone who was equally captivated by the ideas she cared so much about?

She checked her e-mail again. She drew in her breath. Not Maurice but something else.

"We wonder if we have something in our basement that would be of interest to you," the message read.

A curator who had worked on the restoration of a church outside of Boston, which housed La Farge's *Rebecca at the Well,* had discovered a disassembled stained-glass window. It had been taken apart in panels and stored in wood boxes in the basement though no one knew how long it had been there.

In the past Claudia would have dismissed such an e-mail. Even now, she saw it first through the skeptical eyes of her colleagues who would articulate the reasons for its implausibility. It was foolish to stake years of academic research on the serendipity of discovery. Too many times, she'd heard about art historians who eagerly answered queries from people who were sure that the objects in their possession were long-lost works of art. Instead of breaking the disappointing news that the vase or painting or lamp wasn't anything extraordinary, they were pulled into hopeless treasure hunts, seduced into seeing what they wished to be there.

The possibility pressed on her, the word *maybe* cresting repeatedly in her mind. She allowed herself a moment's fantasy in which she was the one who opened a box, broke down a wall. Something lost could still be recovered, something once beautiful could still be revealed. Several years ago, a stained-glass window at Tavern on the Green that had been previously attributed to Tiffany was proven to be a La Farge. Renovations in the Ansonia turned up a rare eighteenth-century leaded window that had been walled over. And during the recent restoration of Trinity Church in Boston, construction workers had uncovered a La Farge mural hidden behind a panel.

Claudia wrote back to the caretakers and agreed to come to Boston for a day to visit the Medford church. She was no longer, if she ever was, the disinterested academic. She felt La Farge's presence. Close her eyes and she summoned him at work, each color both a small jewel of glass on a studio floor and a shimmering indispensable part of a whole. Close her eyes and she felt the genius who knew how to access the part of his mind in which light was visible. Close her eyes and she was with him in his studio, her hand on his, a partner in his majestic creation.

L EON READ ON the couch, but shadowing every word was the pleasurable sensation of being watched. When his curiosity won out, he put down his book and went to the window to check for Nina's presence.

Now that he'd started looking for her as well, he was surprised by how often he saw her. Usually he maintained the pretense that these sightings were accidental, but tonight, after Claudia had soundly closed the door to her office, he wanted to acknowledge Nina, even put on a show. But it was hardly a striptease Nina was after, except of the emotional sort; she'd want him to peel off one feeling after another, to reveal more and more.

Even when Nina wasn't there, Leon felt her presence. She could see everything—in the kitchen, in the shower, in rooms to which she had no access. He had tried to tell himself it would be only that one time—a rash act, a passionate mistake that would be wrapped in the sheaves of memory and taken out to be looked at from time to time. Having grown accustomed to the dormancy of his desire, he didn't know he could feel this way. He'd never before been unfaithful to Claudia. There had been opportunities, but he would have strayed only from boredom, never from sufficient feeling or desire. So why now, why Nina? Maybe he was unable to tolerate this degree of familial involvement. The more he was pulled in, the more

he needed a way out—for every action, an equal and opposite reaction. Maybe Nina was as restless as he, particles in motion that would inevitably collide. Though it had been nice to
think of their burgeoning friendship as primarily her doing, he
knew he had initiated this as much as she had. He'd offered to
lend Nina a book and had shown her Claudia's office, where he
could measure both his proximity to Claudia and his distance.

At midnight, he knocked on Claudia's door—an attempt,
surely, to allay his guilt—but she was still working and didn't
want to be disturbed. He went to bed without her, still jittery
and dissatisfied. There was something to be said, after all, for
the semi-somnolent condition in which so many people spent
their days. But there was no return to that quiet state; all he
could think of was Nina. Everyone knew of the danger—how
many stories had he heard of the wreckage left behind?—yet
so many still ventured off. Even if he could skillfully take apart
his feelings like small electronic devices, he would never be
able to reassemble them; he might understand better how they
worked, but he was still subservient to their power. He was a
teenager again, on edge with possibility. He wanted Nina in his
arms again, against his body. But he also wanted her eyes on his
face, looking at him in that probing way.

In the morning, only partially awake, he rolled toward
Claudia's side of the bed, remembering how the previous week
she had turned to him with an intensity that took them both
by surprise. Usually the sight of her made him feel only inertia
—every day, every feeling, the same. But in a matter of seconds,
she had pulled him on top of her, wrapped her legs around
him, pressed him deeper inside her. At first he had wondered
if she was awake, or if in her mind he was someone else. For
those few moments, they managed to defy the paradox of familiarity, of seeing someone so much you didn't see him or her

at all. He had been reminded, however briefly, that you could never really come to the end of another person.

A few hours later, they'd become the same people as always, which was why he'd preferred to leave unmentioned the passion that had come over her. He was certain that discussion would diminish the memory, equally certain that those who wanted to share everything with their partners, who defined intimacy as full access, did so at their own peril.

Claudia still wasn't by his side, and jarred by her absence, Leon went looking. The door to her office was partially open, which he took as a sign that he wasn't entirely unwelcome.

"Have you been in here all night?" Leon asked. Claudia's normally neat desk was cluttered with manuscript pages. A plate of desiccated chocolate cake sat in front of her.

Her lip was smudged with chocolate, and Leon reached to wipe it off. When she pulled away from him, he felt a stab of anxiety that she wasn't annoyed at him only for hiding what Emma had confided. She knew, somehow, about Nina.

"I'm famous," Claudia said, handing him the *Times* article. "I don't think it makes anyone sound very good, but I suppose the café owner thinks there's no such thing as bad publicity."

"You look very focused," Leon said as he scanned the article, reading of the mothers' outrage at being so publicly shushed, then the café owner's description of the "spoiled moms" who frequented the café.

"These mothers think they know it all," she said, but he was barely listening. At the sight of his patient's picture next to Claudia's, he wanted to laugh, then scream. His world was tied too tightly around him, yet he could reveal nothing. His wife, his patient: their worlds could intersect, but for them at least, those lines would cross unnoticed.

"I sound fairly curmudgeonly," Claudia said.

"No, just tired of the noise," Leon reassured her, though she did sound more caustic than he would have expected. On full display, in the article and on her face, was the anger that he knew was directed, in large measure, at him. At the sight of it, so long in coming, all he wanted to do was duck.

"I should have Emma show it to Nina. She probably knows some of these moms," Leon said.

"Nina?" Claudia asked.

"You know. The woman Emma baby-sits for," Leon reminded her. Though they jointly accused one another of having faulty memories, in his case it was because he wasn't paying sufficient attention to have noticed in the first place. For Claudia, it was a willful attempt to shield herself from sustained involvement with people she didn't know. Though he didn't know how to do it, he felt the urge to rouse her, him, all of them, from this disconnected state. He marveled at his impulse to mention Nina. If he were to tell Claudia what had happened, it would shatter what remained in place between them. The words lined up inside his mouth, waiting for a nod of permission, and then out they would march, small soldiers bent on attacking the stable foundation of their lives.

"Nina knows you, actually," Leon said. "She was your student, at Columbia. She loved your class."

"How do you know her so well?"

"Apparently she once went to talk to you about going to graduate school. I ran into her in the neighborhood," he said, inching his way closer. *I ran into her in this very apartment,* he would say. *While you were in the library, while you had no idea where I was.* And then, what would be left behind? He didn't want to think of the pain that would come a few moments later; all he wanted, for that one instant, was the razing relief of the truth.

"That was a long time ago," she said.

"Yes," he agreed, feeling a rush of sadness. "It was."

Claudia ignored the pained look on his face—as always, they made it easy for one another to retreat to separate corners. He felt a terrible surge of regret—not for any one decision he'd made but for the way they had all accumulated, bringing him to this moment where he was trapped by his own self. He didn't have it in him to start yelling—what true complaint did he have? Only that he could not stand in this room with her any longer, could not bear a silence so laden with disappointment and anger, hers and his own.

He fled her office, the apartment, and went to his car. In this space, which he regarded as a home as much as any other place he inhabited, he would once again become immune to unwieldy emotion.

After he'd been there an hour, or maybe two, Nina walked by and knocked on the window, as though he'd summoned her.

"Nice place," she said, and he smiled at the sight of her. Anyone looking at them would surely know. No one smiled so widely without good reason. No one had reason to look so pleased. She'd told him that when she was with him she felt the space inside her chest widening as though suddenly able to take in more air, and he understood what she meant. He saw her not as she looked among other people, her face coated in a responsible maternal cast that required enormous effort to hold in place. Instead she looked as she had when she was beneath him, flushed pink, her long dark hair strewn against her bare shoulders. In those moments, her whole face opened up into relaxation and her body was both alight with energy yet calmer than he had seen before.

"Have a seat," he offered.

"Where can we go?" she asked, getting into the passenger seat.

"Anywhere you want," he said.

"How about as far away as we can?" she said.

"And then what happens once you get there?" he said.

"I don't want to think about that. I'd rather pretend that whatever comes next doesn't exist. That's what I've always done," she said, and hesitated. "I never thought I was the kind of person who would do this."

"I don't think you know yet what kind of person you are. I don't know if any of us do."

When she smiled, he wanted to bask in the interest and attention she turned upon him. Sometimes a patient gazed at him adoringly, and the mood in the room shifted, an erotic presence making itself known. There was pleasure, undeniable, in being wanted in this way, yet he knew, of course, that what those patients imagined had little to do with who he was in real life. Their longing was mere projection, composed most prominently of longing itself. Even when he felt the tide of his own arousal, he knew where the boundaries lay.

With Nina, those lines had ceased to exist. It was not the idea of her, not what she represented. He couldn't explain with enough precision to make anyone else understand why he was so drawn to her. But why was it necessary to offer rational explanations for everything, especially this? He was tired of the internal voice that analyzed his every move. For once, he wanted to submit himself to life's unknowability, to give himself over to confusion and exhilaration, worry and arousal, guilt and happiness, the messy pile-up of feelings in which nothing fit neatly together and there was always too much at once. He saw into her wild inner plain where she was struggling to free herself from the press of obligation and expectation. It was this fluttering, flapping part of her that stirred the one inside him and made him want to hold her tightly and say, "Take me too."

"Let's drive," she said.

"The bridge or the tunnel?" he asked, because then the whole world would await. With no time to go that far, he instead drove uptown along Riverside to the top of the park where the odds of knowing anyone were lessened. If he looked to one side, all he would see were the grass and trees of the park, then the stone walkways that led to the river. The George Washington Bridge was visible just ahead. If only they had a kayak, a motorboat, a cruise ship: off they would sail.

He dangled his hand, lightly grazing Nina's leg. It was not going to be only that one time after all. He stroked her thigh. He was already starting to lose sight of the path back home; anything dropped to mark the way back was becoming obscured in his mind. Shielded inside his car, safely beneath the line of the windows, his hands could roam across her thigh, to her knee, unseen. All he thought of was the feeling of his hand on her leg. His other hand came to life as well, on her waist, brushing across her breast. Wasn't he supposed to pull away, tell her, "We need to stop"? Wasn't he supposed to remind her in a serious yet kindly voice that they had responsibilities, commitments? He put his hand on her face and brought her toward him and kissed her. When she kissed him back, he allowed himself to fall into the well of his feelings without knowing where he might land.

Hearing the distant honk of cars, he looked out the window and the rush of feeling came to a halt. A familiar figure crossed his line of vision. At the edge of the park, was that a patient staring at him? He'd imagined himself to be so far away, not in another neighborhood but on another planet. Squinting, he tried to be sure, to will her away. He remembered the fantasies this patient had confided, that she would see him on the street and interact with him outside of the office. The wish had surprised him little, but now he worried she was actually following him. He had none of the compassion he felt in his office. There was no escape, not from this patient, not from anyone. His patient had done nothing wrong, yet he was reacting as though she'd banged on his bedroom door in the middle of the night.

"Are you supposed to be incognito here?" Nina asked, pulling away, her face reflecting his discomfort.

"It's not a very good hiding place after all," he said.

"Who are you trying not to see?" she asked.

"It's not important."

"Was it a patient?"

"Even if it were, what can I do? If someone brings it up in a session, I just turn it around and ask what it means to them," Leon said. "Everywhere I go, I get to be the therapist who stays safely out of sight."

"And is that what you want to do?" she asked. Those round blue eyes, so open and waiting: she had a way of staring at him as though daring him to say more, as though her words came with hooks attached and could grab hold of all she wanted to know.

"Who am I kidding? It's not possible anyway," he said. He brushed her cheek with his hand, he wrapped his fingers in her hair. He looked out the car window again. If it had been his patient, she was gone. But if not her, then someone else could have seen them and know. Sooner or later, someone would always know. Fifty blocks from home or five hundred, privacy was generally an illusion. As much as they worried what it would mean to be caught, surely in some small conflicted place inside each of them, they also wanted to be found.

MMA WAS SURPRISED to see Steven's number on her caller ID. Until recently, he'd never called during his writing hours; he didn't answer his phone and was annoyed if she dared to knock on the bedroom door.

"I can't. I'm baby-sitting in half an hour," Emma said when Steven asked her to meet him in the park. She wished someone had told her earlier that all she had to do was retreat and he would come in chase.

She veered from one feeling to another. She wanted to leave him, she wanted to stay and try again. She began to doubt even her own doubt. The worries of the past few months were a mere aberration, little more than the byproduct of having made a firm decision for her future; the terrible fear of the past few months was the belated recognition of what she knew to be true. "Take it slowly," her father had advised. "You don't have to make any decisions yet. You can find your way, as slowly as need be."

"But what if I do that and I still don't know?" Emma asked. "You can push him harder, see what there really is between you. Tell him what you need. He might surprise you," he said, then sighed and looked as confused as she felt. "I don't know, Emma. Sometimes I think the goal is just to endure. It might not sound pretty, but for most people I suspect it's the truth."

Trying to heed his advice, however tentatively it had been

offered, she'd been moving back and forth between apartments. She was no longer sure what she was referring to when she said "home." But having two homes made her lonelier than when she'd had only one. If she weren't baby-sitting, she'd have no idea what to do with herself. When she was with the kids, the future was so far off as to appear fantastical. For Lily, little existed beyond the need to be held and fed. Even Max's worries were cloaked with the shimmer of unreality. Sometimes she imagined that the kids were hers and she felt a momentary burst of clarity. For Nina, there was no doubt that she was wholly needed. If she had kids, she wouldn't have to finish her dissertation. She would have a ready-made excuse for every failing. She would always have something to show for herself.

"Bring them with you. I love kids," Steven said.

"Since when?" Emma challenged him.

"Since right now," he said.

After picking up the kids, she met Steven in Riverside Park by the dog run. She introduced him to Max and Lily, and he immediately adopted the overly friendly voice adults use to mask their discomfort with kids. Emma set Lily down on the ground, where she tried to consume a mouthful of leaves. But Max refused to come out of the stroller.

"Max, it's fine, I promise you. The dogs are playing. They're not going to bite you," Emma assured him, crouching in front of him. She and Max were dressed in matching shades of orange, and she was wearing a plastic bead necklace he'd made for her.

"Is he always this afraid?" Steven asked.

"It's not just dogs. It's balloons, the subway, any kind of noise."

"He's in the wrong city."

To Emma's surprise, Max listened to her. He sat next to Lily, and she and Steven sprawled on the grass beside the kids,

staring up at the leaves which would soon change color. Until
this year, the arrival of fall had always kindled her schoolgirl's
pleasure in new pencils and blank notebooks, as though every
year life really did start anew.

"This could be us in a few years," Steven said.

"You wouldn't say that if they were crying."

"How often does that happen? Come on, Emma. I'm serious. I miss you. Let's get married. Let's have kids."

"Now?" she asked.

"What are we waiting for? Let's do it," Steven said, trac-
ing circles on her palm. "I'm here for you, Emma. I really am,"
he said, as he leaned closer so that their foreheads touched and
their eyelashes fluttered against each other's skin. If the kids
weren't here, he'd roll on top of her, and she'd be unable to re-
sist. He'd press her down until there was no thought of going
anywhere.

She wanted to believe he better understood her. She wanted
to listen to him, even though she could see the flaws; to hold
on to the fantasy of how it might be even if she knew all the
ways in which it would be pierced. Against the backdrop of
trees and sky, Emma saw what her life could one day be. She
would resume work on her dissertation, and begrudgingly it
would open itself to her again. She would set a date for the
wedding. She would have children of her own. Her urge to run
would fade. Her need for something more from Steven might
not ease, but she would learn to live with some parts of herself
unfilled.

Steven was waiting, but instead of meeting his eye, Emma
looked toward the dog run where a man threw a stick. Immersed in conversation with a fellow dog owner, he didn't notice his dog's escape through the open gate.

Off-leash and unfenced, the dog bounded out, ran toward
them, and jumped around Max, who started screaming.

"Stand still," Emma called to Max, who had begun to run. Lily started to cry as well, and Emma wondered if this was when she was supposed to swoop both kids to safer ground. Or call Nina and say, "Your kids are screaming, can you please come get them?"

"Hold Lily," Emma said to Steven. He took Lily reluctantly and shuffled her from one hand to another. Imitating something he'd seen on TV, he held her over his shoulder while patting her back. When Lily continued to cry, he lifted her high into the air, brought her back down, lifted her up again, until finally she began to laugh. He was incurring the risk of being vomited on, but she was happy to let him take his chances.

Max continued to shriek until even the dog was stunned. Emma wrapped her arms around Max, forcing him to be still. The dog stopped running, came up to her, and with his panting pink tongue, he licked her cheek. When she laughed, so did Max.

In the distance, a man was calling, "Churchill," and hearing his voice, the dog began to bark. Exchanging freedom for love, the dog returned to the fenced-in plot of grass, where his owner hugged him. With Max in her arms and Steven and Lily beside her, Emma lay back on the grass, watching the people pass in all directions, strangers alone and in pairs, until she startled and sat up.

Along the path, her father and Nina were walking, and for a moment Emma assumed they were in search of her and the kids, both in possession of a parental sensory device that sounded when their children were in need. From her spot on the nearby grass, Emma waved but they didn't notice. She was about to call their names, but she stopped, because even from where she was sitting, she could sense their degree of familiarity. Nina was laughing at something her father was saying. When she said something in response, his face had a look of immense absorption, which Emma was accustomed to seeing, though rarely in relation to her.

She thought of the loneliness on her mother's face and the dissatisfaction in her father's voice. Steven took her hand, but it was an empty casing. His face came into focus, and she understood. It didn't matter what cracks and imperfections other people were willing to live with. Emma pulled away from Steven. A strong, clear voice was audible inside her head. The words at once so simple and so true: *I don't want this.*

N HIPPO PARK, under the dense cloud cover of distraction, Nina sat with Wendy and a few other mothers around the sandbox, all of them intent on enjoying what could be the last warm day of the fall. A few minutes before Emma was supposed to baby-sit, she'd called to say that she wasn't feeling well. She had sounded uncharacteristically curt on the phone, but there had been little time to wonder why. With the kids waiting to be entertained, the day had quickly remade itself.

"We haven't seen you in a while," Wendy said without meeting Nina's eye and acting as though their conversation in her minivan had never taken place.

"We've been busy," Nina said.

"He's eating sand," Sophie reported, pointing to Harry.

"We don't eat sand." Wendy lifted Harry onto her lap where she tried to wipe the speckles off his tongue. "Come on, honey, spit it out. Do I have to give you a time-out? Okay, there you go. Good boy. The sand can make you sick. You know that dogs pee in here," Wendy said as Harry shoved another fistful into his mouth.

"The last time we talked, you sounded so unhappy that I thought maybe you'd decided to go back to work," Wendy said to Nina.

"I'm thinking about it," Nina said. This wasn't really true, but it felt good to say it.

"You can't go back to work until you help me with the fundraiser," Wendy said. "I've scheduled it for October 27, and I think we should have a bake sale," she said as the mothers around her nodded their agreement. "Why not give Georgia's a little competition? I assume you saw the *Times* article. Everywhere I go, that's all anyone is talking about. There's a picture of a woman with her laptop—the same woman who shushed us, as though we were in her private office!"

Wendy pulled the article from her diaper bag and handed it to Nina. "I was completely misquoted. I wrote a letter to the editor, but it doesn't matter what I actually said. The reaction would be the same. I Googled myself and the article is all over the blogs. Everyone is talking about how terrible it is that kids make a little noise. But you know what I realized?" Wendy lowered her voice and, looking down at her children happily playing, decided not to take any chance of them overhearing. "It's not the k-i-d-s they can't stand. It's the mothers they h-a-t-e."

"Why would they h-a-t-e you?" Nina asked.

Wendy laughed. "Oh, it's not just me. It's all of us. You too. Don't think that if you go back to work, they'll h-a-t-e you any less. They'll just h-a-t-e you for different reasons."

The word *hate,* so easily banished. And what of the other words that couldn't be so easily erased, even if they were spelled out? Nina tried to follow the conversation, but she was continually disrupted by an image of Leon's face. Was that really her, on his couch, in his car, and then the next day and the next day as well? It couldn't possibly be, and yet in those moments with him, it had seemed the most natural thing in the world. When she was with him, she didn't feel the press of thoughts, the ache of being alone. He had a way of looking at her, his eyes slightly narrowed in concentration as he leaned toward her, and she felt that he knew all of her.

She expected Jeremy to question why she seemed so preoccupied; she had waited for him to start calling her during the day. Every morning she awoke to someone who had no idea of the content of her mind. When she was with him, it was hard to remember that this was the person she had married. He looked smaller to her as though the long hours had shrunk every part of him. He had always been thin, but now he appeared almost childlike in her eyes. Standing next to him, she felt irreparably taller.

It had been three weeks, and every free moment was spent in Leon's company, the two of them walking in the park, at his apartment when no one was there, in his car, driving with no destination in mind but no destination needed. What she was doing, what did this mean? There was no time, no space in her head to ask these questions. She didn't have to think, didn't have to know. She had Emma pick Max up at school and babysit both kids every afternoon; it was hard to remember a time when she'd taken care of the kids by herself. She called Leon whenever she had a free moment. "I can't stop thinking about you," she told him. When she was with him, she didn't feel as though the person standing next to her were mere illusion, his mind and body both far away. He called her between patients. "Not in twenty years," he had whispered in her ear, "have I felt this way." She replayed each moment until Leon was displayed across a hundred screens in her mind, each one projecting a different combination of their bodies intertwined.

"I think we should make cupcakes. I've been baking and decorating them every week and it's not that hard," Wendy said.

She should care about this conversation, but her mind wouldn't turn back. While she sat among the other mothers, she was knocking on the window of his car. While she listened to disparate beliefs about the best kind of cupcakes, she was k-i-s-s-i-n-g him in the front seat. While doling out snacks to the kids, she was s-t-r-a-d-d-l-i-n-g him in the back seat. The playground tilted—what was this new world?—and all the boundaries in her mind ceased to exist. She was here with the kids, she was here with Leon, with Wendy, all at once. Her thoughts were known to anyone who saw her. Her every move was visible to anyone who cared to see.

But it's not only her, not anymore. She had magically acquired Maurice's x-ray vision and could see the other mothers' inner terrains as well as she could see her own.

"I don't bathe them. I don't feed them, I don't watch them," calls a mother who is now climbing to the top of the play structure.

"I bake, cook, play, sing because I need to justify the fact that I am home," says a mother who is flying high on a swing. "I want their childhoods to be perfect because mine was not."

"I am here but not really here," Nina says. "I've found the way to both escape and stay behind."

But this confession, alas, is too much. Instead of attracting nods of agreement, there is only an embarrassed silence. On their faces she sees outrage. We would never do that, not us, not ever. Behind the deliberately crafted façade of contentment, they see her treachery.

She has to escape from the stares, the frozen smiles. While one part of her sits here smiling, another part digs her way out of the sandbox. She grabs the kids and never comes back. She finds her resumé and searches for a job she will love. She passes Wendy on the street while she is on her way to one world and she to another, her months at home a strange blip apart from the rest of her life.

"Shouldn't we do something easier? Why not buy cookies from a bakery and have the kids decorate them?" another mother suggested.

But she can't flee so easily. All the well-behaved mothers are chasing her, their strollers clearing the crowds. Nina runs faster and ends up on Broadway, where her kids climb naked and barefoot out of the stroller and take refuge on the riding toys. She fills the slots with quarters, and while they bounce to "It's a Small World," she hails a cab and waves goodbye.

"Last year the moms had the kids make these gorgeous quilts and they auctioned them off for charity. I would hate for us to do less," Wendy said.

At the airport, all the flights are canceled. An early fall snowstorm. An unexpected tornado. A midair collision. The trains too. Even the buses. She calls Jeremy to tell him where she's left the kids. But Jeremy is in a meeting that will last another five years. He doesn't take her call. He doesn't remember her name.

"We want the kids to feel like they've accomplished something. I was just reading an article about how self-reliance is lacking in our kids, and we need to figure out a way to give them more," someone else said.

A different path of escape occurs to her. She hot-wires Wendy's minivan, piles the kids into the back, straps the stroller to the roof, whips out the Benadryl-laced juice boxes, and they're off.

"If we really care about the kids, we should make the cookies ourselves," Wendy said.

There is yet another path of escape. She takes the kids home, dutifully bathes them, smiles sweetly as she tucks them into bed. She bides her time until the next morning when alternate-side rules are in effect and she knocks on the window of Leon's car.

"How about two weeks from today?" Wendy suggested. "Can we count on your help, Nina?"

Nina heard her speaking, but the voice was coming from a distant place that had little to do with her.

"Earth to Nina," Wendy said.

As Nina looked up, startled to hear her name, there was a commotion nearby and Wendy jumped up to see what happened. She returned, carrying Max in her arms.

"I know you have other people you'd rather be with, but I would think you'd be interested to know that Max just vomited on the slide," Wendy said.

"I don't feel well," Max said, his face pale, his body shivering though it wasn't cold out. He'd complained of a stomachache before they left the apartment, but in her distracted state, Nina hadn't really heard him. Now he stood before her with beseeching eyes, certain she would know what to do.

She scooped up the kids and made a run for it. They made it inside the apartment, but before Nina could race Max to the toilet, he was vomiting again. She stripped off his clothes and tossed them onto the bathroom floor as Lily began to heave.

"Come home," Nina begged Jeremy's voice mail, but was no longer surprised she couldn't reach him. Max had flushed the toilet so many times that the water rose ominously to the top of the bowl. Lily lay limp in Nina's arms. Where was Emma's knock at the door, then her cheerful entrance? And if not that, where was the panic button that would summon the cheery band of professional mothers carrying mops and pots of soup?

With vomit all around, there was no path of escape. Her own skin growing clammy, Nina replayed what Wendy had said and tried to interpret the accusing look in her eyes. For a moment in Leon's car, she thought she'd caught sight of Wendy but had pushed away the thought, because she hadn't wanted it to be so.

But now there was no spot of refuge to seek out in her mind, nowhere but the hard, pressing questions before her.

Had Wendy seen her with Leon? And who else had? Was this why Emma hadn't come, why Jeremy hadn't called back? Until now she had managed to trick herself into thinking she couldn't be caught. So many years spent caring what people thought, yet when she was with Leon, it had become shockingly easy to forget. Now, it was not just Jeremy, not just Wendy or Emma, but anyone, anywhere, who might have seen her, might know. Claudia appeared, screaming out her window, not at the construction workers below but at her. Wendy shook a chiding finger at her. Jeremy took up a belated presence there as well. On his face she saw his bafflement, but even worse, it was replaced by a look of pain.

In an increasing state of delirium, she heard the phone ring, but through the haze of her newly feverish state, she couldn't get to it.

"I've tried your cell phone. Where are you? Did you get my e-mails?" a voice hissed into the answering machine. "I don't understand, Jeremy. Nothing has been filed like it was supposed to. I need all the Royalton documents tonight and I have no idea where you are."

She dialed Jeremy's cell phone but got no answer. She knew where she had been of late, but it hadn't occurred to her that he might be anywhere but his job. She couldn't even name the places he might seek out for his own refuge. How was it possible that you could be tied to someone by so much and so little?

Now, her wayward husband, one more worry to add to the swaying pile as she sponged the kids' foreheads, as she dispensed Tylenol and Pedialyte. When her body no longer accepted maternal duty as a valid excuse, she ran for the toilet. Crouched on the bathroom floor, she vomited as Max watched in horror, unaware until now that she was vulnerable.

A SCRAWLED NOTE WAS left on Jeremy's desk. "Your documents are ready. Dress in black and pick them up on the corner of 55th and Park at 11:00 tonight."

Before leaving the office, Jeremy checked his e-mail one last time. He had a message from Richard, but instead of concocting another excuse, he took off through the stairwell door, down thirty-five flights of stairs, dizzy as he emerged into the lobby and ran through the revolving doors. This time, he didn't bother to think up reasons for his absence. The only excuse he could offer: he had finally become unreachable.

At the appointed place, the appointed time, there were three of them, in sunglasses and black trench coats. Had Jeremy not known who they were, they would have been perfect ads for "If you see something, say something." He considered telling Magellan that he'd changed his mind or just bolting outright, but Magellan clapped him heartily on the back.

"Trust me, you're not going to regret this," Magellan said, and handed him his own pair of sunglasses and a trench coat, bringing to mind the games of dress-up Max liked to play, so serious about each of his disguises that it stirred in Jeremy the desire to bolster this imaginative part of his son. Jeremy had shared neither Max's interest in dress-up nor his imagination—this, he must have inherited from Nina. At home, impossibly far away, she was no doubt furious at him. He'd received her message about the vomiting but hadn't called back, lessening his guilt by telling himself that in the time it would take him to survey the scene, she'd have already bathed both kids and tucked them into bed. Instead he'd e-mailed Nina to say there was something he needed to take care of, but even if the kids hadn't been sick, he wouldn't have told her where he was going. If he were to describe his plans, he would abandon them. If he were to hear anyone else's misgivings, he wouldn't be able to evade his own.

They took the 6 train to the Brooklyn Bridge station. On the platform, they waited for the last train to pass before the track work began. Magellan had up-to-date information about the schedule of repairs, having called MTA customer service to discuss how his "daily commute" would be affected. As they waited, Magellan told Jeremy that if you were going to really live in this city, you needed to see the infrastructure, the steel frames, the bare bones. If you wanted to build something, or destroy it, even if you just wanted to truly appreciate a place, this was where you needed to look.

When the train passed through the station and came back into view on the uptown side, Magellan and company walked to the edge of the platform, looked both ways, and jumped onto the tracks. Despite a growing queasiness in his stomach and a tremor in his fingers, Jeremy followed, trying not to wonder whether Magellan had faulty information about the train being out of service at this station; he was trying not to wonder whether the firm's life insurance policy covered a case of accidentally walking on the tracks' third rail. A rat scurried nearby, more afraid than they were, but Jeremy jumped, sure they'd been detected.

A few feet beyond the end of the station, the single set of

tracks diverged, and safely out of sight of anyone in the station, Magellan switched on his flashlight, and Jeremy followed. The white beams illuminated the steel piping that snaked the walls. Posted signs advised DO NOT ENTER. DO NOT CROSS TRACKS. Jeremy's every cell stood at attention. Except for wandering in the Ramble of Central Park, he didn't know the last time he'd been unable to locate himself on the city's grid.

To attract as little attention as possible, they planned to walk calmly. But once they saw the lights of the abandoned station, Magellan began to sprint and Jeremy followed. City Hall station was a hundred yards away, and they hoisted themselves onto the platform and ran back and forth. Magellan's laughter echoed through the station, creating the illusion that hundreds of them had swooped in and were stampeding back and forth. When they stopped running, they looked up at the chandeliers, the intricately tiled ceiling. In the station, Magellan became a nocturnal creature who'd simply been waiting to reveal his iridescent colors.

"Notice the Guastavino vaults. The Grueby tile," Magellan said, shining his flashlight. "And the skylights that lead to City Hall Park, blackened during World War II, though if you know where to look—and I do—you can see them in the park above us."

Jeremy too had read about these details and studied the pictures of the station, but that paled with how it felt to stand here. In this time capsule of a space, he felt not the New York of today, but one that had passed long ago. In Times Square, the Knickerbocker Hotel is two years old. Grand Central Station is under construction. So is the New York Public Library, though it won't be completed for seven years. The Flatiron Building is standing, as is the Vanderbilt mansion, La Farge's work safely inside. It's October 27, 1904, and the first subway riders are assembled in their Sunday best. The city feels ripe with possibility. Finally, a way to escape the overcrowded, polluted streets, the daylight darkened by the overhead trains, the snarled intersections of too many people and not enough space.

The next day, when the IRT officially opens, the city is decorated with festive bunting, and a rush of people descend the steps, holding paper tickets that cost five cents apiece. The train runs from City Hall to Grand Central, then along the West Side up to Harlem, transporting passengers at a speed that until now existed only in futuristic tales. On that first day, they rode the train not because they had anywhere they needed to be, but because they wanted to marvel at the means by which they'd arrive. Their excitement was so close at hand that Jeremy expected the metal gates to rise, the turnstiles to rotate, and those same people to come streaming onto the platform. They would board a train that bore no recognizable numbers or letters, that would take them not to their jobs but to locations that existed only in the outermost boroughs of their minds.

It was as close to a religious epiphany as he'd ever come. Jeremy was reminded of something he was supposed to know: his life lay in his own hands. All the decisions already made, all the encumbering pieces in place, yet his life was still his to shape as he saw fit. No longer squelched, no longer silenced, he had the craving for something fuller, richer, his own. In this closed-off space, there was always more to be uncovered. In a city where eyes had swept over everything, here was the chance to claim what was still unseen, untouched.

"You do the honors," Magellan told Jeremy, and handed him the black flag, which he placed in a corner of the station, hidden enough that it wouldn't be too easily detected, visible enough that it might one day be seen.

Back on the tracks, they ran toward the light of Brooklyn

Bridge station, though it seemed impossible that after where he'd been, he could board a train and eventually emerge a block from his apartment. Surely he'd have to blast through layers of earth in a specially equipped rocket ship in order to return home.

They climbed onto the platform as though they, like the mythical alligators that lived in the sewer system, had simply come up for air. They exited the turnstiles and walked to the next station, where it was a normal night and the subways were running as scheduled. When the train came, they sprawled in the nearly empty car, and Magellan lost his sheen. Once again he was Jon, the sleepy guy from the word-processing center, debating with his cohorts whether their next mission should be to break into the dilapidated insane asylum on Governors Island or to find the still-existent passageway between the 42nd Street subway station and the defunct Knickerbocker Hotel.

"How's your long-lost window?" Jon asked.

"I still think it's there, but Richard thought I was crazy."

"Richard's an asshole. You've got to sneak into the building. Maybe you can break down a wall. We can help you. You'll be our next mission. You should come to our meetings — every full moon, by the base of the Brooklyn Bridge," Jon said.

In the light of the train, Jeremy looked more carefully at Jon. He was older than Jeremy had initially thought; streaks of gray were evident in his long hair, and around his eyes were small forked lines. These nightly adventures weren't a youthful indiscretion that he'd let go of as he aged. They would always be part of who he was.

As Jeremy was about to get off the train, Jon handed him a spare flag. Jeremy began to protest but Jon insisted. "Keep the sunglasses and coat too. You never know when you might need them."

• • •

When Jeremy entered his building, a part of him was still underground. Magellan was probably writing up tonight's adventure for his blog, and for Jeremy, too, the only way to keep his euphoria from dissolving was to tell someone where he'd been. He resisted the urge to rouse the doorman and decided instead to wake Nina. An urgency overtook him, as though there were an emergency he hadn't known about until now. This time he wouldn't let the conversation get lost amid the noise of their lives; he'd shake her awake if he had to, he'd whisper under the covers if need be, pass her a note so as not to awaken the kids. Even though she had stopped calling him as often and no longer urged him to come home earlier, he hadn't wanted to think about what it meant. And even now, when he was late not just by hours but by months, he wanted to believe that she would turn to him eager to hear about his adventure.

Tiptoeing into the apartment, Jeremy was greeted by a terrible smell. His family was asleep on the bathroom floor. He carried Max to bed, and when he came back for Lily, Nina awoke and lurched toward the toilet. He crouched beside her, brushing her hair from her face.

"I'm sorry I wasn't here," Jeremy said as he helped Nina strip down, then get into the shower, her eyes barely open as she stood under the water.

"Lean back," Jeremy said, sudsing then rinsing her hair. Somewhere under the official definition of love, there had to be an entry for showering your sick, naked wife. The only other time he'd taken care of her like this was in the hospital in the hazy days following Max's birth, when Nina had barely been able to stand after her C-section and had been afraid to remove the massive maternity underwear she'd worn to cover the incision. Never had he seen her look so pitiful and never had he loved her so much. She'd leaned her weight on him and together they had inched their way back to the bed. It was so much responsibility, yes, but also so much love. He'd perched beside her and held her and their baby. They hadn't yet endured a single night alone with their newborn. They'd had no idea what awaited them.

After tucking Nina into bed, Jeremy looked around at the apartment and the piles of laundry and wasn't sure what to do. Sleep begets sleep, they were told when each kid was born, and absence begets absence, Jeremy had learned now that they were older. Not thinking about the mess that awaited him at work, Jeremy left a message for Richard saying he wouldn't be in the next day. He looked around, unsure where to begin. It was true that all these years the work had been endless, but he couldn't hide from the fact that so many times, it had been easier to stay in his office than to come home.

Following the scent of vomit, he wiped down the floors. Dishes were piled in the sink and he stacked them in the dishwasher. From underneath the couch pillows he pulled out a lost world of sippy cups. He dug deeper and pulled out a stack of kids' books and, mixed in with these, a book called *Painting in Air* by Claudia Stein. Jeremy flipped through it, wondering why Nina was reading it.

He took the book and all the dirty sheets to the laundry room, where he found Dog Man sitting in front of a dryer, the dog at his feet.

"Do you always do your laundry this late at night?" Dog Man greeted him.

"I never do laundry," Jeremy said.

"So what brings you down here?" Dog Man asked suspiciously.

Accustomed to avoiding any conversation that would waste a moment of billable time, Jeremy didn't answer, focusing all his attention on loading the sheets and towels into a machine.

"You don't want to put them in all together," Dog Man advised.

Jeremy had no idea whether this was true, but he didn't want to take chances. In need of help, Jeremy relented. "My family is sick. It's the least I could do. You live above us, right? I'm surprised you didn't hear anything. I think there was a lot of commotion in our apartment."

"Actually, Churchill and I have had a very quiet night. Not a single disruption," Dog Man said.

"Apparently I missed the worst of it."

"Late night at the office?"

"This might sound crazy, but while my wife and kids were vomiting, I was sneaking into an abandoned subway station underneath City Hall," Jeremy said.

"I imagine you could get into a lot of trouble for doing that."

"Probably," Jeremy agreed. "But have you ever done something that you know is crazy, but you also know that if you keep going, you'll discover something you're meant to see? I'm in my office all day like every other associate and none of them have any idea how much I hate it. I have no idea how they feel either. We're there all the time and I don't really know any of them."

"I was married for two years and I loved my wife very much. I had no idea that I was the only one who was happy," Dog Man confessed. The dog whimpered and stretched at his feet. From a shopping bag he pulled out a white bakery box and took out a piece of decorated cake. As the dog bit into it, Dog Man petted him on the head. He dipped his hand into the icing and let the dog lick his fingers clean.

If Nina were here, Jeremy knew she would take Dog Man's presence as the answer to some great mystery: he was on a stakeout, or he was destroying the evidence of a late-night crime. But really he was lonely, a mystery both easier and more impossible to solve.

"I've seen you around but I don't know your name," Jeremy said, and introduced himself.

"Arthur Grayson. And this is Churchill," he said, extending his hand.

For the next few days, Jeremy stayed home from work. The kids started to feel better before Nina did, and Jeremy took them outside uncombed and unkempt, but it wasn't her problem. Emma had called to say that she was still sick, but though Nina missed her, she didn't need to rely on her alone. There was no greater sound than Jeremy cooking supper, bathing the kids, putting them to bed. He dressed the kids each morning and walked Max to school, as if he were making up for lost time. She'd arrived at that falsely promised future in which the kids were not hers alone. To her surprise, Max and Lily survived without her constant attention. They went to sleep without needing serial feedings and rocking. Only once they sensed that she couldn't meet their every need did they finally stop asking.

In a far-off region of her mind, Nina thought about calling Leon but felt sure her every move was being watched. Trying to return to the approximation of her life at home, she e-mailed him to say she was sick, but she didn't say more, nor did she answer her phone each of the times he called. She would act as though this hadn't happened. If she didn't think about Leon, he would no longer exist. By keeping a tight rein on her mind, she wouldn't have to worry that his name would announce itself when she least expected or that the look on her face would give her away.

But there was no easy retreat. No matter how many times she tried to tamp down her feelings, she felt the shadow of a lie or omission. Leon took his place between her and Jeremy, an invisible presence. In Jeremy's expression, she saw clues that he knew. She couldn't say one word without feeling it was a lie; she couldn't look him in the eye for fear of what he might see.

Nina awoke one day later that week to find Max back home from nursery school, peering at her so closely that she could feel the warmth of his breath; he leaned closer still and she felt the graze of his eyelashes against her cheek.

"Are you awake?" Max whispered in her ear.

She hugged both him and Lily, her airtight alibis. In their presence, no one would look at her and know what she was thinking; no one would see on her face the signs of her duplicity, nor would anyone lean close and hear, beating inside her, a second heart.

Jeremy was folding laundry at the foot of the bed, and she didn't say anything as he struggled with the fitted sheets, bewildered but not willing to ask for directions.

"I think I'm delirious," she said.

"I'm making dinner," he said.

"Now I know I'm delirious."

In his presence, the guilt that she had tried to outrun caught her in its grasp. There had been no unbearable unhappiness to justify what she had done, only the small sharp slivers of loneliness and discontent. These, it turned out, were the most dangerous of all. She wanted to give in to the child's fantasy that to confess would make it all better. She wanted to hug Jeremy and console him; she wanted to wake and find none of this had happened after all.

As soon as Jeremy fell asleep that night, Nina went back to her usual spot in the living room. How wrong she had been to think she could gaze out unaffected. How wrong to believe that you could always find your way back. When, she wondered, had her betrayal truly begun? Was it when she first kissed Leon, or was it weeks, months before, when she'd allowed her gaze to linger, her restlessness to swim toward the light?

Tonight, as she looked out, all the windows were dark except for one. In a lit room she thought she saw someone in Leon's arms, on his couch. Staring into that room with the same scrutiny she'd once turned on other people's lives, Nina realized that she was looking at a version of herself, one that until now she hadn't known existed. She had unrestricted access, yet she was looking at this person, supposedly herself, with the same curiosity and wonder as she would a stranger.

ITTING IN THE back row of a community meeting, Jeremy clapped, even though the protest being planned would infuriate the client and cause him countless late nights. He would be forced to draft memos reminding the neighborhood groups of the developers' legal rights. He'd be the ruthless lawyer who cared for nothing but the bottom line.

He'd come to the meeting as Richard had instructed. Richard had stopped giving him substantive work, treating him as though he had come down with an unmentionable disease. The junior associate, whom Richard had recently recruited for the deal, would normally have been dispatched to cover the meeting, but Richard claimed that he was busy on a document that needed to be drafted right away. As far as Jeremy knew, the junior associate didn't have a family, wasn't yet jaded or used up. That he would be one day didn't matter — there were thousands of billable hours to be wrung from him before this happened. And when, inevitably, it did, there would be other young associates to replace him. Jeremy was sure of this, because when he first started working for Richard, there had been an older associate whom he'd pushed out of the way. The defeat had been present in his eyes, though Jeremy hadn't yet known how to recognize it.

"Why don't we get started?" said Barbara Kaufman, a

woman whose name he recognized from the irate e-mails she wrote that the client forwarded to him.

Barbara began her presentation by wondering aloud what would happen if every neighborhood looked alike. What if all the stores were identical, all façades the same towering glass, endless reflections of each other but of what else? Jeremy listened, hoping she would announce that they had unearthed the presence of a major work of art hidden in the walls of the building. But she admitted that she had found no rationale to stop the construction. He alone knew about the possible presence of the window.

When several elderly people in the back shouted that they couldn't hear her, Barbara spoke more directly into the mike, telling everyone assembled how, if the developers were allowed to construct this building, it would send the message that West Siders no longer cared about preserving their neighborhood. In the future, she would push to have the neighborhood rezoned, but it would be too late for this site.

When Barbara stopped to take questions, a man with a nest of white hair spun a conspiracy theory involving Metro-Cards, transit police, and old cable car wires. It was easy for Jeremy to laugh him off as one of the crazies, the marginal people he walked past and thought little about. Richard portrayed all the local activists as rabble-rousers or gadflies, but at least they cared about their neighborhood.

"Thank you, but we need to move on," Barbara said in a voice firm enough to dissuade everyone except the owner of a persistent hand in the front row.

"I've looked over the information you handed out, and it's clear to me that if you want to put a stop to this building, you need to take action," the man said, standing as he spoke. "You have to know how these developers think. They'll let us have our meetings and hang our signs, but they don't think anyone cares enough to fight. Hanging signs is nice but trust me, it's hardly enough."

Jeremy recognized Dog Man, or Arthur as he was trying now to think of him. When Arthur asked for a show of hands for who would attend a protest, he was met with nearly unanimous support. When the meeting ended, Arthur was surrounded by people wanting to congratulate him on his speech, so Jeremy walked home by himself. In front of the building across the street, he noticed for the first time the grizzled gargoyles adorning the prewar façade. The lover with his curlicue mustache, flowing long hair, and soulful eyes. Next to him, the explorer whose face peeked out from underneath a triangular hat; the mercenary, decorated with gold bullion and crossed swords. Long ago he might have simply enjoyed their decorative presence if he saw them at all, but now he wanted to grab a crowbar from the nearby construction site and wrest them free.

Inside his apartment, Jeremy sat on the living room floor, spreading out the documents he'd been bringing home in the hope that one day he would know what to do with them. They were supposed to be confidential, but he was letting go of all those years of hard work. He no longer wanted to pay the price, nor did he want the reward. He took the copies of the documents he'd drafted and added to them the piles of research he'd compiled. Using Max's Magic Markers, he copied passages from Claudia Stein's book which he'd unearthed from the couch. He e-mailed Magellan asking for help and pulled from his briefcase the flag and sunglasses. He'd intended to give them to Max, but he had found someone who needed them more.

Remembering his elation at being underground, Jeremy ran up the flight of stairs and left a thick envelope outside 14B's door.

N THE BASEMENT of Grace Episcopal Church, in a suburb of Boston, six wood boxes lay covered with dust. They were in a back corner on the dirt floor, near a pile of discarded books and broken chairs where for decades they had been ignored. The caretaker of the church led Claudia inside and left her alone.

She opened a box and held her breath at the cloud of dust. After all these years, her window might be here in this basement. Slowly, she removed the white sheeting covering the first panel. With a brush, she removed the layer of dirt. Cherubic angels. Garlands of flowers. Squares of bright blue glass.

She released her breath and fought back tears. The handiwork was visibly clumsy, the glass dimmer, the color painted on. Claudia looked at each of the panels, trying to maintain hope. But she wasn't fooled; she knew his work too well to mistake it for anyone else's. This window might have been made by one of La Farge's followers, an honest attempt at imitation, but it wasn't the work of the artist himself.

Claudia wanted to extract each piece of glass until the floor was a shimmering mess. She wanted to smash each piece into jewel-colored dust. The window was lost anew, as though it had already belonged to her. She thought about calling Leon, wishing he could offer her consolation. "I thought you didn't believe that the window existed anymore," Leon had said when she told him she was going to Boston. "I never said that, not definitively," she had said, unable to hold back her anger. "You haven't read my article. You don't care about my work. How could you possibly know what I think about my window? You don't know what I think about anything."

She carried with her the skeptical look in his eyes, the pity that had taken shape as he looked at her. All he saw was her hopeless search. But he had turned out to be right. In more arenas than she cared to admit, she had let herself be fooled by hope. She had given in to the fallacy of believing that what existed in her mind also existed in the world. She had been fooled into seeing what she wished to be there.

She needed to see the windows again, the ones that had first kindled her love. For the first time in decades, she drove to North Easton. She'd forgotten how close it was to Boston where she'd been so many times over the years. She went first to Unity Church, where the *Wisdom* window was visible from the street, although from the exterior, it looked like a study yet to be completed. But once she walked in, the world was recast with color. The windows were living creatures, and she approached them as though she were greeting someone she loved. It didn't matter that she could lecture about each plate of glass, or that she knew the minute painstaking process with which such creations were made. A part of her still believed that these windows had always been in existence, as though someone had dug deep enough and extracted them from below the layers of earth, or built high enough and found them hidden in the far reaches of the sky.

In the *Wisdom* window, made in 1901 and La Farge's largest, a Madonna-like figure was seated, haloed, on a throne. The rose lines of her dress were so supple it appeared to be made of cloth. Some of the shards of glass were so small, so brittle, that few glassmakers would be daring enough to use them today. A verse from Proverbs surrounded the window: *Wisdom is more precious than rubies and all the things that thou canst desire are not to be compared unto her.*

The *Angel of Help* window, across the room, was done in 1882, its background made of broken glass jewels, blue stones embedded along the bottom, ridged nuggets of purple stone along the top, fractured bottle-green roundels of glass at the base. The eye was immediately drawn upward by the jeweled sarcophagus which rose to heaven surrounded by a flock of angels. And at the center was the Angel of Help, bearing a face so gentle and lifelike, Claudia had always felt sure she had been seen by her.

Were there words to describe the shock of so much color, the feeling of having entered into a supernatural world in which there existed such light? It was like falling in love, only the feeling didn't fade. Both windows were commissioned as mourning icons for members of the Ames family, yet these blazing colors were a celebration, not just of familial loss but of love, not just of death but of life.

She traced the path she had taken every day toward home. The same ten-minute walk, the same quiet, winding street. The leaves were already changing color, the sky dappled with orange and red. She passed the factory buildings of tan stone that had once housed the Ames family shovel companies, and the stone Romanesque-style buildings; they were so heavy that they seemed to have sprouted from the rock on which they were built, so solid and impermeable they could never be knocked down.

She turned the corner onto her former street, but the house in which she'd grown up wasn't there. In place of the small, nondescript white Cape was a gleaming McMansion with pillars and a portico that looked as though they were made of plastic. The intended style may have been Greek Revival, but the result was American gaudy.

All these years she thought she had left this house behind, and though it no longer existed, it had been fully preserved in her mind. Her regret surged. What if she and her mother had, for one moment, stopped fighting? What if they had found some other way to see one another? She thought she had run, but however winding it was, the path led her back to this very place. The mother she had become was inextricably tied to the daughter she had been. She had wanted to give her daughter so much. Yet Emma wasn't a window through which she might have seen all the different possibilities of who her daughter might become. She had viewed her as a mirror, in which she had primarily seen herself.

Claudia called Leon and left him a message that she was staying in Boston longer than planned. She didn't ask if he minded, didn't say she would call back later. After living for so long with his absence, she wanted to inflict her own.

The only way to feel better was to sink inside her work. She spent her days at the Boston Public Library where the words flowed as though emanating directly from her hands, her fingers containing her thoughts, as if she too were a craftsman fashioning a majestic work of art. At night, in her hotel room, she propped herself up in bed, her computer perched on her lap. She fell asleep with her books spread open around her.

She took breaks only to walk around Boston. She went to Trinity Church, where she gazed at La Farge's famed *Christ in Majesty,* the astonishing blue background of which made the actual sky seem like a poor imitation of itself. She went to the MFA and stood before La Farge's *Peonies Blown in the Wind,* staying until the museum closed. She wanted to disobey the museum guards and run her hands along the glass; she wanted to believe that when no one was looking, the guards indulged this urge as well.

When she had been away for four days and still didn't want to return home, Claudia sat at a table in the library where, next to her, was a copy of an obscure American history journal someone had left behind. Leafing through it, she found an article that traced the more recent generations of Cornelius Vanderbilt's extended family.

She knew most of what was recounted there, but on the next-to-last page of the article was a footnote that she almost skipped over. There was one little-known branch of the family in whom Vanderbilt had taken a special interest. A niece, a young woman whose husband had died young, was left penniless, and she and her newborn daughter were taken to live in the 58th Street mansion. Eventually it became clear that the woman was mentally ill, and though the family tried to keep her from the public eye, they had allowed her to remain in the house. Later her own daughter too began to show signs of this mental illness—a form of paranoid schizophrenia that would continue to be passed down from one generation to the next. After Cornelius died and the mansion was demolished, the family honored his request to care for his compromised relatives and moved them into an apartment on the newly developing Upper West Side. No one knew how long that apartment had stayed in the family, but it was probable that it, like the mental illness, had continued to be passed down.

There was no escape from the bonds of family. Even when you tried to stay away. Even when you thought you could set yourself free. Everything, ultimately, was passed down.

THE HANDWRITTEN NOTE inside the manila envelope directed Arthur to the microfilm room of the New York Public Library. It had a date and the title of an article and instructed him to be there the following day at 9:00 a.m. Accompanying it were a pair of sunglasses and a black flag.

The sound of applause still resounded in his head, as did the image of all those approving faces. He was no longer someone to avoid; he was a man who knew how to get things done. He wouldn't have even gone to the meeting if not for the fact that when he got to the gym for his nightly swim, a sign on the door had announced that the pool was closed for emergency repairs. The stinging rebuke he delivered to the woman behind the desk came naturally. He would be lost, he realized, without his outrage; in its throes, he felt most recognizably himself. But what surprised him was how badly he craved the freedom of the pool.

He had gone home to another evening with nothing to do but prowl the apartment. Except for the brief interaction at the gym, he'd spoken to no human being the entire day. He felt trapped inside each room, a prisoner in his home. Churchill was no comfort, not even when he nuzzled against his leg. All he could think of, all he wanted to do, was stand before Georgia's café. This time he would not simply gaze inside those windows, forlorn. He wanted to smash his hand through the glass and upend each gorgeous cake, leaving behind icing covered with shattered glass. Let her customers eat them that way. Let them see that though the cakes looked gorgeous on the outside, their secret ingredients were disloyalty and betrayal.

He had run downstairs, where in the lobby he'd looked for anyone to talk to. But the lobby was deserted, everyone else having places to be. He had noticed a sign hanging where his flyer about the missing laundry had once been. *Save our neighborhood!!!!!! Let your voice be heard!!!!!!!!!!!! Come talk about the plan to build another luxury high-rise building in our neighborhood!!!!!!!!!!!!!!!!!!* He'd seen these posters before but had been too preoccupied with the issues in his own building to get involved. He'd also been annoyed at whoever hung these signs on bus stops and the barriers to construction sites despite the warnings there to Post No Bills. But with more urgent outrages to confront, he overlooked these minor infractions. Arthur had glanced at the date and time, excited to see that the meeting was that night.

After the acclaim his suggestion had received, his anger was still there, but now it gave him purpose. Though he opted not to wear the sunglasses, Arthur went where he was told. In the main reading room, another black flag was detectable, high up on the coffered ceiling. He found the article about the demolition of the Vanderbilt mansion on the corner of Fifth and 58th Street, and despite his misgivings, he went to the site where this house once stood. The buildings there were so immense that it was hard to imagine anything else ever existing in their place.

As he looked at the bald mannequins in Bergdorf's windows, someone jostled him from behind, and when he spun around to rebuke the careless offender, he realized that he had been the opposite of pickpocketed. Sticking out from his back pocket was a black flag, and at his feet was another envelope containing a list of all the places in Manhattan where certain stained-glass windows were installed. The same scrawled hand-writing instructed him to visit each one, in the order in which they appeared on the list.

He considered whether he was being subjected to com-pulsory art appreciation. If he looked closely, he wondered, would he catch his neighbors following at a safe distance, hands cupped over their mouths to stifle their laughter? But remem-bering the good feeling of the previous night, he continued on to the Church of the Incarnation, followed by four more churches. Inside each was one of the stained-glass windows on the list. By the time Arthur reached the Met, he was eager to get home to Churchill, who would be whimpering by the door. The museum was closing soon, which gave him an excuse for paying only a dollar of the suggested admission. He couldn't re-member the last time he'd been there. Did New Yorkers ever go, or was it just tourists who clogged the place?

He asked a security guard to direct him to the American Wing, getting lost along the way among the mummies and sar-cophagi. In the nearly empty courtyard was the window he was supposed to be looking at.

The *Welcome* window was more interesting than the oth-ers, and the shimmer of glass and color allowed him to mo-mentarily forget his accumulated list of slights and grievances. When he was swimming, he had the same sensation of having shed, however briefly, the parts of his body that weighed him down. An unfamiliar feeling jolted him. He realized, with sur-prise, that he was having fun.

At one of the café tables nearby, a skinny man with a pony-tail was staring at him as he ate a piece of cake. Arthur scowled, but unintimidated, the man stood and held out another en-velope. "Don't think we're not aware of your efforts," he said, clapped Arthur on the arm, and was gone.

The note inside instructed him to go to the Department of

Buildings and request the file for 2687 Broadway. When the office opened the next morning, Arthur was the first in line. He asked the clerk for the file, surprised that it wasn't harder to gain access to a building's floor plans and renovation records; it was like walking into a hospital and requesting the medical records of anyone you were curious about.

Arthur photocopied the pages and took them home. He read about the townhouse that was subsumed into a larger building, then attached to another building with a party wall. When he found the scribbled note about the stained-glass window being covered, he understood his mission.

He took a break only to walk Churchill and to swim. When he returned home, he looked for Barbara Kaufman's phone number, steeling himself to the possibility that she was besieged by calls from people wanting to get involved. Though she remembered him from the meeting, she sounded guarded and skeptical. But no one had ever accused him of being insufficiently zealous.

"It's recently come to my attention that there may be a long-lost stained-glass window boarded up between these buildings," he said.

She agreed to meet the next day, and as Arthur hung up, he suddenly realized how he knew her. She was the owner of the terrier that antagonized Churchill on their morning walks, the dog's small size belying its ferocity. He'd always assumed the owner to be as obnoxious as the dog. He'd responded to her with hostility because that was what he'd seen on her face.

The first impression he'd had of her softened. At the meeting, he'd recognized her like-mindedness, and all that evening, when he thought back to the window at the Met, her face replaced the one depicted in stained glass.

N HIS OFFICE Leon sat across from his patient, unsure of what to say. After seeing her from the window of his car, he had hoped that she wouldn't show up. He'd wondered if he could come up with a good reason to tell her he couldn't see her anymore. Gone was the feeling that at least with regard to his work, he remained in control.

She too was quieter than usual, but instead of directly addressing the discomfort, she launched into her customary account of her every interaction with the kids. He tried to listen but he couldn't sit there for one more moment, not when he wanted her, him, all of them, to give in to the onslaught of feeling she was so afraid of.

"And what do you think would happen if you got angry and screamed, 'I've had it'?" he interrupted her.

"But that's not who I want to be. That's not how I want my kids, or anyone, to see me," she said.

"I know, but even then, how bad would it really be? Would Sophie and Harry survive? Would you?" he persisted. He had pushed her before, but never with as much conviction.

Her face took on a wild expression he hadn't seen from her before. "I saw you in your car. You were sitting in it with a friend of mine."

He startled. Of course she and Nina were friends. Even in this city of so many people, there was no escape from the expanding web of intersections. He fumbled to regain his calm, reminding himself that even if she had seen him and Nina talking in the car, what would that really mean? He had looked out the window before kissing Nina; he was sure of that. There was no way she had still been there. Only his guilty conscience would have him believe otherwise.

"First I thought I was imagining you. But I know it was you. I can't stop wondering. How do you know each other, what does it mean? But now I realize. I have no idea who you are. I don't know anything about you."

"We can talk about what was actually happening in that moment, but I think it's more important to talk about what it means to you," he said, invoking the old formula he'd been taught to recite.

"Why were you in the car with her? Please, I really want to know."

He could continue to turn the question back at her, ask her again why she was so interested to know. What had been her wish, that she was the one in the car? What had been her irrational fear, that they had been discussing her? Had she felt a child's slight at being left out? Had she felt this way with her own parents? Had she felt the urge to break in and join them?

He was tired, too tired. All he wanted to do was step out from behind the screen.

"We have something in common, actually. I'm also used to being in control of my feelings. I'm not sure what to do otherwise," Leon said.

"So what if you weren't? What would happen? Would *you* survive?" she said, her voice growing more playful, lighter.

"I don't know. That's what I'm trying to figure out," he admitted.

Before his guard was back up, she leaned closer and took hold of his hand. What fantasy was he participating in now, what gaping hole inside her being filled? He allowed it to happen, unnerved by what she had seen and the questions open between them. He didn't know how he would feel toward her in their next session, what meaning this would hold for either of them. But nowhere, not even in therapy, were there blank slates. Not even the strictest of boundaries, the most impermeable of barriers, could contain life's messy drama.

He was rescued by the end of the session, life broken down in fifty-minute segments. But an image of Wendy screaming in anger, in relief, permeated his day. What if he were not to remain in control? The self unleashed: it was to risk the loss of who you knew yourself to be. For the rest of the day, he couldn't put aside this feeling. Every patient who sat in front of him seemed on the verge of upheaval. Screaming, all of them. The pain in the room was more acute than ever, as though all his patients had descended upon his office at once and formed a chorus of lament. Their lives entered his; there was no protection.

At the end of the day, Leon left his office but didn't want to go home. With this pocket of free time, he wondered if he should call Claudia—she was still out of town and hadn't called, though until now he'd been relieved. The night before Claudia left for Boston, he reached for her out of guilt, knowing all too well the substitution he was making in his mind. But she pulled away, as if she knew as well.

He went to the park where he walked down the cobblestone pathways to one of the playgrounds Nina often mentioned. He couldn't tell her what Wendy had said—he was ethically prohibited from confession—but he needed to see her nonetheless. It was cooler out than he'd realized. Soon it would be too cold to spend time here, but the mothers were determined to make use of every last day before being forced into their winter hibernations. He was the only one without a child, potentially closer to grandparenthood now than young parenthood, and he assembled excuses for his presence in case he saw anyone he knew. He came up with no good explanation, but it didn't matter: it seemed impossible that anyone would recognize him when he hardly recognized himself.

From afar, he tried to pick Nina out among the swarms of mothers. In the past two weeks, he and Nina had exchanged a few e-mails, but she hadn't called him, a silence he wasn't sure how to read. He had become so accustomed to her regular presence in his day that he checked his phone messages and e-mails with great urgency. He stared at his phone, as though expecting it to change form, become her. He looked out the window in the hope that some coded message might flicker.

He knew all too well the part of himself that would feel relief at her retreat. Less required of him, less expected. A brief flash of excitement, but overall, a complication averted, his quiet life unimpeded. He would go forward, impassively, into whatever the rest of his life happened to hold. Nina would be a memory of something that had happened long ago. He walked through Riverside Park, from playground to playground, in search of her. All around him, children screamed, in the avid throes of life. When he looked up, above the rocky outcropping of the park, he saw the rising spires of steel. Last week, as he and Claudia happened to walk out of the building at the same time, Claudia had marveled that cranes dangled lethal beams, yet they all went about their lives oblivious to what was above them. At the time he had been only half listening and had murmured his disinterested assent, but now he stopped to think. What if they did look up, what if they really saw what was around them? He stopped walking, newly aware of an idea that had started to take shape.

ERE'S WHAT WE'RE going to do," Wendy said to Nina and her children, who were assembled around the table, awaiting instructions. Wendy passed out small tubes of icing, bowls of sprinkles and sparkles, and Nina looked on as she displayed pictures of cookies that were perfect replicas of clowns and cats, houses and dogs, the icing as smooth as a potter's glaze.

Since she and the kids had been sick, Nina had been hiding from Wendy. She left nursery school pickup early. She took the kids to distant parks where they knew no one. They stayed home and ate Wacky Mac in front of the TV. Except for the few hours when Max was in school, she was alone with both kids all day. Emma had called to say that she still wasn't feeling well, and Nina had felt hurt at her excuses, having allowed herself to think that they were friends. She told herself that the closeness had been in her own mind; Emma had probably lost interest, her kids one more thing to take hold of, then let go. But the possibility that it was something more complicated pressed at her. *Don't think about that,* Nina told herself. Don't wonder what Emma knows, don't try to imagine the betrayal she would feel if she did know. Think of nothing but the kids, nothing but the demands of the day. She didn't call Leon, making every effort to stay inside the narrow fold she had constructed for herself. If she busied herself with the children, she wouldn't have time to think—this, the path of escape so many of them had chosen.

"I ruined mine," Sophie said, her tears spilling onto her dog-shaped cookie which looked nothing like the one in the picture.

Wendy surveyed what her daughter had made. Both the icing and the children were more willful than anticipated. The cookies were becoming increasingly unrecognizable. The cookie cutters seemed incapable of doing their job.

"Come on, honey, don't give up! You can do it! Try again," Wendy urged her, and glanced over at Harry, who seemed unbothered by the mess he'd made. She smiled at Nina. "They usually love baking with me. I don't know what's gotten into them today."

Max crawled on the floor, pretending to be a dog. After his encounter in the park, which he'd told her about though Emma had neglected to mention it, his love of firemen had been transformed into a love of dogs.

"Max, don't you want to make cookies?" Wendy asked.

As Lily licked the crystals off Max's hands until her face sparkled blue and green, Wendy's expression became more grim.

"I hope he Purelled," Wendy said.

"Actually we forgot," Nina said. Let Wendy accuse her of squalor. Let her cast a downward sweeping eye. Absent the rules and all the expectations, it no longer felt as hard to be with the kids.

Wendy made a face, but there wasn't time to linger on this trespass when there were greater ones happening all around. "Come on, Harry, not like that. I know you can do it like I taught you. A little more icing, Sophie," Wendy said, her voice rising in pitch. "Do it like this. Try it again. Good. Once more."

Sophie threw the dough onto the floor and stared her

mother down. She swept out her arms, knocking the bowls of edible glitter onto the floor. "You always make me do it your way," she screamed.

"I see how angry you must be feeling but edible glitter is not for throwing," Wendy said. Her smile looked like it could rip open at any minute and become a scowl. "Do you want to draw your feelings? Do you want your alone time? Do you want me to get your special chair?"

"Can you please please please stop talking!" Sophie screamed, her face bright red, her hands pressed against her ears. Looking her mother in the eye, she overturned two more bowls of glitter, her hands and the floor now dusted with sparkles. A bowl of hot-pink glitter landed on Harry's head.

Nina sat still, enjoying the sight of other children's meltdowns. She tried to squelch the rise of laughter, but she couldn't help herself. She laughed until her shoulders shook and tears sprang to her eyes.

"What's so funny?" Wendy asked.

"Nothing," Nina tried to say, but that made her laugh more.

Wendy tried to grab her kids, but Sophie, Harry, and Max were jumping in a pack, a tangle of arms and legs. They tossed glitter in the air, licked it from their hands, from the floor.

There was a tussle, then a scream. Nina stopped laughing and Wendy froze, both of them anticipating everything from a snatched toy to a severed limb.

Max's arm was imprinted with a bracelet of tiny teeth. Nina stood to console him, as Wendy leaped toward Harry and grabbed him by the arm.

"What is wrong with you! Why are you biting? How many times do I have to tell you?" Wendy screamed.

"It's okay," Nina said as she hugged Max. "I think he's fine."

"How can you say that? We both know it's not fine." She took hold of Harry by the shoulders and shook him. "People are not for biting. How would you like it if someone bit you? We only bite food, okay, okay, OKAY? Apologize to Max right now," Wendy insisted as she held him in front of Max.

The words were right, but her face was distorted by rage, her eyes bulging, her mouth twisted into a grimace. She turned on Sophie as well. "What did I ever do to deserve this? Do you not see how hard I work for you? Do you not realize that I've given up everything for you?"

Instead of apologizing, Sophie began shoving handfuls of sprinkles into her mouth, trying to clean up the mess as quickly as she could. Still in his mother's arms, Harry shoved his hand toward his mother's mouth, offering himself up to be kissed. For a moment, neither of them moved. Wendy was silent, her color drained. Even when she put her arm around Sophie and dutifully kissed Harry's hand, it was too late. The embers of hot, red rage had flared and Nina had seen it all.

THE SPARE KEY to her father's car was in the kitchen drawer, and Emma borrowed it without permission. Her whole life had been transported in this car, from camp and then home, from college and then home, and to her apartment with Steven. Now she needed to borrow it once again, though this was a move she was going to do on her own.

She had found an apartment on Craigslist, a share with four other people in what was once a two-bedroom subdivided by portable walls. It amazed her that basically you could get your whole life from Craigslist. She'd also found a job in a nursery school, working as an assistant in the toddler room. When she went for an interview, the two-year-olds were awash in finger paints, slapping colorful hands onto their papers. Emma had crouched down next to two girls who were leaving their gooey marks on each other's arms. Maybe when she was their teacher she would have to put a stop to their behavior, but in that moment, all she had done was join in their laughter.

She'd told neither of her parents what she'd decided, because somewhere along the way, she had shed her belief that they knew best what she should do. If she told them, they would pretend to be accepting, then try to reframe her decision into something more comprehensible: she really wanted to develop curriculum in children's foreign language instruction or eventually get a degree in child development. Maybe one day, but for now, she wanted to live not away from the noise and the mess but as deeply inside it as she could. She would be changing diapers, wiping noses, life broken down into the tiniest moments.

Emma parked the car in front of the apartment she'd shared with Steven. She ran up the flights of stairs and went inside, afraid that if she paused, she would back down. She was scared of what she was about to do, but as she stopped to catch her breath, she realized that it was a new kind of fear. Rather than holding her back, it pushed her forward, inevitable, exhilarating. She wanted to see her life through her own eyes. If she was wrong about this choice, she would have no one to blame but herself.

It was the middle of the day but Steven was asleep on the couch and stirred as she came in, the pattern of their couch pillows imprinted on his cheek.

"What are you doing?" he mumbled.

"Go back to sleep," Emma whispered, hoping he'd awake hours from now and think he'd been robbed.

"I didn't know you were here," he said plaintively, expecting her to come sit beside him and offer consolation.

"I'm a figment of your imagination," she said, and began filling every stray knapsack and shopping bag she could find, the kind of leave-taking most people did only when they were being chased. Most of the clothes she stuffed into her bags either no longer fit or she no longer liked, but she didn't want to leave anything behind. The bags were so heavy that she struggled to lift them, but that was a good thing. Once she moved out, it would be too much work to return.

Emma made a few trips to the car, refusing to slow down. She was glad that she had somewhere she needed to be. After

a few weeks of pretending to be sick, she'd called Nina and offered to baby-sit that afternoon, having missed Nina and the
kids more than she'd anticipated.

Emma had stayed away out of anger, stayed away because
she didn't know how to understand what she had seen in the
park. Having continuously reconstructed the image of her father and Nina, she could play it back from every angle, supply-
ing alternative endings, like the "choose your own adventure"
books she'd once loved because you could always backtrack and
start again. At home, she searched her father's face for signs of
guilt, but he betrayed nothing. Even if she confronted him with
what she'd seen, he would claim that he and Nina had simply
run into each other and taken a walk, making Emma think she
had misread what at the time had seemed so clear. She knew
him so little that he could get away with almost anything. But
it didn't matter, she realized, because this problem wasn't hers
to fix. No one, not her parents or anyone whom she'd envied,
had lives as orderly as they made it appear; she might have run
wildly, uncontrollably, until she twisted her ankle and fell, but
how many of those who gaped at her from the seeming safety
of their own lives had wished to join in?

"Wait," Steven said, as Emma dragged a final bag across the
room.

She expected another fight, but he shocked her by burst-
ing into tears. He was barely recognizable in this rumpled pose
of love. She understood now the problem with this game of
chase, or hide-and-seek, or whatever it was she and Steven always played. Once you were found, you had to be the one to
go looking, shouting in vain to *come out, come out wherever you
are.* She'd rather take her chances: stand alone behind the curtains or under the bed and endure the terrifying thrill of having
chosen the best hiding spot of all.

Standing in front of him, she had no way to comfort him. She needed to do this, yet she knew that it wasn't true that you could always run—or if you did, you couldn't get away unscathed; there would be casualties left in your wake. He was waiting for her to offer some fuller explanation, and she forced herself to take in his look of betrayal. What could she say when she could hardly explain to herself the feeling that she had arrived suddenly at a wall and she could not move forward, could not continue. "I'm so sorry but I can't"—this was the only thing she could offer for upending the future they had planned.

She pulled the engagement ring off her finger, which bore a red-lined impression where it had been. All along it had probably been too tight, but she'd told herself that it was supposed to feel this way.

"I should give you this," Emma said.

"And I was going to give you this," he said, and handed her a rubber-banded manuscript. She looked at the copy of his book as if he were belatedly handing her the uncensored, wide-open access to him that she'd craved. Flip the pages, and there finally he would be. Read his words, and she would no longer feel as though she had to chase him down. Despite his protestations that he couldn't work in her absence, he had managed to reach the ever-receding finish line. The jealousy she felt wasn't enough to make her want to return to her own struggling sentences. Everyone around her was blinded by work, but she knew that she could be happy without it.

She didn't want to be swayed, didn't want to be reeled back in. Emma tossed his manuscript into a shopping bag but didn't slow down, even when Steven pleaded with her to stay. She lugged the last bag down the four flights of stairs. In the car, her bags were piled so high she couldn't see out the back window. She drove to her new apartment and unloaded everything into her bedroom. Then she got back into the car, so she could get a few more things from her parents' apartment. The few blocks she drove felt like a thousand miles, a cross-country journey undertaken alone.

WHEN CLAUDIA RETURNED home after a week away, Emma was standing in the doorway, holding a duffel bag.

"I found an apartment," Emma told her. "I just came to get the rest of my stuff. You're not going to like it, but I'm not going back to school. I got a job in a nursery school, in Queens, right near my new place."

Claudia opened her mouth to speak, then closed it again. She shook her head in disbelief, but then she laughed. All children were surprises, even those who once seemed to know where they were going.

"And what about Steven?" Claudia asked as she looked at Emma's bare finger.

Emma shook her head. "I know you liked him. Or at least the idea of him," she said.

"Emma, it doesn't matter if I like him or not. I wanted you to be happy."

"I know you think this is crazy," Emma said.

"I don't," Claudia said, and it was true. A new version of Emma was taking shape in her mind. More than dismay, she felt envious that her daughter wouldn't quietly withstand what left her distressed, unhappy, alone. She was capable of acting on what she knew to be true instead of quietly living with dissatisfaction.

"I need to go. I'm supposed to be baby-sitting soon," Emma said, but when she made no move to leave, Claudia reached for her.

"Do you really want to know why I'm leaving him?" Emma asked. "I don't want to get married so I can be alone. I don't want to be with someone who can't see who I am."

Emma's words sank in. Claudia tried to hide from them but she couldn't.

"I don't understand. Why do you let him ignore you? Why don't you care?" Emma asked.

"It's so much more complicated than that," Claudia said.

"Do you ever wonder where he is? Do you even care enough to go looking?" Emma asked, motioning to the window, to the great expanse outside.

"Do you think you're the only one who's ever felt this way? Do you think you're the only one who's ever wanted to run?" Claudia asked. She wished there were some way to shield her daughter from her pain, anyone's pain, and yet make her understand that no one really knew the inner workings of anyone else's marriage. Even inside, there was no way to see it entirely; even to your spouse, you couldn't fully explain the relationship you were in.

"Why didn't you? Please tell me. I need to understand," Emma said.

Why for so many years had she tucked away the feeling that she was invisible? Why had she told herself she did not really feel what she felt, why did she hide so much of herself away in order not to rouse anyone, shake anyone? She wanted to offer Emma some confession or revelation, to boil down her love and pain into a shining, essential truth. When Emma was a child, Claudia had wanted to hand her the world in its safest, most comprehensible form. But now, she wanted to offer Emma the truth about the imperfection of marriage, and the consolations sought in other people, other places. She would allow her to see not a mother's smooth, protected façade, but the all-too-human reality.

"Your father and I," Claudia started to say, and stopped, scared to put into words what she knew to be true. "It's hard," she admitted. "Sometimes it's very hard."

"Is what you have enough?" Emma asked.

"No. Not anymore," Claudia said, and took Emma in her arms and wrapped her in, tighter than she had in years. Emma leaned forward into the hug, not wanting to be released either. Claudia drew closer to Emma, then farther away, to see her both up close and from a distance.

When Emma left, Claudia went to her office. The glass bottles along the windowsill were shaking from the construction. When she was away, she had forgotten the sensation of being besieged by so much noise. She had barely been gone a week, yet it felt like months had passed. In no time, the building seemed to have progressed from steel frame to a nearly completed structure.

She lifted the window, planning to scream once again. But as the words assembled in her mouth, the urge dissipated. She was screaming at the wrong people, asking for the wrong thing. All this time, she had been demanding peace and solitude when it was engagement and interaction she so badly desired. What if she had asked for more? Her loneliness swept through her, emerging from the hiding place so deep inside her that not even she had known it was there.

She picked up a glass bottle, the most delicately formed, the brightest blue, and cradled it to her body. She tried to stop her hands but couldn't. Anything to free herself from the rising pain, anything to change the way she felt right now. She threw the bottle out the window, to the construction site below. One day, when this building was deemed outdated, the shards of blue glass would be discovered amid the wreckage. She was deprived of the pleasure of hearing it shatter, but she reached for the next bottle, and the next one too. How easy it was to destroy something she'd cared so much about preserving. But for what end? Why save what had no purpose? She wanted to shatter every illusion, false promise, false hope.

Claudia went back to the living room and grabbed the keys. Outside, she walked down the street until she found the spot where Leon's car was parked. As she unlocked the door, she hoped an alarm would sound. In a rush of sirens and lights, she would be arrested for breaking and entering. For far too long, she had accepted Leon's need for solitude. Until now, she hadn't thought she had the right to intrude.

N A BRIGHT, noisy procession, Wendy marched Sophie and Harry uptown. The cookies, packaged in white bakery boxes, were in the bottom of her stroller, safe from the jostles and the pleas that *we promise we won't touch, we just want to look.*

How perfect they must look to everyone they passed, the kids dressed in bright fall jackets, their hats festooned with tassels and pompoms. But Wendy couldn't stop replaying the fury that had overtaken her as Sophie screamed and Harry bit. Her smile was a growl. Her teeth had become fangs. Determined to wrest an apology from Harry, she had been overcome by an impulse to sink her teeth into his arm, to show him how it felt. He'd put his hand near her mouth, as though offering himself up, and in that moment, she had wanted to consume him alive.

A second later, she was mortified. No one else had ever felt such an impulse, no one ever. If another mother confessed to something half as bad, she'd have called Child Protective Services. Only at the last second had she pulled herself back: she'd kissed Harry's fingers and smiled, but in that moment, she'd become newly, exquisitely aware of her children's vulnerability.

Positioned within screaming distance of Georgia's, Wendy pulled out one imperfect cookie after another. They didn't match what she had envisioned or what she could have produced had she made them alone. But she was worried less about the cookies than she was about the kids. She searched their faces for signs of damage; with every flicker of expression that passed across their faces, she wondered how she had changed in their eyes.

On the walk uptown, they'd passed a familiar-looking woman sitting in a parked car. As Wendy laid out cookies and talked to the other moms who'd joined her, she realized it was the woman whose picture had appeared beside hers in the *Times.*

She couldn't tolerate the vulnerable looks on her children's faces. She was not the selfish woman portrayed in that article; she was not the screaming mother her kids had caught sight of.

"Come with me," she announced to the kids, who were awaiting their first customer.

Holding one of the boxes of cookies, she marched Sophie and Harry over to the car.

"You're 'the art historian who frequents the café,' aren't you?" she said when Claudia rolled down the window.

"And you're the mother who doesn't want to have to stay away from cafés until her kids are grown," Claudia said.

They stared at one another. All her anger, all her readiness for a confrontation, so long stored up. Here was her chance to unleash it. The woman looked so different from the way she remembered her, softer, with kind, forgiving eyes. At the café she had seen a woman who had wanted to offer rebuke; in the article, she had read of a woman who had no tolerance for anyone besides herself. But which was she, which role did she play? She wasn't sure of herself anymore.

"Do you have any idea how hard it is?" Wendy asked. Her voice was shaky, not her own.

"Oh, I do," the woman said, sounding surprisingly rueful.

"Do you know how hard I tried to make them be quiet? What is it I'm supposed to do?" Wendy said.

"I'm sure you don't want to hear this, but in the end, you have no control over who they're going to be. Eventually they do what they want," she said.

The woman may have intended her words as a warning, but Wendy felt only relief. She had lost control with the kids and they had survived. In this moment, she wanted to silence the constant thrumming, chiding voice in her head. She wanted to hold up her hands and call the time-out to end all time-outs.

Balancing the box of cookies on her hip, Wendy opened it and pulled out a dappled creation.

"Would you like one?" Wendy asked. "The kids made them. They're delicious."

Claudia took the peace offering, and Wendy and the kids ran back to Broadway, to the table laid with their creations. She pulled out a CD player and turned on *101 Disney Favorites*. "It's a Small World" came blasting out, loud enough to be audible over the small crowd across the street, holding placards. Wendy too had come with signs, hand-painted and decorated with stickers and glitter, which read *The Outside Voices Café*. The children wiggled and laughed, touched the merchandise, licked it when no one was looking. None of the pedestrians who spied this infraction reported them, nor did they mind the space they occupied or the noise they made. Who could pass without stopping, without smiling? They were children, noisy, messy, delicious.

H OP IS GONE," Max announced to Emma, who had arrived to baby-sit in the midst of their frantic searching. Through some extraordinary combination of will and desire, the frog had catapulted out of its bowl.

"We'll find him, don't worry. When I was little, I had a bird that escaped from its cage and it flew around the apartment until bedtime, then happily went back in," Emma said, and took Max's hand. Nina tried to catch her eye, but she was focused solely on the kids. She had missed Emma but assumed the kids had forgotten her, their love for her temporary and fickle. But Max and Lily saw no betrayal in her absence; they were thrilled when she walked in the door.

"He'll show up," Emma promised Max when they had searched the apartment and there was no sign of the missing pet.

"What should we do now?" Max asked, ready to call off the search.

"We're going out," Emma said. "I have a plan. Is it okay if we come home a little late?"

Nina agreed, still trying to catch Emma's eye. "The kids missed you. I missed you too," she said as Emma bundled the kids into their jackets.

"There's been a lot going on," Emma said. "Maybe you already know. Things are very hard at home, with my parents.

But I'm not staying there anymore. And I'm not going back to Steven either. I found my own apartment. I'm moving in today. And I got a job. I don't know if I'm going to be able to baby-sit as much."

Nina was surprised though she shouldn't have been. The haze of indecision, the grip of paralysis, eventually lifted. Sooner or later, everyone moved forward in their lives.

"The kids will really miss you. So will I," Nina said. "I guess we won't be neighbors anymore." Inadvertently she glanced at the living room windows, almost wishing she could restore Emma to the image she had seen through the window. How badly she wanted to say to Emma, *Did you know I was there watching you, or did I simply see what I wished to be there?*

Emma was trying to get the kids out the door, but she followed Nina's gaze to the window, then finally met her eye. "When I first came back home, I used to stand by the window and imagine that someone looking in might understand me. But why would anyone be standing there watching me? Why wouldn't people be focused on what's going on inside their own apartments?"

Emma hustled the kids out of the apartment before Nina could think of how to respond. Alone, she prowled the apartment, tossing toys into baskets in an attempt to create order. She looked across the way, but in the daylight, she could see little. Emma's words replayed in her head. She had tried to escape her own life by immersing herself inside the lives of others. If she didn't seek refuge in other people's lives, what would she finally see?

N O SWELLING CROWDS overtook the sidewalk and blocked traffic, no chorus of voices was wrapped together into one. But Arthur wasn't dissuaded. Afraid of being late, he had walked swiftly, weaving purposefully around those who were in his way, carrying the posters he planned as a surprise for Barbara: black-and-white replications of John La Farge's most famed works, and underneath, the proclamation SAVE THE WINDOW!!!!!!!!!!!!!!, the exclamation marks for Barbara, the bold letters and all caps for him.

Beneath each picture, he'd listed facts about La Farge, along with the information about the newly formed Committee to Save the La Farge Window. Arthur handed signs to the ten or so people assembled and looked up and down the block, hoping to see throngs of approaching supporters. A man was lingering with a look of bewilderment but didn't join them. A woman who did join was disheveled, and instead of holding the sign Arthur handed her, she stared into it, mesmerized.

When he and Barbara first met at her apartment, he had been distracted by the lingering memory of Georgia, with her long, tousled hair and creamy, freckled skin. But the harder they worked, the more he was drawn to Barbara, fiery and energetic, short and clipped, tough and knowing. He awoke each day with renewed purpose. He came to Barbara's apartment brimming with ideas. And then, one night, as they wrote press releases and drafted letters to lawyers and local council members, he realized that his ever-present image of Georgia had faded. He could see only Barbara.

He didn't dare believe that his feelings might be mutual. But Barbara looked so happy when he arrived at her apartment and invited him to stay for dinner. Accustomed to being disliked, he hardly knew how to interpret her apparent interest. So as not to jeopardize the pleasure of their newfound friendship, neither he nor Barbara mentioned their previous encounters until the morning they decided to walk their dogs. Lacking their owners' polite reserve, the dogs began barking furiously. But dogs don't get to choose their friends, and though he and Barbara each offered apologies, it was easy to laugh them off and chalk them up to the fact that dogs will be dogs.

"Is anyone here from the press?" Arthur whispered.

Barbara shook her head. "They're not coming."

"It's still early," he said, lifting his sunglasses.

"Do you know how many times I've stood here and waited for someone to show up? You haven't been out here like I have. Trust me. They're not coming," she said, and looked as though she expected him to walk away. He looked at her searchingly, trying to understand what he had done wrong.

Her anger turned to fear. She turned her eyes upon his and her voice became hesitant. "I don't want to do this alone anymore," she admitted.

"Then you're in luck," he said.

There were seven of them, then four, the slogans tepid when chanted by so few people. But they'd outlasted the nursery school kids across the street, who, despite meltdowns and accidents, managed to stay in business all afternoon. Soon, Barbara and Arthur were the only ones left.

"We're not done yet," Arthur said. He took her hand and shyly interlaced his fingers with hers. Then from his knapsack he pulled out two rolls of masking tape. From a small bag he produced two cookies he'd bought, both shaped, however vaguely, like dogs.

T HE CAR WAS gone. Leon knew exactly where he'd parked it and yet, when he walked past that spot, a black Camry was in its place. He walked up and down the block, past children selling cookies, past a small group protesting some unknown offense. He was becoming increasingly concerned that his car had been towed or stolen—but his spot was good until tomorrow and who would steal an antiquated Volvo?

He looked around for someone who might help him. The street was crowded, but no one cared about the distress on his face. He felt an unfamiliar yearning to stop a passing bystander in need of help or comfort; they could sit on the curb and he would tell all.

He tried calling Claudia, who, for all he knew, was still in Boston. As he left a series of messages, he became increasingly worried about the meaning behind her absence. He should have known, of course, her travel plans; he should know why she had gone, what she had learned. There was no hiding from his own culpability. Claudia had made no terrible transgressions, nothing he could offer to justify the fact that he did not want this any longer, nothing except the feeling of falling into an inescapable slumber. He could no longer look away from the slow seepage of his feelings for Claudia, over months, over years.

He stopped trying to reach her, stopped trying to try. He

thought instead of Nina. He had counseled himself on all the ways it was improbable, impossible, a path surely paved with pain. Until now he hadn't been sure that he would have the courage to tell Nina the idea that he was holding on to as though it were a life raft. But that practical restraining resolve was gone. So many of his patients came to him seeking permission to act in accordance with what they felt; they paid him to reassure them that they were not bad, to bolster what they knew to be true of their lives. They came to him, like people strapped and bound with ropes, wanting to know: were you allowed to change course?

He had to find Nina, talk to her. The two of them could be together. Not for a few weeks, not just for the tenuous uncertain present. In his mind, he created the story they would tell themselves and others: *We fell in love. We were married to other people at the time but we were both unhappy. We wanted to be together.* His life was once again before him. In so many ways, his life was his to start again.

W E'RE RIDING THE subway," Emma announced. "Come on, Max. It's going to be fun. If you want to be a real New Yorker, you've got to take the train."

Max's eyes pooled with concern, but avoidance worked for only so long. Eventually you had to face your fear. Max slipped his hand into hers, offering his agreement. Her good mood was infectious. Emma had half expected her mother to try to talk her out of her plans, but to her surprise, there had been no such impulse. The permission she had been after had been hers to grant all along. It might be a little late to be making such a discovery, but there it was nonetheless.

They bought a MetroCard, planning to ride the trains as far as they wanted. Emma showed Max the subway map and let him choose the route. Lily sat in the stroller, happily licking her shoe. Giddy with relief, Emma laughed at the sight. On the train, Max lost himself in the view out the window. Amid the crowds, they were the only ones not in a hurry. The subway car's placards advertised a buffet of possibilities. *Learn English. Lose weight. Report suspicious packages.* And *If you see something, say something.* And *There are sixteen million eyes in the city. We're counting on all of them.*

Max was so engaged by his conversation with Maurice that she decided it didn't matter that she'd forgotten the diaper bag.

"It's part of the adventure," she said when he held out his

hand for his regularly scheduled snack. "We have to see if we can survive—at least until we can buy something at a newsstand."

She too was hungry, but in her own bag she carried no Ziploc baggies filled with food. All she had was Steven's manuscript, which she'd brought along on this journey to nowhere.

She pulled it out and started leafing through the pages. Despite Steven's claims that he was nearly done, whole sections were missing, and in their place were typed notes to himself, in bold and all caps. Fragments of sentences appeared next to those perfectly hewn. Paragraphs that began beautifully trailed off into blank white space. He'd given her the novel, imperfect, unfinished. Whatever struggle with his work he was engaged in he had kept hidden from her. She was tempted to call him, to ask him what it meant that in the face of her own difficulties he had pretended to be effortlessly working. It was so easy to grab this chance to ply him with questions, to seek out the closeness she had so badly craved. But she wasn't going to do it. Since she was a teenager, she'd gone from one boyfriend to another; there was rarely a stretch of more than a month or two when she was not connected to someone. Now she was ready to be truly alone—she wasn't even sure yet what this meant. Nothing to anchor herself inside of, nothing that gave the feeling of being held down. She had thought that when she was finally an adult, life would be firmly rooted, but she was learning what a wishful illusion that was.

"Tell me about the zoo," Max begged.

"Didn't I tell you already?" she asked.

"More," he insisted.

She thought for a minute. "Okay, here's the part I didn't tell you yet—and remind me when we get home, we should tell this to your mom too. I have a feeling she'd appreciate it. Once you see the night zoo, you can never really go back to how you used to be. For some people this might not be a good thing, but it's true. You might go home, but you never go back, not for long anyway. Do you know what happens the next time you go to the zoo? You always have in the back of your mind what it looks like at night and you can't help but wish you were there again. It's not just the zoo that's different. It's you that's changed."

She held Max more closely in her arms, and he nuzzled against her. If she peeked inside his head, surely she'd see images of those animals running free at night. Kids knew the pleasure of such sprints, yet where along the way did they forget? It was one of the reasons she wanted to be around kids. That night she had run from her apartment, it was from fear, from panic, from a desperate need to make something change. But there had also been an unyielding sense of her own capacity for forward motion and speed.

When they reached Times Square station, Max tugged on her arm, needing to pee.

"You're wearing a pull-up, aren't you?" she asked.

He shook his head. "I have my practice underwear on."

Not only had she forgotten the diaper bag, but she'd forgotten to change him before they left. They could survive without snacks, but not without pull-ups. If he peed in his pants, she'd have to ride the subway with a kid who smelled like the subway.

"Max, you can wear diapers for the rest of your life, but just this one time, can you use the toilet?"

Emma looked around for anything that resembled a bathroom. Next to the Shuttle tracks, she pushed on a door labeled Knickerbocker Hotel, but it was locked, leaving her no choice but to look for a token booth and ask a clerk for the key to the nearest bathroom.

"Okay, Max. Let's do this as quickly as possible. And do

yourself a favor and try not to touch anything," she said. Holding Lily in one arm, she pulled down Max's pants to the layer of Bob the Builder underwear, and he peed into the toilet as though he'd been doing it his whole life.

"Are we all here? Do we have Maurice?" Emma asked when they were back on the platform, waiting for the train.

"Maurice isn't here anymore," Max said.

"Oh, God, where did we lose him?" Emma asked, envisioning a city-wide search for a missing imaginary friend.

"He decided to move. He left a few minutes ago."

"I thought he was afraid to leave the laundry room. Last I heard, wasn't he planning to live down there?"

"He got over it. He moved to the country. And he took Hop with him. Don't you think they'll be happier?"

She took his hand. "You know what, Max? I do."

MY CAR WAS stolen," Leon said when Nina answered her phone. She couldn't help herself. She told him she was home alone and waited for him to come over.

When Leon came into the apartment, he looked around at what he knew only from her descriptions or had glimpsed from across the way. She wondered, briefly, how her life appeared in his eyes. But mostly she marveled at the strangeness of having him here inside her apartment as if until this moment, he was a figment of her mind. For the first time, she saw him in the light of her real life.

"Maybe it sounds silly, but I love my car," Leon said.

"What are you going to do without it?" Nina asked.

"Claudia has always said that if something happened to my car, I'd have to invent some other excuse to be alone."

"Did you call the police?"

"I will but I don't think anyone is going to help. I can't even reach Claudia."

"Maybe she took the car," Nina said.

"Maybe she left me," he said, trying to pass it off as a joke, but his voice faltered. "My family life is a mess. I tried to be more involved, but that only made things worse. I have very little idea what any of us really need. I know you went looking for a vision of a happy family, but I told you, I'm not good at this."

She shifted, excruciatingly aware of her body. Where should she put her hand, rest her gaze? There was no escaping the desire in Leon's eyes and in her body as well. Once she had touched him, once she had felt the weight of his body upon hers, there was no other way to see him.

"I've been looking for you," Leon said.

"Out the window?" Nina asked.

"On the street. In the park. In my mind."

"In my mind too," she said.

His hand swam through the air to find hers. His fingers laced through hers.

"I've tried to pretend that nothing happened. I told myself, 'This is not really you, this is not really what you feel,'" she said.

"Why?" he asked.

"Look around," she said, gesturing to the evidence of her already-made life all around them. "I'm scared," she said. "I don't know what to do."

He came closer until his forehead met hers, so close that she saw not him, but her own face in the reflection of his eyes. He came closer still, until she saw only a single distorted eye. Their bodies brushed against one other, so many points of contact flickering at once.

"I can't stop thinking about you," he said. "Every day, you're all I think about. What if we decided that we're going to be together? What if we took a chance and changed our lives?"

What if, a game she had played in her mind since she was a kid. What if every possibility could be brought into existence? What if no pathways were yet closed off? She listened to his idea. The two of them were trapped in the shells of their lives, but what if they pushed them open? They could leave their marriages and be together. It might seem impossible at first, but they could find their way to the other side. As improbable,

as insurmountable as it sounded, it did happen that people discovered they were with the wrong person, in the wrong life.

And then, what would she find on the other end? This
imagined life where she lived free and unfettered, not just in
the privacy of her mind. Would it be there waiting for her, finally real, attainable?

The Leon of her mind, the Leon who stood before her. Her
own life to think about, yet all she had wanted to do was hide
from it. What would happen as she drew closer to Leon still: In
her attempt to escape the press of her own life, would she end
up in an all-too-familiar place? Was he, at least in part, a figment crafted from the rib of her longing? A mirage of escape
that would vanish if she drew too close?

What she imagined crashed up against what she saw. What
she thought battled with what she felt. The life inside her mind
beckoned her forward. Her real-world responsibilities came after her with nets, with hooks. All she'd felt was the urge to run.
Nowhere in her mind was the thought of where she might arrive.

A T THE END of the workday, Richard was waiting, and this time there was no way to avoid him. At his request, Jeremy went to the office in which he had spent so much time. Richard was joined there by Tom Markowitz, the head of the personnel committee, whom Jeremy had seen only in passing.

As they motioned for him to sit, Richard gave him a surveying, critical look. Here was his chance for the grand rebellion—run naked through the halls, throw the documents in Richard's face—which he and Nina had joked about on those late nights when they'd concocted impossible plans of escape.

"Why don't we get right to it," Tom said. "You were due for your midyear review in a few months but given the recent circumstances, we decided to move it up." He began to recount the filings that had not been done on time, the embarrassment Richard had suffered assuring the client that the deal was under control. "It's become abundantly clear that you no longer have a role to play here."

"You should also know that we're planning to get the disciplinary committee of the city bar involved," Richard said, and handed Jeremy a copy of one of the documents he'd given to Arthur. At the bottom of the page was the client matter number which, in his haste, he had forgotten to cover.

"I wonder who could have given this to the community

groups. The client was very interested to know this as well," Richard said.

He startled though he knew he shouldn't be surprised. At least in some part of himself, surely he had intended this to happen. It had been the only way he could make his escape, yet he hadn't expected to see such betrayal on Richard's face. He felt bad about what he had done, but somewhere along the way he had forgotten that he could have just quit; there might have been illuminated signs marking the exits but he had stopped believing he could walk through them.

With one last withering glance, Tom left him alone with Richard. "I thought that you were going to be one of the few who made it to the end. I thought you had a future here. But you know what the trick is? You have to want it badly enough to be able to make it through all the hard work. You have to decide that this"—Richard held his arms out wide to take in his office and all that lay inside it—"is worth it in the end."

"Worth what? My whole life?" Jeremy asked.

He was about to leave, but remembering something, he turned back. Draped over Richard's chair was the familiar swath of khaki. "What's with the vest?" he asked.

In response, Richard gave him a stony stare, a facial impasse. That was all he was going to get. With nothing left to say, Jeremy started to leave the office.

When Jeremy was halfway down the hall, Richard stuck his head out the door. He checked to make sure no one else was in earshot.

"Bird watching," Richard called after him.

Jeremy waited to laugh until Richard was back in his office with the door closed. Several months ago, he would have viewed this admission with shock; now it made him sad that in all these years of working together there had been no available language to speak of any outside interests. Like his father with his models of planes and trains, Richard had room in his life only for a costume that was small enough to be tucked away like an airplane's life preserver under his seat, taken out and inflated in a moment of need. Jeremy had initially thought that this would be enough for him as well—he had hung the trench coat Magellan had given him on the back of his office door, planning to put it on when he needed something all his own.

He had an hour to clear out his office, surrender his card key, return his BlackBerry. The reality of what he'd done began to sink in. Even more so, the fact that he would have to face Nina. How could he tell her that he had felt as trapped as she, consoled only by the fact that one day, this office, this building, would feel as distant as a dream? He would be missed by no one. He had worked so hard yet mattered so little.

There was nothing he wanted to take except the trench coat. When he left the building, it was late afternoon, but the moon was already visible in the blue sky, full and hanging so low over the city that the peaks of skyscrapers seemed like they could pierce it.

At the sight of the full moon, he remembered. He could go home; he should go home, and he would, soon enough. But first he got on the subway, in the direction of the Brooklyn Bridge.

THE GROUPS ON both corners had dispersed, but the streets were still crowded with people enjoying the warm October day. The city was awash in color. Calves and elbows, cleavage, necks and waists sailed across Leon's frame of vision. After leaving Nina's apartment, he walked to clear his mind, but he could no longer ignore the press of faces, the bombardment of bodies all around him.

"I don't think I can," Nina had said to him in her living room, even as she looked longingly at him.

"I know," he had said as they held one another. He felt her pull toward him at the same time as he heard her words taking her away. He considered what to say: the unknown future before all of them. She was in battle with herself, so much still unexplored. Eventually she would find a more definitive answer. Life itself was reckless. Despite all attempts to the contrary, no one made it through unscathed.

"Can you?" she asked.

"Yes," he said. "I can."

He had been about to leave Nina's apartment, but before he closed the door, he stopped, because what would she do now—take care of the kids as though none of this had happened, live beside Jeremy with a part of herself sealed away?

"Do you really think you can go back?" he asked her.

She looked stunned, as if the question had never occurred

to her. He saw the road ahead more clearly than she could. She might spend years, maybe her whole life, discovering what he knew. You couldn't go back. So many tried, so many even stayed at least with their bodies, but in their hearts, in the widest, deepest parts of themselves, did anyone really go back?

He'd left Nina's apartment though he hadn't wanted to. "Where are you going?" she'd asked, and all he could say was that he didn't know. As he walked, he looked at the jigsaw of buildings above. He wanted to steal one of the bulldozers perpetually parked on his block, demolish every old building, every piece of stone and terra cotta, and replace them with a glass city built entirely anew. He didn't want to let go of the feelings Nina had sparked. It would be easy enough to do what he decried as impossible, go back and let the days of his marriage pass quietly by. He would live as most people did, perched between acceptance and resignation. So much of life was behind them, so much already shared. To take it apart at this stage was to cling to the idea that enough still lay ahead.

On a corner, Leon passed the two warring dog owners, and he expected a fight to break out. But they were working together, leaving him to wonder whether he'd misread the hostility of their earlier interactions.

When Leon came closer and saw what was written on their posters, he stared in disbelief. It was impossible, yet here it was. Not just Claudia's windows, but her name. Her work, out in the world. He'd formulated multiple explanations for why she so badly wanted to find the window, but he'd rarely considered the possibility that it actually existed. In his mind, she was someone who would always toil in vain, and he'd felt not compassion but pity at how long the work had taken her and how lost she was inside it.

"Barbara," he called. "Does Claudia know you're doing this?"

"I told you to have her call me," she said. "Don't you remember? I said that she might want to get involved, but I never heard from her so I assumed she wasn't interested."

"I never told her," Leon admitted.

"Why don't you give her one of our flyers. It's her work, after all. We'd love to talk to her," Barbara said to him, but her attention was on her fellow dog owner, both of them bearing the stance of shared purpose.

His envy was aroused and he felt stabbed by loneliness, a condition to which he'd thought himself immune. He didn't know what Claudia would make of these signs. The simplest of questions, yet it felt hard to imagine asking her, as though he would be prying too deeply into her private world. For how long had he and Claudia mistaken silence for companionship, how long had loneliness been dressed up to look like anything but? Now that he felt such loneliness, it was hard to bear for a single moment, yet he had borne it unknowingly all these years.

He went home to an apartment that was as empty as he'd always wanted, yet he longed for distraction or disruption. He went into Claudia's office where the window was open, and her glass bottles were gone. On the ledge, one bottle remained though it was cracked. He leaned out to retrieve it and tried to see the site as the impossible intrusion that Claudia had. When he'd come upon Claudia yelling out the window, he'd assumed that she was embarrassed to be seen, though now he realized that this was precisely what she wanted.

He looked around her office for some understanding of what she was feeling, but there was nothing more legible than her Post-its. Leon tried to decipher what Claudia had written, but even if he could make out the words, he'd no longer know what they meant. Once, long ago, soon after they'd met, he'd asked her why stained glass mattered so much to her. Eager to discuss her work, Claudia had gathered photographs of her favorite windows. "Stained glass is an art form that's never static," she'd explained. "It's entirely dependent on the time of day, the quality of light, the direction of the sun, and where you're standing. As long as it's exposed to light, the colors are in a continual state of creation."

When she'd said that to him long ago, he had been moved by the look on her face, so flushed with excitement and ambition. Once upon a time, he had enjoyed the fact that he was as comfortable in her presence as he was when he was alone. But how far past that point he was, and how late it was to recognize this. Only now, when he'd come to the end, did he wonder if she'd always made the connection between the windows she loved and the people around her. Had she always known that they were equally in need of having sufficient light cast upon them?

It wasn't simply that he had wanted to be alone. He hadn't wanted to be with Claudia, not nearly enough. He had tried to protect himself, and her, from this knowledge. But after this gasp of dizzying wakefulness, he wouldn't settle again into the approximation of love, of life. It was far easier, of course, to leave with someone—to jump off while holding on to another hand. But he was willing to do it alone, because once you were aware of how else it might be, going back was far more terrifying than moving forward.

ARKED ON A side street, Claudia contemplated what to do. She had been sitting in the car for what felt like hours, unsure of where to go. She pulled out of her space and drove through the neighborhood, aimlessly. She had once conjured a city that opened itself up, the streets leading to wooded trails that would take her into green pastures, but those had closed down not because of the noise of the streets but the sadness inside her. So many people stayed where they were because they thought that was the only option.

When she could stand being in the car no longer, she found a parking spot near the construction site. She'd felt such hatred toward this site, but in early evening, with work done for the day, it seemed like little more than a ghost town, a harmless, dusty remnant of a place people had once lived.

It took her a moment to see the posters. Taped to the scaffolding was the *Welcome* window, La Farge's iridescent rendering of Andromeda, the mythological daughter punished for her mother's sins. On light posts, pictures of *The Angel of Help* and *Wisdom*. The captions under each picture were drawn from her descriptions and attributed to her. At the bottom of each sign was information about the Committee to Save the La Farge Window, a group she hardly believed existed, unless it sprang from inside one of her dreams.

She drew in her breath. The buildings, the sidewalk, tilted.

Was it possible that the window had been located, that these neighborhood activists might have used her work to uncover what had eluded her? Without knowing it, her work had gone into the world, making contact on her behalf.

Next to her, staring at the signs, was a man wearing a trench coat, and he smiled when he saw her.

"They're your windows," he said.

"How do you know who I am?" she asked.

"I met you at the New York Public Library. You gave me your article."

Finally, Maurice. If he hadn't said something, she would have walked right past him. She'd thought about him so many times, yet he barely resembled the person she had created in her mind.

"I didn't recognize you," she admitted. "You're in graduate school, aren't you?"

"That's just my fantasy. In real life, I'm a real estate lawyer. Or at least I used to be. Now I'm not really sure who I am."

"I wondered if you were really in school," she said.

"How did I give myself away?"

"I went looking for you," she admitted. "I was hoping we could talk some more."

"It was your article that made this happen," he said.

"How do you know?"

"Because you gave it to me, and I gave it to them," he said, gesturing to the posters, to the names listed at the bottom. "E-mail me, I'll tell you the whole story," he said, and gave her his real name, which she wrote down. The interaction might not match what she'd created in her mind, but then, what of that image had been real? Here was the actual possibility of a friendship. It couldn't fill every space inside her, but if she opened herself up, one small piece of emptiness might be colored in.

Before going home, Claudia turned back to Broadway,

where on bus stops and storefronts more signs were plastered. She walked to the red brick building above what used to be the dollar store and lingered out front. It was one of the last low-rise buildings on the block, and it was a wonder it hadn't been torn down earlier. At some point it had been attached with a party wall to the building next to it, but except for that addition, the building appeared to have gone untouched for decades, which made it more likely that the window could actually be there. Only a structure so nondescript could quietly house something so magnificent.

She came into the apartment where the door to her office was open and Leon was reading at her desk. He jumped up when she came in, but he didn't look like himself, his expression uncharacteristically pained, anxious.

"Where have you been?" he asked.

"Where have you been?" she countered.

"I was worried about you," he said.

"I assume you already know that Emma found an apartment. And she got a job in a nursery school," Claudia said.

"I didn't know. When did she decide this?"

"She told me a few hours ago."

"Are you upset?" he asked.

"I'm glad she knows what she needs," Claudia said, struck by the quiet of the apartment. Emma was taking one more step on the path toward becoming herself. The two of them would be standing here, sooner or later, alone in their lives.

"Did you see the signs?" Leon asked.

"They're everywhere," she said.

"Do you think it's possible?" he asked.

"For all I know, it could be a ploy of neighborhood activists to attract attention to their cause," Claudia said. "In all likelihood, the window would have belonged to a family member who lived up here. Cornelius Vanderbilt was known for giving works of art to his family, and it's likely that those gifts would go unrecorded, especially if the family members in question weren't worthy of public notice."

She was trying to keep the hopefulness from her voice because she expected him to tire of the conversation and wander away. And now, at this late date, where should she even begin? How could she cram years of work into a single conversation? Lecture him about the origins of La Farge's work for the Vanderbilts? About the way in which the works of art were divvied up before the mansion was demolished?

"I'd have to see when the buildings were attached, but I would guess it was done in the fifties. It's actually not a bad way to preserve a window. If it is there, I would expect it to be in good condition, certainly better than if it was removed and stored elsewhere. It would need to be cleaned, but it stands to reason that the glass could be intact."

"But why does it matter?" Leon asked.

"Because it might have been one of his most important works. Certainly from the sketches, it appears as monumental as the Ames windows—"

"No. Why does it matter to you?" he asked.

Long ago, he'd asked her this, on one of the many occasions they'd been introduced, each seemingly for the first time because he never remembered her. She'd answered the question with such passion, hoping he would finally see who she was.

Claudia met his gaze. "Because they're alive." Covered over for so many years, yet they would still maintain their beauty. Deprived of light, yet a blast of sunlight would change all that. It mattered so much to her, then and now, because no one had seen them in so many years. Because she had persisted even when she felt like giving up. Because despite the many painstaking hours, she hadn't lost her love for the splendor of the work.

It was hard to recognize Leon, who was staring at her with something new and unsettling in his eyes.

"You don't see me," she said. "You haven't for a very long time."

"I know," he admitted, and held out one of her broken bottles which he'd rescued from the ledge. Was it a peace offering or an admission of all that was wrong between them?

"When did this happen? How did we become this way?" she asked.

"I haven't been here, I know."

"Why do you always want to be alone?"

"I haven't wanted to be here," he said, "at least not enough. Not like I should. But I'm tired of being unhappy. I'm tired of wanting to be alone."

"What are you saying?" she asked.

"I can't hide from it anymore. I don't want what we are."

She opened her mouth to protest but had nothing to say. It was so much easier to believe he had neither the desire nor the capacity for anything more. It was impossible this was what he was saying, impossible this was what he wanted. His words sank further in. After so many years together, it was unfathomable that a decision like this could be his alone to make. Her whole life, upended, and she had so little say. To be alone: not in the way she had been until now, but truly on her own. Until now, there at least had been someone to sit across from her at a table, there at least had been the warm body in bed next to her, even if she rarely found comfort in it.

She knew him well enough to understand that his mind wouldn't change. Here, finally, was the bare truth, shearing away a part of her, but with that came a small measure of relief, because it was the truth nonetheless.

NINA CAME HOME into the night of her very own living room where it was quiet and still.

After Leon left her apartment, she'd walked up the path of Riverside Park, weaving around the dog walkers, through the flocks of strollers. She stared at everyone she passed. Why uphold the façade of strangers, why pretend to keep her distance? All those who would have you believe that you were the only one who searched for a way out of your own life; all those who smiled and said, "Not me, not here, not ever." She was no longer fooled: there might be protestations of contentment, fronts of well-being, but scratch one surface, ask one question, and it would come tumbling out. If she spoke honestly of her own feelings, she would hear a chorus of others. If she were to name her treachery, confess her truths, the streets would be lined with people eager to do the same.

The question Leon had asked her spun around in her mind, each word growing larger and brighter, each word coming loose from the rest of the sentence, each word louder, sharper, unrelenting, each word encircling her, prodding her. Can she go back from this precipice? Can she go back, from this place where she had gone yet had stayed? Can she tuck away what she had done and felt, can she disclaim herself—not me, not anymore? Leon and all he had unleashed in her would be hidden safely inside. Her own urge for some deeper, darker more

would bide its time, maybe forever, maybe until some unknown later date.

At 116th Street, she cut back to Broadway and went through
the gates of Columbia, to the campus that was the reason she'd
come to the city long ago, with infinite variations on how her
life was going to be. How young the students looked; how
much older she had become. How had she ended up inside a
life where there was simultaneously too much and not enough?
Until now, she had believed that the only open path of escape
was inside her mind; only there could she come and go as she
pleased. She had believed that it was sufficient to travel only on
the rails of her imagination. But she hadn't been able to live inside the one square of her mind. She hadn't been able to remain
inside the boxed life she'd crafted for herself.

She waited for Emma and the kids to return home; she
waited for Jeremy. An hour passed, then another. Finally the
door opened and Jeremy came in. Instead of looking exhausted,
he was invigorated in a way she hadn't seen in a long time. But
it was hard to meet his eye. He'd been away for so long, and so
had she. All she had come to see in him was the perpetual exhaustion that coated their lives.

"You might not believe this," he said, "but I was at the
Brooklyn Bridge."

He sat down next to her on the couch. "I wasn't working
the night everyone got sick. I went with someone from my office to an abandoned subway station. It's an empty, gorgeous
space that no one ever gets to see. For weeks I read about it
in the library, when I was supposed to be working. And then,
when I was standing there, I felt like I'd stepped into a different
city. I became a different person.

"There's more," he said. "I got fired. It wasn't just that
night. I haven't been working very hard for a long time. And I
don't know if I'm going to be able to get another job as a law-

yer, at least not right away. You probably don't want to hear this but it's possible I could get disbarred," he said, and told her the rest of the story.

"Is it time to buy the RV?" he said, plaintively.

She knew what she was supposed to say. Move to the country, backpack through Europe. But she couldn't do it. It was their familiar refrain, but her heart wasn't in it. These fantasies had simply sustained them, enabling them to avoid what they didn't want to see. So long as they could dream of doing something else, so long as they could assure themselves that one day it would be different, they hadn't needed to look at what was before them. They hadn't needed to go anywhere at all.

"No. Really. What are we going to do?" she asked.

"I don't know," he admitted.

"I don't know either," she said.

"There was this moment when I was in the station, and I realized that I could still decide. It's not all fixed into place," he said.

She searched his face to find the meaning behind his words, wanting to set forth on the hope, if not the promise, contained inside them. For the first time in ages, he looked awake, alive. Could she go back, fold his words, and shape them into a small pointed roof under which they could live, fold them again into a boat in which they could set sail?

Jeremy was waiting for her to respond, and the words assembled at the edge of her mouth. She could confess all that she had felt and done. Or she could hide away the secret and live with the wisp of unease between them. The prospect of concealing scared her as much as revealing. Would she rather stay hidden or be found?

Nina stood up and went to the window. She couldn't force the words from her mouth. It was dark out, and she expected to see Leon and Claudia in their usual spots. But there was noth-

ing to see. The curtains to their apartment were closed. There
was only this life, only her own.

Jeremy came up behind her, encircling her in his arms. Leon's question asked itself again and again, like streaks of light in
the sky, whizzing continuously past, dangerously close.

The crash was so loud it physically jolted them. It rang in
their ears, pounded inside their chests. They both jumped up,
looked out the window, ran down the stairs of the building,
and went outside.

FROM UP AND down the block the neighbors came running. A stream of people as the sounds of sirens grew closer, fire trucks arriving, police officers rushing in, directing everyone back, back.

But there was no way not to look. "What happened, what happened?" everyone asked, their minds constructing scenarios that spanned the largest tragedies to the smallest mishaps. Except for the scared, hushed tones, it was like the block party that would never take place. Everyone stood together, looking up and at each other, waiting to see what seemingly solid structure would fall next.

It was the construction site on their block. One of the newly built columns had given way, falling backward onto the scaffolding and collapsing it, resulting in a shower of dust, a tangle of metal and wood on the sidewalk. They had built too high, too quickly, placed too much weight, unsupported, on too fragile a structure.

Recognition coasted over Nina and Jeremy at the same moment. Both kids in Emma's arms, screaming but shockingly, achingly, fine. They grabbed hold of their children as Claudia and Leon came running, people crowding around Emma, all asking questions of her at once. Her face scratched, her hand cut, she recounted how, on their way home, she and the kids had stopped to look at the construction site. To their surprise, lingering in front had been the woman bedecked in an array of colors, whom both she and Max recognized.

"We know her but we don't even know her name," Max had said, unable to comprehend how this could be. Determined to rectify the situation, they'd gone up to her and introduced themselves, then asked her name.

She had looked shocked at the question. "Myra Vanderbilt," she said, then ran from them, into the site. They had waited for her to come out, but then, the crash, the noise, the rainfall of dust. Emma had grabbed the kids and run, keeping them safe.

"The woman was definitely in there," Emma was saying. "I think she still is."

The firefighters rushed into the site as rescue trucks arrived and the media swarmed. Nina held Max, Jeremy hugged Lily; Claudia and Leon hugged Emma. They looked up at each other, Claudia at Jeremy, Nina at Leon, then went home, to their own families, into their own nights.

ALL THOSE WHISPERED bedtime promises that there was nothing to be afraid of. All those assurances that everything bad or frightening existed only in the realm of make-believe. And yet, the cordoned-off site across the street. The woman whose inert body was carried from it. Only tomorrow would they find out more about her, when it was too late. Only tomorrow would they pay attention to the signs protesting the ever-present construction.

But for this one moment, it was quiet. Nina and Jeremy slept with the kids curled between them. After a late dinner and quick baths, after books and songs, after futile efforts to soothe, to rock, they'd taken the kids with them into bed, not as adherents of Family Bed, but simply a family in bed.

Every time Max rotated, Nina shifted to accommodate his new position. Lily awoke for a moment, needing to be held or changed. Sensing the shift into wakefulness, Nina awoke as well and cradled her closer. Eventually they would all be awakened by the demands of the day. There would be newspaper articles about the building's collapse and streams of phone calls once their friends heard how close they had come. There would be the questions Max would inevitably ask, the images from which neither he nor Lily could be shielded. But none of that would be for hours.

Nina got out of bed and stood in the doorway of their

room, to capture an image of the peaceful faces immersed in their respective dreams. This close, the characters from those dreams mingled, crossing on strands invisible during waking hours. In Max's dreams, Maurice settles happily into his quiet country life. Having experienced the momentary thrill of freedom, Hop finds a quiet spot to hide. Max lifts the lid of the toilet, and there he is, eyes bright and bulging. Next to him, Lily's nightmare of a loud, terrifying boom gives way to dreams of the mouse running up the clock and a cow jumping over the moon, a very hungry caterpillar and a brown bear and all that he sees.

Nina closed the bedroom door and went into the living room where all the lights were off. She walked to the window, the city lit before her under the full moon. In windows above them and below, she saw the dazzling, dizzying array. All these people, all these lives. In the window one down and two across, Leon sits alone on the couch. Then he is gone, and Claudia sits in the same spot by herself. Loneliness emanates from that window, but then, it had always been that way.

Nearby in a suburb, on a block, in a house, Wendy has driven out to take a look at what will soon be her home. Alone in the car, alone in the dark, she is bothered by the silence. Except for the all-night Super Stop & Shop, the stores have been closed for hours. Within a year, she was told, all this will seem normal. In two, it will feel like home. She will send back happy dispatches from a land where the grocery stores are huge and the parking is plentiful. In the meantime, she gets out of the car and walks across the backyard to the adjacent soccer field of the nearby elementary school. There are no hockey rinks, not this close to her house, but even in the dark she can see the white goalposts and the nets rustling in the air, and then, in the light of the moon, something else.

A caravan of silver Honda Odysseys pulls up at the field. From a distance, they look identical to those that exist everywhere, but as they approach, Wendy sees that each of them is emblazoned with a racecar's streaks of fire. From the drivers' seats the soccer moms emerge. They come from work and from home, from PTA meetings and board meetings. They put down their purses and briefcases, they pin up their hair, pull out their cleats. While the kids sleep and the husbands clean, while the moon and the headlights of their cars illuminate the night, they run. For this one hour it doesn't matter that the kids' homework has been left undone, that rotting under the car seats are the remnants of month-old chicken nuggets, that rotting in the kids' unbrushed teeth are the remnants of month-old gummy bears. For this one hour, there are no rules, no worries, no constraints. They run until their feet lift from the ground, run until they become the wild, unfettered girls they once were, the fearless, confident women they'd always believed they would become. They run until the stroke of midnight, when from somewhere far away, a whistle that sounds suspiciously like the cry of a child blows. Out of breath yet surprisingly awake, the sweaty, elated moms throw their arms around one another as they meet for a huddle and congratulate each other on a game nicely played, a job well done.

In a rent-controlled apartment on Broadway, an elderly husband sits beside his elderly wife, clutching her hand. Having screamed at each other in public all day, it's easier now to sit in silence. Behind them, the back wall of their living room is yellowed and bulging. The super has promised to plaster and paint, but now it's too late, because soon they will have to move out of this apartment in which they've lived for over thirty years. After a lifetime of renting, their red brick building is being torn down to make way for the young and rich. They have nowhere to go. Instead of making a decision, they fight. He thinks they should refuse to leave; she worries they will be put out on the street. If they were younger, he says, he'd buy a sledgehammer and hack through the wall, past the pipes and the wiring. Were he to do so, he'd find, sandwiched between his building and the one next door, a window unlike any they had ever seen, one that would make them rise from the couch and gape in awe.

Underneath twisted piles of metal, inside storms of dust, a woman dressed in shades of sapphire, topaz, and garnet is still trying to gain entry to the apartment in which she once lived. Several times each day, she'd circled past all the buildings that could be hers, but for reasons she still doesn't understand, the doormen always refused to admit her. If she stood for more than a minute, trying to locate the window that used to be hers, she was told that it was time to move along. But now she doesn't have to worry about the eyes that stare at her, people everywhere glancing maliciously at her or feigning smiles to hide their derision. Now she doesn't have to yell at those who look, because now no one can see her. She is set free from the eyes that create pinpricks of pain on her skin.

As her body ceases to belong to her, in her mind at last she returns to the apartment that was once hers and at last she sees the window. The colors are even brighter than she'd remembered, the light more abundant. The garlands of flowers and the children's faces come to life, opening her eyes to the shifting, shimmering world that lived inside. If Myra ever talked about the window, people treated her as though she were crazy. They didn't believe that she could descend from a family that was once considered the city's royalty. They didn't believe that anything so beautiful could be real. They didn't believe that anything unseen could so long survive. But she had always known that the window existed. She never doubted what she knew to be true, not when she had seen the dazzling colors with her own eyes.

In the window one down and two across, a lone figure is now standing in the light, waving to her. Nina recognizes the bright smile, the long, curly hair. The gestures grow more insistent: she points at Nina, then at the sky. Instead of hiding, Nina reaches over to a nearby lamp and switches it on. Her corner of the room is flooded with light.

In an instant, Nina is out the front door, taking flight in her pajamas. There is no time for shoes. Outside on the street, Emma is standing.

"The moon," Nina said.

"You remembered," Emma said.

"Should I get the kids?" Nina asked.

"No," Emma said. "Just us."

The two of them take off, in step with each other, bare feet slapping against the pavement. Perhaps the kids are waking up, perhaps Jeremy is looking for her, calling her name. She doesn't stop. Along the way, they pass a man and woman walking their dogs. The dogs are playfully barking; the couple hold hands. Along the way, they pass lampposts and bus stops bedecked with glimmering signs, colored photos of jeweled windows.

Inside the park, they run over the branches and the stones, onto the grass. The full moon lights the way. She has never been alone in the park at night, but there is no fear, not tonight. It's a cool night, a reminder of winter that's on its way. They run deeper into the park, to the Central Park Zoo, which is closed and locked, but Emma knows the way in. Nina follows her to the spot where the fence is slightly lower, and she grabs hold of the top and hoists herself up. Nina tries, and she struggles and falls. She tries again, and this time, she swings one leg over, then a second, until she is perched on top.

"Do you want to turn back?" Emma asks when she sees her

trepidation, but Nina shakes her head no. There is no way but forward. She leaps down and is inside.

"It's just like you said," Nina says.

"It's even better than I remembered," says Emma.

The animals are awake. The bars of the cages have ceased to exist—those were mere illusion, present only for those who believed they were there. At night the animals know better. They are sitting on benches, swinging in trees. The colors of their fur have brightened. Horns, teeth, tusks, and claws have grown longer, stronger, sharper. The animals cry out, they caw roar squawk growl. Every animal is aflutter, afoot. Everywhere, the whoosh of wings, the pounding of hooves.

Emma runs from one end of the zoo to the other, her arms outstretched as if she too can take flight. Then she extends her arms, one at each side, and she spins. Her hair is set loose and spins around her, her mane, her feathers, her wings. Nina joins her, her hair loose too and flapping against her face, the two of them spinning around.

Spin past the internal assault of should and could; spin past all you were supposed to do, to be. All these efforts to hide inside other people, to tuck away what she did not want to feel, to know. There was no turning back from what she had done, from who she had become. For how long could she hold this inside her? Could Jeremy widen the space inside his mind where she lived; could he turn himself into new shapes as well, and could there be ways, like an ever-turning kaleidoscope, to find those shifting points of intersection?

And if not, then what? She didn't yet know. She would not turn back in fear, not desperately reshape herself to fit into old, tightly wedged spaces. She had never thought of herself as someone who would do anything other than what was expected of her, yet there was never really an arrival at any fixed point. All that wishing for certainty, all that belief in the clear path always visible up ahead. Here she was with life before her unknown, a reluctant yet inevitable traveler on the path still uncharted.

No longer spinning, Nina regains her balance and steadies herself. She turns around to look for Emma, but she has gone home ahead of her, leaving her to take in this vision alone. She is the only human in a dark world lit with eyes. But as soon as she leans her head back and looks, she sees that the entire city has become visible. Shades are pulled open. Every window is lit. People inside wander from one window to another. They cut holes through their walls and connect this living room with that bedroom. They extend hallways to create passages from one building to another. But not even that is enough. The windows are flung open and people shimmy on ropes, swing acrobatically down to the street. Doors everywhere are open. Neighbors, on every street, on every block, spill out of their buildings, in masses, in hordes, all of them like she is, loose on the streets. They take over the sidewalks, stop all the cars, fill all the parks. On a night like this, no one can bear to be inside.

Acknowledgments

I would like to thank the Massachusetts Cultural Council for their support and the Hadassah-Brandeis Institute for the gift of time and space. I am enormously grateful to Julie Barer, my agent, and to Lauren Wein, my editor, for their extraordinary insight, intelligence, and vision. Finally, I am deeply appreciative of my family and friends who have sustained me with their love, support, and enduring belief in this book.